A Light of Her Own

A Light of Her Own

Carrie Callaghan

Amberjack Publishing
Chicago

First hardcover edition published 2018
First paperback edition published 2020
Amberjack Publishing
An imprint of Chicago Review Press Incorporated
814 North Franklin Street
Chicago, Illinois 60610
ISBN 978-1-94499-590-4

The Library of Congress has cataloged the hardcover edition as follows:
Title: A light of her own / by Carrie Callaghan.
Description: New York : Amberjack Publishing, 2018.
Identifi ers: LCCN 2018017976 (print) | LCCN 2018019558 (ebook) | ISBN 9781944995911 (eBook) | ISBN 9781944995898 (hardcover : alk. paper) | ISBN 9781944995904 (pbk. : alk. paper)
Classifi cation: LCC PS3603.A44188 (ebook) | LCC PS3603.A44188 L54 2018 (print) | DDC 813/.6--dc23
LC record available at https://lccn.loc.gov/2018017976

Cover design: David Provolo

Printed in the United States of America

To Patrick, my love.

Chapter 1

FEBRUARY 1633

JUDITH LEANED AGAINST THE SMALL window ledge and looked inside. The frigid twilight air seeped past her cloak into her many layers of tunics and her well-worn bodice, and the painted ledge below her numb fingertips had dulled to the gray of a low sky. Behind the glass, the inn's golden light beckoned, and though it was not yet suppertime, already drinkers dressed in shades of brown sat at small tables. Her teeth chattered with cold and nerves. She scrutinized the scene for any telling detail, but she saw nothing unusual, to her disappointment.

She wished she could step out of the back garden, around the corner, and through the inn door, but entering would be too risky. Even though the inn was public, anyone who knew her would realize she wasn't visiting for the ale. Respectable women didn't socialize in taverns or inns. But an artist showing up the night of a clandestine auction? Someone might recognize her and report her to the Guild, whose leaders would delight in an excuse to ban her. No artist, particularly not an apprentice like herself, could sell outside approved Guild channels. She stamped her feet against the cold and watched.

Inside the inn's common room, located at the back of the building, a trio of musicians played in the far corner. Judith anxiously tapped her finger against the windowsill along with the muffled beat, until the cold pinched her skin too deeply and she hugged her hands against herself.

Nothing suggested an auction was taking place, illegal or otherwise. No art, no passed canvases or wooden painting supports. Only pewter tankards and a few plates moved from hand to hand while bearded men gulped down ale or, less often, wine. A knot tightened in her stomach. The man with the misshapen nose had deceived her. For a moment Judith pressed her fingertips—smelling of linseed oil and ochre—against her eyelids. If he had misled her, stolen her painting, he would cost her four months. Or longer. She was twenty-three and still a student.

She opened her eyes and watched as, along the side of the room, a thin man dressed in an azurite-colored doublet stood up from a bench. She didn't recognize him, but his distinctive clothing caught her attention. He seemed to be speaking, then bent down and straightened again, and as he did, he lifted a linen draping and revealed a painting beneath. Judith exhaled.

She wondered which artist had produced that credible painting of a shepherd strumming a lute. Earth tones, with flashes of soft green. Who else would need to resort to illegal auctions? Obviously not the city of Haarlem's most prominent masters, like the brothers Frans and Dirck Hals. They sold under the St. Luke's Guild auspices. Maybe a mature apprentice like herself, someone on the cusp of recognition. She hoped the artist on display now was reputable, or close. If the other paintings fetched high prices, hers might as well. Twenty, even thirty guilders would be enough. She had never earned that much money before, not at one time. That is, assuming the auctioneer gave her a fair share.

The man with the canvas carried the painting to another table, where four card players frowned at their hands. Judith conjured up every detail of her own painting. Her woman holding a wineglass aloft had precisely the right tilt to her head. But the magenta wine glowing behind the etched glass had been tricky. Judith had struggled with the refracted light, and she had resolved her difficulties by moving the woman's fingers to block the view a bit. She loved how paint granted her mobility, the power to reshape the world in the most beautiful way she could imagine, but she hoped none of these buyers would notice her correction. They were shopkeepers and petty merchants hoping to display a little luxury alongside their wares or in their once-bare visiting rooms. It wouldn't matter to the merchants if they were displaying Judith's paintings, those fragments of her soul, or some mediocre depiction of a rustic cottage along a winding road. Judith needed her own workshop soon, a chance to establish herself as a serious painter before the public's fascination with paintings as ornaments for their homes faded. So many young men had left Frans de Grebber's workshop to set out on their own, but Judith still lingered there in her apprenticeship. Even though she was just as good as them.

Her fogged breath clouded the glass, so she stepped back. She bit her lip and rubbed at her rough woolen sleeves to spark some warmth. The light revealed the paint still stuck to the back of her scrubbed hand, and doubt wound through her veins like a cool fog. She should have offered the coarse man a different work, like the picture of the two men at cards with the boy chasing a dog nearby. Three figures made the canvas far more valuable, and the subtle critique of games—the warning implied in the boy's foolish play—would appeal to buyers. But the man made her wary. He had sidled up to her as she exited church one Sunday morning, both of them jostled by the crowd streaming from the echoing central cathedral. He offered no money up front, and he gave her a nearly illegible receipt, as if he had not expected her to be literate. Only after she delivered her painting did she realize he had let her assume when, and thus if, she would be paid. That night she cried silent tears into her threadbare blankets.

The first canvas the auctioneer displayed had disappeared in the room's haze. Judith shifted. The setting sun turned the glass into a mirror for a moment, and she was irritated to see her small face and thin lips instead of the room. Judith knew she was no beauty. She moved again, trying to see past the reflection. At her height, she had to stand on her toes to see around the heads of the drinkers in the elevated room, and this was the only window. The auctioneer sat at a table with two older men, and their backs obscured his face, though his doublet's unusual color glowed—a reason for optimism. To wear clothes of that hue, the man must make money doing this. Maybe he had traveled to Haarlem from bustling Amsterdam, and certainly he would know how to extract a high price for her painting. She shifted again. Her toes were growing numb from cold inside her battered shoes.

"You're plain for a strumpet, but I'll give it a try," said a voice behind her. She spun around, and a waft of alcohol enfolded her. A man with greasy brown hair pasted to his forehead below his wide-brimmed hat stood between her and the narrow street that ran along the side of the inn. He leaned toward her and tried to prop an arm against the wall, but missed and stumbled.

"I'm not a whore, you fool." Judith stepped away from the

window, further into the shadow of the kitchen garden. She glanced behind the man at the street and saw only empty dusk. Her heart surged, as if to run away without her.

"Don't be coy, now. That won't earn you a penning more. Come on, where's it to be? Not here, I hope. Though," he looked her up and down, "I'd manage."

"Leave me," she said. "I'm not for sale. I'll call the watchman." She had no idea where the patrol might be at the moment, but she hoped she sounded confident. Her blood rushed in her ears. "Get out of here, or you'll regret it."

The man gave her an appraising look and spit on the muddy stones lining the garden patio.

He reached out toward her. She stepped back again into the dark, and her eyes widened. She needed to go forward, toward the street and anyone who might be walking past. He grinned and shuffled closer.

She took a deep breath and shoved him.

The man shook his head, surprised. He gave her a sneer, and she held her hands up, ready still. Then he spat again. He walked away, muttering. The ribbons tying his breeches off at his calves were orange, and for a moment, the color flooded Judith's mind. She leaned her shoulder against the inn's freezing wall and, with her eyes pinched shut for a moment, tried to steady her breath. The cold air ripped at her lungs.

Judith peered again into the window, but each time she turned away from the street, she felt the gaping, uncertain evening lurking over her shoulder. The auction inside had continued, and, for a moment, she glimpsed painted fingers around a glittering wineglass. Or so she thought, but the crowd swallowed the image. She should have thought to bring Abraham, her younger brother. During the day, women in Haarlem could easily wander alone, but as the light faded, so did her safety. She scanned the garden and adjacent side street again. At twenty, Abraham was old enough to protect her and canny enough not to ask questions about the auction.

She looked back inside the inn, but now she couldn't locate the auctioneer. The tables were still crowded with half-emptied tankards, stacks of ivory gaming tiles, and even a few women. But there was no sign of the man in the azurite-colored doublet.

She dug her fingernails into the windowsill, and her gaze fluttered between the street and her anxious search for the auctioneer. Shame held her fixed, yet a panic began to circle in her gut. The supplies for that painting were expensive, and each week she remained trapped in her apprenticeship with Frans de Grebber was a week that saw another young painter set up shop. Soon, the blacksmiths' and bakers' walls would hold all the moralizing paintings and Bible scenes they could hold, and no one would take a chance on an unknown woman artist. The evening's low light eased toward darkness. She had not brought a lantern and would have to leave before curfew and winter's early sunset consigned all law-abiding citizens to the safety of their hearths. A church bell tolled, but she lost count of the chimes as she switched her attention back and forth between the street and the window. A cloud of male voices rumbled somewhere nearby, and she froze. After the sound passed, Judith counted to twenty, mustered her courage, and walked around to the front of the inn. She stepped through the door.

Inside, a chaos of voices and music greeted her. She whispered a prayer that no one she knew would be present, or none would recognize her. Still, a few heads turned, likely surprised at the sober brown dress and simple white cambric cap covering her chestnut hair, so different from the brightly dressed women scattered about the room like harvested flowers. And the fool had taken her for a whore.

She paused and blinked, overwhelmed for a moment. She grabbed the elbow of a passing serving girl.

"Excuse me. Is the man in the azurite doublet here? With the pictures. Do you know where he is?"

The girl held four empty tankards from her fingers as though they were misbehaving kittens caught by the scruff of the neck. She tilted her nose upwards while she looked over Judith's head, evidently weighing the balance of courtesy and her pressing work.

"I didn't see any pictures," she said finally. Her eyes settled upon Judith. "It's been busy, we don't always notice those things. Unless you've got a name? Maybe it's someone I know." She gave a smile but took a half step away.

"An azurite-colored doublet. Blue, I mean. With a touch of green. He was wearing a blue doublet. He was here." Judith reached toward her but did not have the courage to grab her again.

The serving maid shrugged. "Sorry." She walked away.

Judith looked around and tried to quell the distress rising in her throat. Brown doublets and moss-green bodices filled the room, but she saw no auctioneer. She had been foolish to imagine she could monitor the sale.

The drinkers made the room throb around her. She must be wrong, he must be here, and she searched through the flushed crowd. A face caught her attention, but it was a young man who painted in Dirck Hals's workshop. The sort of man to ask questions and tell tales about her presence in the inn. She spun on her heel and rushed outside.

She rubbed her arms and wished her safety did not depend on abiding by the curfew. The auctioneer could not have gone far. She could look for him. Then a stranger strode past her and gave her a lurid glance. She turned toward her master's home in the smothered light.

There was nothing left to do but try to sleep and hasten dawn's arrival. Judith quietly climbed the stairs to the room in Frans de Grebber's loft that she shared with his daughter, Maria. Without lighting a candle, she pulled on her nightdress. In Maria's bed, a few feet away, her friend's breath ebbed and flowed in peaceful sleep. Barefoot, Judith crossed the cold floorboards to Maria's bedside, where she could see her friend's form in the shadows. She reached out and held her hand over Maria's head, and Maria's wayward hairs brushed her palm. Maria exhaled and stirred but did not wake. Judith turned away and crawled onto her own straw-stuffed mattress. She pulled the quilt to her chin. Maria, her only real friend, would not have to worry about scraping together enough coins for the St. Luke's Guild fee. Her father was a successful, prominent painter. Though no woman had yet joined the Guild as a master, Judith suspected Maria, if she worked hard at it, could gain the other members' approval. But as far as Judith knew, Maria had no interest in a painter's life. Judith had little else. Of course, she could try to find a husband. She was plain but hardworking enough to attract a weaver or cobbler, some humble man. But she hoped for something far better than a husband: a life spent turning colors and oil into wonder. She stared up toward the invisible ceiling, concealed by the dark night. She had her talent and her dreams, but if only she had not lost that painting. And it was gone. The agony of those vanished hours and coins pressed upon her, and she exhaled a near-growl that caused Maria to murmur in her sleep. Judith clenched her jaw and watched the darkness.

Chapter 2

THE MORNING LIGHT WAS STILL low, and Maria squinted in concentration. She tapped the painting with her tiny brush, leaving more air than pigment on the small flame she was coloring. A little brighter. She had forgotten to put on her extra sleeves and the new woolen stockings, and her skin prickled with goosebumps beneath her two tunics. The house was too cold for her to be up painting, yet she had no choice. She had little work time left, as her father and the apprentices were rumbling about the house and beginning their morning habits and breakfast. Soon they would wander into the workshop, and her brief solitude would end.

The household knew by now how she spent her mornings, up to seize the sun's light at the first hint of late dawn, while everyone else dressed and ate breakfast, but still she insisted on keeping the painting veiled in their presence. The portrait was for her eyes, and her purposes, only. Maria could not explain her project to anyone, not even Judith. She took a deep breath. She looked at the sheen of the wet paint upon her wooden panel, and she wished she could allow herself to show Judith. But, no, someone else's eyes upon the painting would stain her work. Every night, Maria silently invoked her intention as her fingers roamed the circle of her rosary, and she prayed nothing would happen to her before she could purge her sins with this painting. Now, more than ever, she needed an offering. She could not marry Samuel Ampzing. The poet was almost two decades her senior and, worse, a minister in the Reformed Church. His affection was a punishment she deserved, yes, for her endless litany of failings. But she hoped to earn herself a way out.

She intensified the black behind the flame to sharpen the contrast. With her brush poised, she nibbled at her lip and examined the whole painting. Perhaps she had exhausted her inspiration for today. But she could work endlessly, seize the muscles in her wrists with the agony of precision, and the painting might never be good enough. With less than two weeks left before Samuel was coming to Haarlem, time was running out.

The woman's large eyes were pools of ebony surrounded by soft gray. The picture displayed Maria's full lips, heavy eyebrows, and long face. She had used a mirror to paint this portrait, but she did not think of the woman in the painting as herself. When Maria had started the work, she wanted to ask Judith to model for the portrait, even though she doubted her friend would rest her own brush and sit. One morning, while the two women dressed in the cool dawn, Maria had opened her mouth to ask. But she saw Judith's sure fingers tying the knot on her bodice before rushing to her latest picture, and Judith's lips murmured the list of painting tasks she recited each morning. The question disappeared back into Maria's throat.

Now, across the room, the floorboards creaked. Judith stood in the entryway, a slice of bread still in her hand and a crumb upon her dark bodice. The smell of the morning loaf wafted after her, and Maria could hear the hum of young voices coming from the kitchen at the rear of the house. She draped a cloth over her painted wood panel, but left her fingers resting at the edge.

"I won't spy," Judith said. She took a step closer and held out the bread. "You've been so busy, so I brought this for you. And there's a little cheese left in there. In case you wanted some."

Maria took a step forward, then stopped. "It's kind of you, but I'm fasting today." She gave an apologetic smile. "Thank you."

Judith looked away and tucked the bread into the waist of her skirt. "Is it a saint's day?" she asked without lifting her gaze.

Maria shook her head. "No." She did not know how to explain the pleasure of hunger's sharp knife cleaving her body. "Are you starting now?"

Judith pushed a strand of chestnut hair back under her white cap, rubbed her hands to warm them, and walked over to the long table of painting supports. Six wooden boards lay there, drying after receiving the first layer of chalk and glue grounding, and ready for the second layer of lead-white and ocher. Above the table, rising almost to the ceiling, a window glowed with the timid light.

"Yes, I've got to finish these today." Judith's tone was neutral, but Maria knew she hated the work. The drudgery of preparing the wooden surfaces irked her, not because she thought herself above it, though Maria suspected perhaps she did, but because the task fell to Judith regardless of who else was in the workshop. Even the youngest of the apprentices who had cycled through the workshop over the years mostly bypassed that work. Boys, all of them. Judith never complained, and Maria loved her the more for it.

"Will you show me the painting you're working on?" Judith asked as she pulled on her long-sleeved smock. "It's obviously important to you. I'd love to see what it is."

Maria bit her lip and dug her fingernails into the easel's wood. Judith waited.

The two other apprentices barreled into the workshop and filled it with laughter and the scratch of their new men's voices. Judith remained looking at Maria with her eyebrows raised for another breath, then she shrugged and turned to her work.

Maria's father, Frans de Grebber, entered and sat on the stool in front of his easel. He had curly gray hair cropped above his ears, and a beard that was more silver than brown. After a moment of dabbing at his portrait of a spice merchant, he looked up.

"Judith, I'll need you to sit with Herold this afternoon to supervise his sketch of the new client we're doing the portrait for. The wine-seller."

Judith frowned, but she nodded in agreement. Herold, the younger apprentice, flashed the other boy a triumphant smile. Taking the first sketch was a prestigious prize.

Frans de Grebber shifted in his chair and then adjusted his easel to better catch the light. The light always seemed insufficient during winter.

"Maria, this painting of yours. You'll have to show it to me soon, so I can discuss it with potential buyers." Frans ran a thumb down his silver beard, still seasoned with brown like sparse wood dust on a tile floor. "Soon." He narrowed his eyes, and then returned his gaze to his own work.

Maria wanted to argue, but it was easier to say nothing. She couldn't show the painting to him, and she certainly could not let him think he was going to be able to sell it. He wouldn't understand. Once, after her mother died, Maria had asked her father if she could join a convent. She wanted to spend her hours walking through ancient stone hallways and kneeling in prayer to the Holy Trinity. But there were no religious orders in the United Provinces, and her father laughed when she asked if she might travel to the Spanish Low Countries to find a sisterhood there. He needed her help, he said, and insisted she would grow bored with such an isolated life. He was wrong, but she would not defy him.

The midday meal brought the household together around the large table. Maria ate nothing, and no one remarked upon it. Across the rough-hewn tabletop, Judith picked at her plate of stewed duck and vegetables, and then stood and begged Frans de Grebber's pardon for departing early. Maria sought some explanation in Judith's expression, but the other woman's face was a mask. She said she would return for the afternoon's work, then turned and left.

"Where's she going?" asked the oldest apprentice, the son of a United East India Company official who was taking advantage of his newfound wealth by sending his scion to dabble in painting.

Maria waited to hear the others' speculation before she realized he was addressing her. The boy, some six years younger than her, had both elbows propped on the table and was leaning toward her, his full-lipped mouth slightly open while he waited.

"I don't know."

The other apprentice, Herold, laughed. He brushed his fingers over the linen piping decorating the seam of his doublet. "Of course you do. We know you girls share all your secrets up in that room, whispering into the night." He was young but had never shown any fear of Maria, even though at twenty-five she was old enough to have her own household. She turned to give him a sharp retort, but what came to mind was too embarrassing to say. She didn't know because she and Judith didn't talk much now. Their exhausted exchanges now were nothing like when Judith had first joined the household, when she was thirteen and Maria fifteen, and they could talk until the night seemed endless. Then, the young, skinny Judith whispered with such fierce passion about her dreams of being independent that her eyes seemed to glow in the dark. And when the strain of missing her family grew too great, Judith would crawl into Maria's bed and beg the older girl to tell her stories. With their hands intertwined, Maria would tell tales from the Bible, or gossip she had heard from the servants, or, when the night stretched so long that it seemed the two girls were the only ones left in Haarlem, she would make up her own stories about two friends whose love was so sound they might give their lives for each other. Always, Judith held her hand and whispered, "One more, Maria. Tell me just one more."

Herold laughed again.

"I don't know," she repeated, keeping her voice even.

Maria's father interrupted with a cough. Meals were typically quiet, and he rarely got involved in any apprentice chatter. He sat at the end of the table, where he used his fingers to peel the duck flesh away from the bone. He looked at each of them, gave another shallow cough, and returned his gaze to his plate.

When he was not looking, Maria dipped her thumb into her beer flagon and ferried a drop of the weak brew to her lips. The drink did not count as breaking her fast, and it gave her something to consume so as not to draw attention to herself while everyone ate. She loved quenching her thirst drop by bright drop. It was yet another secret pleasure, and of course the secrecy enriched her delight. Like the painting. Or like the clandestine Mass that she and her father attended, along with the handful of other Catholic families who refused to join the Reformed Church. There was a visiting priest in town this weekend, and when he held Mass in this week's secret house, Maria would taste the consecrated Host, the actual Body of

Christ. She closed her eyes and savored the anticipation. When she looked up, her father was still intent upon his duck, and she dipped her thumb again.

After a few minutes, Maria wiped her hands on a napkin, the purchase of which was a rare concession by her father to her deceased mother's French-influenced tastes, and she stood. The household was still lounging around the table, and she had time to look at her painting.

Alone in the workshop she uncovered the portrait. She sighed. The flat images held nothing of the sublime she aimed for, nothing of the deep and physical joy she had hoped to capture, the way a sail catches and harnesses a salty sea breeze. Here, on her painted panel, the woman's eyes did not gaze at the flame held in her hands, but rather at a spot to the side of the candle. And Maria had only outlined the woman's dress, which needed to fold softly over her arms and waist and display both the woman and her light. It had taken Maria four weeks to get this far in stolen moments and rare bits of solitude, and now only the two weeks before Lent remained to perfect her painting. She could not let herself fail, not with this chance to atone for how she had failed her mother, grown distant from Judith, and somehow misled Samuel into affection. She heard footsteps and swung the cloth back over her work.

Chapter 3

JUDITH HAD LITTLE TIME TO herself that afternoon. She hurried down Korte Barteljorisstraat, just off the broad main square, to the three-story brick linenwares shop between the bakery and a cobbler's house. The street was rather wide here, enough for two small carts to pass each other, and she examined the way the low sun's rays struck the windows of the upper floors, while behind her the musical tap from the cobbler's hammer skittered across the air. She stood shivering in the cold outside, just beyond the wooden awning at the front of the house, and waited for the linen-seller to finish with the customer blocking his doorstep, a stern woman in saffron-colored skirts and dark fur with fine lace peeping out at the cuffs. The cobbler's sound reminded her of driving nails into a coffin, and she shuddered. This room might be her only chance. Rooms in this part of town, a safe neighborhood with handsome brick frontages where she could invite customers, rarely came on the market. Most deals were made between friends and acquaintances, men who already knew one another and would never think to advertise publicly. But Judith knew no one. She was alone and, worse, a woman. She stood up straighter. It didn't matter that she lacked connections, or that her family's name was disgraced by her parents' behavior. That didn't mean she was worthless. She squeezed her palms shut, relaxed her fingers, and looked up at the window again. The paint was peeling from the black shutters.

She stepped closer. Linen the color of fallow fields lay piled under the wooden awning, but the craftsman kept his finer pieces inside the house's dark entryway. Beyond, as was customary, lay the man's living space. The linen-seller was raven-haired and thin, with an uneven gait, yet still he reminded her of her father: a thick, sixty-some-year-old man. Or so he was the last time she had seen him, five years ago. Her father was once a linen smallworker. He'd created delicate pieces for years, and there was something about the trade that infused the manners of its practitioners. Maybe it was how they turned their wrists, ready to flick a shuttle between fine threads.

The customer walked out, and Judith laid down the fold of cloth she had been examining to pass the time and distract her thoughts. She took a deep breath and lifted her chin.

"I'm about to close for midday, but I can help you if it's quick," said the proprietor.

"I'm Judith Leyster," she said. Her hands began to shake, and she clutched them together. "I sent you a note. About the workshop."

"Judith?" He let his mouth fall open for a moment, and then closed it before he might be accused of being rude. "I had assumed the J stood for Jan. Or something. Like the other applicant."

"It stands for Judith. Not that it makes a difference, I assume." She paused, and he said nothing. "Women can rent spaces too. Catharijne Cuijpers has her linenwares shop the block over." She knew she sounded defensive, but she couldn't help it.

"Yes, fine work she does too. But she's a widow. I hadn't thought . . ."

"I'm not a widow. But I'm entitled all the same. My master, Frans de Grebber, will hear of it, if you don't give me a fair chance." She did not want to tell Frans she hoped to rent her own workshop, but the painter was well known. An empty threat, but it was all she could think of. She dug her fingernails deep into her palms.

He pressed his lips together, and resistance began to cloud his face.

"Please?" She held her palms out, open, and prayed the crimson half-moons from her nails wouldn't show. "I'm honorable. I want to rent the space for my painting."

The linen-seller brushed his hands against his trousers and thought for a moment. He coughed. "It's no matter, I suppose. Tenants are tenants, and you're right, women do run businesses. I hadn't expected . . . but, no, you're right. Would you like to see the space?" He walked to his front door and closed it.

"Yes, of course." Judith tried to smooth her expression and conceal her anxiety about his mention of another applicant. With other interested renters in the market, she would have a difficult time negotiating any reduction in rent. And Jan—Jan who? They passed the linen-seller's living quarters, and then she followed him to climb a creaking staircase. The shopkeeper introduced himself as Chrispijn de Mildt. From her vantage point a few steps below him, Judith appraised his well-made but worn leather boots and hoped he needed a renter at any price. Which Jan, though? Which of the many aspiring young artists could he be? And men, all of them, that was certain. A tremor of nerves coursed through her stomach.

At the top of the stairs, Chrispijn de Mildt pulled a set

of brass keys from his waist pocket and unlocked a door. The hinges creaked as he opened it, and a wall of stale air rushed out.

They entered the room, and Chrispijn stood at the entrance with his hands clasped together near his waist. Judith walked across the dusty floorboards to the two wide windows facing the street. Below, the street was quiet, even though the main square was half a block away. The brick frontages and white-washed doorways of the neighbors' shops were not as close as she had feared. She took a deep breath before turning to face the wall to her left. There, she ran her fingers over the bone-white plaster. Already she wanted the place so badly her voice grew weightless.

"I'd be able to hang items on the wall? Props, supplies?" She kept her fingers to the cold plaster but chanced a glance over her shoulder at him. He had touched a thumb to his nose in thought.

"What would you use to hang them?"

"Nails." What else could he be thinking of? The plaster was rough beneath her fingertips, and she raised her hand to her nose to sniff them, but she could only detect the sharp bite of linseed oil and pigment permanently infused in her skin.

"Nails. I suppose nails would be fine. I might need to charge you some for it, though."

She turned to face him. "How much?"

"We'll discuss that in a bit. Downstairs, after you've finished your look around."

Judith nodded, as if money were of secondary importance, and as if she had not heard the peremptory tone to his voice. She reached into her pocket, the pouch hung from her waist, and took out a handful of buttons. It was a habit of hers to carry around the components of a painting so she could consider them, learn their curves and secrets, whenever she had a free moment. She crouched down to place the buttons on the floor. It was the best way to examine the light.

Her skirts circled around her as she knelt in front of the small collection. The sunlight washed over the buttons, and they seemed to grow in response, losing their boundaries in the lustrous sheen of their colors. One, a shell button, swirled like the light had unlocked an ocean hidden within. The light was perfect. She had to have this space.

"The light is dim," she said with a frown. This was how people negotiated, or so she guessed from seeing Frans de Grebber with his customers. She scooped up the buttons and dropped them back into her pocket bag. "And the noise isn't ideal for working conditions."

Chrispijn de Mildt clasped his hands together again. "I would have thought it was ideal, but the other fellow also . . . Well, that doesn't mean much. Look at this. It's a great space. Where else in Haarlem can you find a whole room available?"

Judith shrugged. "Plenty of places." Of course, that wasn't true. She blushed and fingered the buttons through the cloth of her pocket. "What are you asking for it?"

"No, no, not here." He waved for her to follow him out of the room. "Business downstairs, where we can sit, be comfortable. You artists. I swear."

Judith frowned as they descended. This Jan, then, had also gotten so far as to discuss the rent. But he must not have signed an agreement, since Chrispijn was still offering the place. The linen-seller might even be leading her on, intending for her to think she had competition. The thought gave her hope.

Twenty minutes later Judith exited the linen shop, and she had to press her lips together firmly to keep a smile from escaping. The rent was enormous, beyond what she could even in her most optimistic scenarios hope to earn in a month, but he needed a tenant. She could tell. He had held his breath, for an instant, after he told her the price. As if he needed her approval. And he did not, in the end, seem to mind she was a woman. Outside in the cold street, she sidestepped a frosted mud puddle. All she needed was to save a little more, to pay the first few months in advance, and then negotiate with him after she had signed. The other artist who had looked at the place did not have the resources to rent. Though, neither did she. Not yet.

Chapter 4

Still smiling, Judith walked south through the winding streets, toward the weaving district. She crossed a bridge over one of the smaller canals, and at the other side, she stopped.

A funeral procession turned from a narrow lane toward the bridge. The silent mourners wore the customary black robes, and the coffin was draped in a black cloth ornamented with the mallet insignia of the Masonry Guild. Tears wet the pall-bearers' cheeks. A few wilted daffodils were scattered on top of the coffin, the flowers indicating the youth of the deceased. Judith stood still and watched. Would the St. Luke's Guild someday be responsible for burying her? A number of the mourners trailing after the coffin had pale, wasted faces. She couldn't tell if they were contending with grief or illness. Maybe both. She clasped her hands together and waited for the small procession to pass.

She continued walking, past smaller houses and through the mud-coated streets. Outside the inn where the illegal auction had been held, the boards covering the gutters that ran along the sides of the street were bowed and filthy, and she hesitated to step on them. In the faded light two nights ago she had not noticed their poor condition. She lifted her skirts, bringing a rush of cold air against her legs, and stepped over the little bridge to push the battered door open.

Inside, the place was warm and surprisingly bright. An amber fire hummed in the hearth to her right, and men clustered around the handful of occupied tables. A large man in an apron carried a crate over his head and set it down by the rear door with a clatter.

"Sir, you work here?" Judith plucked at the starched lace collar around her neck and then, realizing how nervous she looked, pulled her hand to her side.

"That's right. I run the place." He looked her up and down. "You're not looking for work, are you?"

"No." She stood up straight. "I'm looking for someone. Well, two people. Either one of them will do."

He used the apron tied around his gut to wipe each of his hands in turn. He arched his eyebrow and waited.

"One of them was in here two evenings ago, selling some paintings. He had an azurite doublet. I couldn't say what cut, exactly, but the color was a deep blue. Like the ocean at the horizon, or . . ." She closed her mouth and paused for a moment. "The other man worked with the first one. This man was tall, taller than you even, with blond hair and a nose that looked screwed on crooked. One side larger than the other. Have you seen either of them?"

His eyes flickered at the corners when she mentioned the crooked nose. Judith saw details in faces others might have let glide past unnoticed. It was a product of her training, her hours staring at the angle of a model's smile and discerning the exact color of a curl lying damp on a forehead.

"Maybe a stuiver to make up for the time you've taken out of a busy day." She held out a coin and, after a moment, he took it. His fingertips were rough.

"I remember the man in blue, but I don't know anything about him. Probably not from Haarlem, if I had to guess. But that nose, that reminds me of a type who lives on my brother's street. A few blocks over. Not the best place for a lady, though."

She shrugged. He considered her for a moment, and then told her the street.

"The man I'm thinking of," he said, "he has an accent. French, or something. Sound right?"

"I don't know. Maybe. I'd like to get a look at him and see."

The innkeeper nodded. "Don't mention me. I don't need any trouble."

"Trouble?"

"You never know these days." He gave her another calculating look and then walked across the room to heft up another crate of dirty dishes. Their conversation was over.

The bells tolled the hour. It was too late now to continue her search, and she was almost late for her appointment to oversee Herold's sketch. She turned back toward the De Grebber house. After a few blocks, she stopped at a small intersection, where one corner was occupied by a cooper's shop, as advertised by the yellow cask painted above the entrance lintel. Her breath gave a frosted cloud, and she looked down the narrow street to her right, toward the home and workshop of Frans Hals, Haarlem's most prominent painter. He painted lively figures whose emotions throbbed beneath the layers of pigment. Judith did not like to admit it, but she was jealous of the man's skill. And his success.

"Judith, there you are."

She turned around to see her brother, Abraham, regarding

her with that half smile she loved and his arms crossed over his chest. He was tall and thin, and his eyes had the shape and silver flash of minnows.

"Were you looking for me? I'm not as hard to find as you are." She tapped his cheek with her index finger, and his smile broadened for a moment. Abraham didn't have the constancy to hold an apprenticeship, so he skipped from job to job, like the oar of a boat dipping in and out of the water. He seemed afraid to grow attached to anything but Judith, and sometimes she feared he was drifting from her too.

He glanced behind her at Frans Hals's workshop. "Are you going in there? I'd rather not join you." His hands, pink from the cold, plucked at his mended breeches.

Judith gave him a quick kiss and nudged him into motion, walking toward the main square.

"No, no time for Frans today. I was looking for someone, but now I have to head back to the workshop."

"That's mysterious. The someone, I mean."

"Not really. He's a man I have some painting business with."

"What's his name? Maybe I know him."

Judith pretended to be distracted by a few swallows whose flight dipped over their heads, and then she laughed. She couldn't lie to Abraham, no matter how embarrassed of her dealings she might be. "I don't know his name," she said finally. "But I can take care of it myself."

He nodded. "You tell me if you change your mind." He stopped walking and held her elbow, pulling her to a halt beside him. "Help was what I wanted to talk to you about. I was hoping I could borrow a few coins. Not much, maybe fifty stuivers or so. I had to miss three days of work, I was sick, but the rent is due and . . ." His voice trailed off.

"Fifty stuivers? 'Sblood, Abraham, that's nearly three guilders. That's a lot of money."

"I know." He looked at his feet. "But if I don't pay the rent this month, I'll lose my bed."

Judith sighed. "No, I'm sorry. I can't now. And you still owe me from last time."

"I know, I was almost ready to pay it off, and then—"

"Don't, Abraham. I can't."

He looked down again at his feet, and her eyes followed down to the cobblestones. His left boot was cracked and nearly split along the side. He scraped some mud from the sole onto a protruding stone.

"If I don't pay the rent, the landlord'll have me at the magistrate's. It's enough to lose a hand."

She shook her head. "It's more than rent, isn't it?"

Abraham pulled his arm away. "If I don't pay him, he'll find a way to collect his price."

Judith stepped back. She tried to set her expression, but her younger brother sagged in the street, and he wouldn't meet her gaze.

He could, she knew, decide to leave Haarlem. Like their parents, who five years earlier had accumulated such debt that the city declared them bankrupt and the Reformed Church expelled them. God condemned the irresolute and insolvent, the minister had declared. So Jan and Trijn Leyster packed their few belongings onto a borrowed cart and drove out of town, as the sun was setting and the town gates closing. They gave their two children no farewell and only sent a scrawled letter, written by some literate stranger, some weeks later. By which point Judith was frantic with worry. Even while she lived away from Jan and Trijn's home, she had attended church with them every Sunday. Her parents were her touchstone, and then they had disappeared. When she showed Abraham the letter, he grabbed the small bit of paper from her hand, crumpled it up, and threw it into a nearby canal. Judith gasped as the precious paper, the reverse side of which she could have used to draw, floated away half submerged. Their parents did not deserve a response, Abraham said with tears in his eyes. He swore he would never contact them again, and to Judith's knowledge, he had not.

No, she would not be her parents. Money was not more important than family. She took a deep breath.

"It's fine, Abraham. I can lend you the money. It sets me back, you understand? I'll get you the coins in a few days."

"Thank you." His face glowed rosy for a moment. He gave her a brief embrace, and resumed walking, his arm entwined with hers. "I'll pay you back soon, I promise."

They walked together for a few more blocks, and Judith steered their path away from the linen-seller's house with the clear light on Korte Barteljorisstraat. She didn't tell Abraham about the workshop, though ordinarily she would have. She couldn't think about the rent money she would need to find, not yet. For it would be her rent. She would find a way.

Chapter 5

March

It was midday, and Maria had the workshop to herself. Everyone else was either resting or elsewhere, so she stole away to work. She lifted the cover off her portrait and frowned. She'd had to restrict her palette to mostly ochres and grays, the less expensive pigments her father did not mind giving to her. The somber colors suited her, mostly, for there was little in her concept of pain and penance that merited a lush blue or vibrant green, and the modest colors of earth and flesh reflected better her concept.

In all her years helping in her father's workshop, this was the first time she had tried to capture an aspect of herself, or even anything personal. Her labor had always been rote and in her father's service, and that satisfied her. She loved the soaring feeling that filled her when she regarded others' fine artwork, but there was little need for her own. Until now.

Samuel's most recent letter had arrived three Saturdays earlier. He had written to her on and off in the five years since he surveyed Haarlem's art community for his book and had thus spent more time in his hometown. Then, she and Judith had been thrilled to read of themselves in his account. For nights, Judith would read out loud: "Again. 'And also the daughter I have to praise. Who ever saw a painting made by the hand of a daughter? See here another'—that's me—'who paints with a good, keen sense.' Do you think I have good, keen sense, Maria?" Judith would hug the book to her chest and fall back onto the straw mattress, smiling.

Maria wrote him a brief note of thanks, and to her surprise, he responded with an avalanche of affection. He had seen her as a girl, certainly, but now that she was a young woman, he was struck by her beauty, he said. And though he kept his courtship respectful, writing letters even when he was in town, Maria was baffled. She mentioned it to Judith, who laughed. "You could certainly do worse," her friend had said, and though Maria protested she wanted nothing to do with the man, Judith persisted in teasing her about it. Eventually, the letters stopped coming, and Judith's jokes tapered off.

Until last year, when Maria saw Samuel in the Grote Markt. It was summer then, and he was listening to an itinerant preacher at the edge of the square, in front of an ornately carved doorway. When Samuel saw Maria, his face brightened into a smile.

"It's a pleasure to see you again," he said, approaching before she could disappear into the crowd. "I'm sorry I troubled you with my correspondence so long ago. I married, you know, but my wife died two years past." He paused to watch her reaction, and she dipped her head in sympathy. "I would have told you I was back in Haarlem permanently now, but I wasn't sure the news would be welcome."

"It's pleasant to see you," she said, and there was some truth to it. He was a charming man, in his earnest way, with large brown eyes and a well-trimmed beard. If only he weren't a heretic and wanderer.

He coughed, and then again, and a spasm took over him. She looked at her feet.

"I'm sorry, I seem to be recovering from something," he said when he regained his voice. "Can I walk with you?"

They strolled around the market, and Maria told Samuel what news she had heard recently of Haarlem's painters—that Frans Hals was once again mired in debt, and that Jacob de Gheyn had died. She suspected he already knew all this, but Samuel listened, then asked about her own painting.

"I do little now," she said, fixing her eyes on the roofline over his shoulder. "I mostly help my father."

"I'm sure you're a good helpmeet," he said. He reached over and drew his thumb down her cheek. She froze. "I must attend to some business, but I'll visit later."

Maria was too startled by his touch to object. Samuel nodded then left her. In spite of the warm sun, her cheek felt frozen as she walked home frowning. She went directly to her father in his workshop and told him she had seen the poet. To her surprise, he was delighted.

"It'll be good to have him back in town. Was he writing another account? The last was so helpful for business. Did he say anything?"

"He said he would visit me here later, but mentioned little about painting," she said.

Frans de Grebber raised an eyebrow. "He seems fond of you. That's wonderful, Maria. Think of the advantages such a connection would bring for us."

They spoke little more about it, and Samuel never came. He sent a letter apologizing, but wrote nothing else until this latest letter. He was again ill, he said, and he could think of little else but her. That he would cry to leave this world without knowing her company better. And he begged her to marry him. She burned the letter in the hearth before anyone else could see it.

Maria prayed the rosary every night, but now her entreaties needed greater strength. She hated to injure the man by turning him down, yet she could never marry a preacher of the Reformed Church. So she needed God's help. One night, during her cycle of the rosary, a remembered image came to her. One of her father's copybooks held a woodblock print that had long intrigued her: it showed a young woman clad in rags and holding a single, glowing candle. As a child, Maria had brushed her fingertips over the ink and wondered what the flame illuminated, and what it did not. What lay beyond the candle's gift of light, outside the printed lines? Or was it simply the light itself that mattered, like the light within the soul? The darkness beyond might be as meaningless as death. Or meaningful? She loved that she could not decide. And the vision of that woodblock inspired her. God was asking for an offering.

Clearly, that old, adored print was the appropriate subject. It was not vanity to paint herself onto this flame-bearing woman. The woman was a sinner, and so was she. Painting herself into this image was acknowledgment, which was, in turn, humility.

Now Maria sat on her stool in front of the easel and considered the panel in the clouded light. She strove to capture an acknowledgment of both sin and redemption, shadow and flame, in the piece, yet the painting fell short. She closed her eyes and felt wrung out, with an empty, bitter feeling in her chest, as if a hound clawed at her soul. Her father would have had the skill, certainly. Judith too. Maria squeezed her eyes shut more tightly. This was her sacrifice and her struggle. She would have to make the painting sufficient using her own resources.

Perhaps some blue, a hint of rich indigo in the black shadow behind the woman's head might be enough of a hint at redemption. A reminder of the Virgin's celestial robes and of the purity of Heaven. She stood up from her stool by her easel and walked over to her father's pigment cabinet. A jar of smalt rested on a nearby tabletop, but the resulting blue wouldn't have the depth that azurite could grant. No, smalt wouldn't serve. Azurite was expensive, and Frans de Grebber kept it all locked away. Maybe she could borrow some. She jiggled the small latch, but the lock held. Maria placed her hands on her hips and regarded the wooden cabinet, and then the empty room. She could ask her father, who likely sat in his bedroom down the hall working on his ledger book. Or she could buy her own. She liked the idea of having her own little pot of azurite, a tiny stash for her own artistic extravagances. If she spent her sparse coins, the painting would have even more meaning.

Maria had a few guilders she had saved over the years, and she dropped the coins into the cloth pocket tied at her waist. She left the house without saying a word to anyone, easily done as the boys were resting and listening to her older brother Pieter, who was visiting and playing the lute. Outside, the street was peppered with shoppers, vendors, and children. She nodded at a neighbor and hurried on. A few blocks from her home, a rectangular placard covered in black silk and edged in lace hung from the front door of a house. The device meant that a baby had been born, but stillborn, as indicated by the black. Maria had to stifle the urge to make the forbidden sign of the cross. That poor family, burdened by broken hopes—or so she imagined. She thought of her mother, weakened from the stillborn death of her last child. She had never seemed to recover; the heartache, which Maria had been powerless to remedy, eventually dragged her into the grave four years later. How Maria had cried at her mother's deathbed, wishing she could have been enough to anchor her mother in this world, even if the stillborn baby had departed. Maria gave a heavy nod in the direction of the house.

The shop was near the docks, on the northeastern side of town, a fairly long walk. She skirted the edge of the busy Grote Markt square and crossed a tree-lined canal. Judith had grown up in this northern neighborhood. Her father's brewery, bought with the ambition of leaving linen work behind, was once there, on the corner where Maria turned from Bakenessergracht to the quay that ran along the Sparen River. Now Jan Leyster's low brick building was a warehouse, leased to the United East India Company, judging by the round smell of nutmeg lingering near the door. Sea birds swooped overhead, and among the crowd was a beautiful woman who tilted her head and grimaced as she walked with mincing steps.

The supply shop was the lower level of a broad house, and the front door hung open, in spite of the cold. A young boy threw a rag ball against the wall at a small spot not covered in wooden panels or finished art: displays for the merchant's fine quality pigments. The rest of the wall radiated colors, from the carmine red of the precious cochineal to the blinding purity of the lead white. The boy stopped when he noticed her and stood looking expectantly at her.

"You work here?" she asked.

He nodded.

Maria raised an eyebrow, but the boy said nothing else.

"I would like some azurite. The smallest bit."

He nodded again, walked into a room deeper in the house. He returned quickly with a bronze key held delicately in his fingers, which he used to open a trunk lying next to a large table, bare except for two sets of scales. After rummaging around in the trunk for a moment, he lifted a pewter scoop filled with coarsely ground radiant blue pebbles. He poured it out, almost shard by shard, and scrutinized the needle on the scale.

"That look right to you?" he asked her, in a soft, ringing voice.

"Yes." She glanced around, hoping no one she knew would enter the shop. Especially no one from her house.

He told her the price, and she paid it without hesitation, even though it was nearly the amount of all the coins in her pocket. He twisted it in a scrap of paper, and Maria left.

She felt as if the small package emanated warmth into her cold palm, and she let a smile play across her face. She decided to return home a different way, to avoid the busy riverside and cut through a smaller street. A few dogs scampered ahead, tussling over a picked-over bone. They were sleek enough to belong to a home, although she was not sure any of the modest households nearby would want to feed a dog. Then one growled at her, baring its teeth, and she froze. The dog turned away, and she walked on, unsettled.

She turned down a narrow side lane, where the tall buildings cast the cobblestones in shadow, and the chilled air grew still and quiet. No windows faced out onto this street, and the mud coating the street's stones swallowed the tap of her footfalls. She quickened her pace.

Without any sound or warning, a hand smashed over her mouth. A wide, rough palm drew her, smothered, back against a man's body.

"Come on then," a rough man whispered in her ear.

Maria tried to scream but his palm stifled it. Every inch of his body pressed against her back, and she writhed and tried to pull away. She had never felt another body like that, not against her entire length: her thighs, spine, buttocks. She was horrified.

He pushed her over to the wall, and she held out her arms

to keep her face from smashing against the brick. Her knuckles scraped against the rough wall, though she hardly felt the burn. He kept one hand on her face, pulling her head painfully back, and his other hand began fumbling around her waist. Even then, drenched in fear, her first thought was a plea that he not take the azurite, and she kept her fingers wrapped around the package. But then, his hand moved lower, grabbing at her skirts, and she would have gladly given him the blue pigment.

He tried to thrust his hand between her legs, and she thrashed about. In doing so, his other hand slipped from the vice grip on her mouth, and one of his fingers plowed, filthy, into her mouth. She bore down. The sharp taste of blood arose on her tongue, and the man cursed. But still he held on to her.

He pulled his free hand back and then bashed her on the side of her face. She reeled, yet he kept his hold on her. She was halfway facing him now, and she glimpsed blond hair and an unshaven face. But his features were only a shifting shadow of a man, not a portrait.

"Come, let's see that cunt," he said and grabbed at her breasts. The hand slipped again from over her mouth.

She screamed.

He grabbed at her body, and she stumbled. She screamed and twisted, and he thrust one hand at her neck and the other below, where her legs met. He swiped at her face again, although it did not hurt as much. She felt snared in a moment that would never end, an eternal struggle cycling through waves of fear and pain.

Then, there were voices. Many voices cascaded into the street, and someone yelled. The man stopped squeezing her. He stepped back and ran.

Two men chased him, and a woman trotted up to Maria.

"Are you all right?" the woman asked in a rough voice. "He knocked you about a bit, he did."

"I think I'm fine." Her heart was pounding, and she had no idea how she felt. Her body was suspended, somewhere out of her mind's reach.

"It looks like you're no worse for the wear," the woman said. She had dusty brown skirts and broken fingernails. A scent of fish clung to her. Perhaps the woman sold fish.

"Did they catch him?" Maria asked. She did not know what else to say. She wanted to fall into the woman's arms and sob.

"I don't know, dear; I'm here with you. Look, you're fine. Go on home. Would you like me to walk some with you? We'll tidy you up, first. There we go, tuck your hair back under that cap. And no one will know. No one will be the wiser, will they? You're lucky that way, dear."

The woman's words washed over her, and Maria obeyed without registering the conversation. She needed not to think but rather to cling to this malodorous woman and her arm while she took Maria's wrist and turned her back toward the center of town. They walked slowly together, and Maria indicated the direction of her home. She held fast to the package of azurite in her sweaty palm. Maria ran her thumb up and down the rough twist of paper while the woman walked over the canal with her and a few more blocks, toward the massive Grote Kerk and the large square adjacent to the church.

"Lucky girl, you," the woman said. "No harm done. No one needs to know anything, do they?"

"No, nothing." She tried not to cry. "Thank you."

The woman nodded, patted her arm, then turned back toward the north and the lake. Maria wished she would stay. The woman carried away the easy comfort of a witness with the intuitive knowledge that Maria needed a gentle touch and kind words after a horror. To find understanding elsewhere, Maria would have to speak of what had happened. While she watched the woman walk away, she cringed at the thought of telling her father, or even Judith. The man's body had pressed against her as if she had been something to be used, like a horse or chair. She could not confess that. And even if she could bring herself to tell the truth, her father would ask why she had been walking in that part of town and what she had bought. No, she could not explain this. She took a deep breath. The violation was another trial, and perhaps it would make her sacrifice more meaningful. Tears welled up. Maria rubbed her cheek and wondered if the punch would show. Her fingertips brushed over her skin, and to her surprise, her face did not hurt. Perhaps his hand had grazed her. Then no one would ask any questions.

When she reached the house, she stopped to look at the familiar brick frontage with its tapering top, like steps leading to Heaven. She closed her eyes then entered. In the cold entryway, the sounds of her father's humming and the scratch of his quill drifted from his open door a few steps away.

"I'm home, Father," she called softly from the hallway, without approaching his door. She heard a grunt of acknowledgment. "I don't feel well; I'm going to rest." Her throat tightened at the pain of diminishing her injury, but she kept her voice even.

"Feel better, dear." His distracted tone suggested he had not looked up from his writing.

She blinked back some tears and went upstairs, where she closed herself in her room. A wave of self-pity threatened, but she sat on the bed, wrapped her arms around herself, and tried to still her thoughts. She would channel her guilt and manage her wounds, as she always had.

Chapter 6

During the midday meal, Judith sat at the large table a few seats down from the men. Maria was sick and confined to her room, so Judith swallowed her roasted carrots and parsnips without tasting them and then left the house. When the heavy door shut behind her, she turned the key in the lock and took a deep breath of the frigid air. She knew such air bred illness, but she liked how she could feel the heft of it reach down into her lungs. She rubbed her numb hands together and turned toward the main square. An industrious maid swabbing the mud from a nearby home's entryway splashed her ankles with ice-cold water, and Judith muttered a warning.

She was walking past a shop of used crockery and dishes when a man grabbed her elbow.

"I hear you've been looking for me." He dropped her elbow and narrowed his eyes at her for a moment. Then he picked up one of the heavy earth-colored cups piled outside the shop on display. He held it in the palm of his hand, but kept his gaze fixed on Judith. His black hat had once held some shape.

She took a breath and planted her feet. "That's right," she said.

There were a few people in the street, but they were dressed in worn trousers and skirts. No one she knew. She lifted her chin. "Good of you to find me instead. I'm looking for my payment. Or my painting back, if it didn't sell."

The man with the misshapen nose flipped the cup over, as though searching for the maker's mark, and pursed his lips. He had a wide mouth nearly the same color as his sun-leathered face.

"Sorry lady, but I don't know what you're talking about."

"You do. My painting, the one with the woman and the wineglass. It was a good one."

"Oh yeah? Sorry, but I'm still coming up empty. I think you'd better remember that, and stop looking for people you don't know."

"No." Judith stamped a foot, though the impetuousness of the gesture embarrassed her. "I saw the auction. I know my piece sold. And if you don't give me my money, or find a way to get me my painting back, I'll report you." She hadn't seen the piece sold, but it must have.

"Oh, you will? To whom?" He smiled, a twisted grin that looked more like a tear in his face. "Last I heard, you weren't a Guild member, and I had the impression you did not have permission from your teacher, your *master*, to sell as much as a painted piece of dog shit. So who, exactly, are you going to report me to?"

"My brother." She crossed her arms. Perhaps that would conceal the trembling in her hands.

"Now that's droll."

He dropped the cup, and it shattered on the gray paving stones. The shopkeeper rushed outdoors, but after one look at the broad man standing by his display, he shrank back inside the dark doorway.

Judith stood and waited.

"I'll have my money," she said, trying to keep her voice from shaking.

The man smiled a bit, turned, and walked. She stood, her arms still crossed, and tried to remember to breathe. There must be something she should say.

After a few steps, he paused and plucked his fingers at his dull white sleeve. Then he turned back around.

"You must be one of the only lady painters around here, right?"

"Yes."

"You're odd, then. A novelty."

"I am not odd." She stood up straight. The menace left his eyes, but it was replaced with a sharp cunning.

"I'll grant you've got painting talent. And if you're a lady painter, you might be of interest to some. Though, at a discount." He coughed. "How about we make a deal? You make me another painting, one of something specific. A commission. And I'll pay you for both."

"Something specific? I won't paint anything obscene, you know."

He grunted, a sort of laugh. "Some*one* specific. Gerard Snellings. You know the man? The fellow who plays Peeckl-haering so well. A picture of him doing his act."

"A merrymaking picture? I've done Peecklhaering before, but it wasn't Gerard. I don't know if he would pose for me." She lifted her chin. "Why him? And I'm not considering anything until you tell me how much you'll pay me. For both paintings."

He bent down to pick up a shard of pottery and ran his thumb down the edge.

"Ten guilders. For both."

Judith laughed, in spite of her nervousness. "That's absurd. You're not negotiating with Peecklhaering himself, now. One of my paintings alone is worth near twice that."

He closed his fingers over the pottery shard.

"Fifteen. Take it or leave it."

She swallowed. "Fine. But it won't be any larger than the first."

"Three weeks from now."

With Shrovetide only a week and a half away, Judith was not sure she would get Snellings to sit for her. His character Peecklhaering, the "pickled herring" fool, was in high demand during the revelries. "I don't think—"

"Three weeks. Or there's no deal."

She tucked her cold fingers inside her fist, in an effort to warm them against her sweaty palm. "Fine. But I should know your name, or how to find you, in case . . ."

"It's Lachine. That's all you need to know. I'll come get the painting in three weeks, Judith Leyster."

"I won't be swindled, Lachine," she said. A woman in a splattered brown dress walked by them and clucked her approval. "I want an advance payment. To cover supplies."

Lachine rubbed his uneven nose and sighed. He dropped two guilders in her hand, plus the shard of shattered cup. "I'll find you in three weeks. And if you can't deliver, you'll owe me. With interest."

He touched his hand to her elbow, a gentle and chilling gesture, and walked away. Judith watched him pull his floppy hat down low on his face and turn down the next street without looking back.

Chapter 7

SHE WAS ALREADY SPENDING THE commission money in her mind as she walked away from the crockery shop. That much money, plus what she had, would pay a few months' rent in the room, barely, and by then she could sell more paintings. She would need every penning to purchase the workshop supplies, but she knew how to be thrifty. She might become a Guild member soon. Then, she could paint as she pleased and sell her beautiful images to the world. She smiled to think of it.

When she arrived at the linen-seller's shop, Chrispijn de Mildt was in the large entryway, speaking to a man with curly hair and a wide hat obscuring his face. It was chilly, even inside the house, but better than waiting outside in the lingering winter's cold. Judith stood to the side and occupied herself by looking at Chrispijn's wares—some he had made and other pieces had been woven elsewhere. Possibly by laborers in the southern part of town. Judith rubbed the fabric between her fingers. In the texture she could imagine the looms, shuttles, and calloused hands that had made such a humble thing.

"Judith. I can guess what you're doing here." His tone was jovial, but when Judith turned around, Jan Miense Molenaer's face was still and serious. Or it was for a moment, until he gave a half smile. His pale skin had the gentle tint of a peach.

"Shopping?" She lifted one edge of indigo linen from its roll.

"After a fashion, yes. Exactly what you're doing." He tugged at the full sleeve of his dark green jacket, the velvet of which matched the bows tied beneath his knees to ornament the hem of his breeches. He had a head full of curly, dark blond hair, a strong nose, and an incipient belly straining his doublet. Not a handsome man, but he had his charm.

"Judith, I'd like to speak with you outside," he said.

"I'm sorry, but I don't have time. I'm shopping, you see, and—"

"It will only take a minute." He winked. "Excuse us, Chrispijn." He took Judith's elbow and turned her toward the door. His touch was firmer than Lachine's.

She glared at Jan as he held the door open for her.

"What are you doing, ordering me around like that?" They walked out past the cloth displays and down past the cobbler's shop until they were well out of the linen-seller's earshot. She crossed her arms and gritted her teeth.

"I know why you're here. And you know what I want too. Don't try to pretend otherwise." He leaned a hip against the red brick wall of the house adjacent to the cobbler's house.

Judith exhaled loudly, and her breath plumed out in a cold mist in front of her. She once spent a few weeks of her apprenticeship on loan to Frans Hals, and Jan had been an apprentice there at the same time. They struck up a sort of friendship, casual and competitive, as friendships between students often were. Though she had few friends to compare him to.

"What do you want to discuss, then?" She rocked back on her heels and waited.

"An idea. Look, I know you don't have the money to afford that lovely room with the gorgeous light up there. You know it's true, no matter what you've saved or what you're dreaming you'll earn some day. No apprentice or student does, nor even a newly minted master like myself. But together . . . we would have enough." He smiled, and she felt her cheeks warm. "We could have enough to convince him not to rent to the toymaker. Ah, you didn't know about that, did you? See, you already need me. Or he could rent to another artist, one of the bottom-dwellers like Karel. The sooner we finalize this, the better."

Judith shook her head. "You have no idea how much money I have, or how much I can earn."

"You're not in the Guild yet, so I know exactly how much money you can earn—hardly any."

Judith looked at her feet, her scuffed boots barely visible below the hem of her skirt, and she kicked some dirt away.

"People would talk, you know. It's not appropriate for me to share a space with one man." Nor would it be comfortable, she knew. A distracting heat sometimes overtook her when she was alone with him. She needed to focus on her painting. And though she often found herself seeking his face in a crowd or smiling like a farm girl when she encountered him, she knew to keep her distance. Men and marriage were like a greedy black pigment, transforming whatever they touched into their own hue. Judith did not want to disappear into a coupling, no matter how pleasant.

He waved his hand away. "We'll invite other artists for inspiration. And the models will be around. All the usual bustle of a workshop. Plus, think, we can share painting props. I have a violin, and you have that fine crystal goblet. It's for the best. Really. You'll see."

Judith wondered why he was not making this offer to one of the other young masters, who must be as interested in the room—and male, a less controversial partner. He seemed to enjoy her company, but she doubted he felt anything more than a brotherly affection. Maybe he thought sharing with her would be easier. That as a woman she would be no threat to his work. Or that she couldn't influence his choice of subject matter or imitate whatever style he imagined himself inventing. She snorted.

"It's funny?" He raised his blond eyebrows.

She smiled. "I'll admit, Jan, it's an attractive proposition." She wondered if the flush that she felt upon her cheeks was visible. She should be more careful about her choice of words. "From a financial standpoint. It would be easier to split the rent. But, as you say, the key is finding a space of my own to do my own work. And I know I can't do it by sharing with another artist."

"Judith, you must—"

"Consider it a compliment. I need to focus on my painting, and your work would detract from that. I would be too drawn by your lively figures to concentrate on my own. It's true, you know. Your figures are quite good." She was putting him off, but she meant what she said.

His mouth curved up into a sad smile.

"We can still help one another out," she said. "I'd be glad to borrow that violin of yours. I've got a merrymaking piece in mind. I'll trade it for the goblet. But I can't share a workshop."

"So are we to compete for the space?"

She shook her head. "Neither of us can afford that."

"Indeed."

A silence fell between them. Nearby, a dog barked, and a boy cursed at it.

"I suppose I'll have to pray for some guidance then," he

said finally.

"If you think you need it. Me, I'd like to rent this room."

He laughed. "And if I still do, as well?"

"I think you'll be a gentleman, and let the lady have her way." She smiled.

He sighed and shook his head. "I was hoping to convince you. It would have saved us both a good deal of money. But, fine. I have another possibility, to tell the truth. More light, but more money. Someone else asked me to share that one."

A flame of envy flickered in her chest. Should she consider sharing the other space, wherever it was? No. This light here, the soft blanket—this was destined for her. All alone, to arrange as she pleased and manage as she liked. She would make her finances work. She knew she could. As long as she started painting soon.

"Thank you, Jan. It was a good idea. Now, if I may?" She gestured toward the shop's closed door.

He sighed again. "Go on."

She nodded and knocked on the linen-seller's door. A grin tugged at the corner of her mouth while she waited, and behind her, Jan walked away. No matter the circumstances, she enjoyed talking to him. Even more when she got what she wanted. When Chrispijn opened the door, she forced a small frown onto her face.

"I'd like to discuss terms," she said.

Chapter 8

Maria spent a day confined to her room where she huddled, ashamed and trembling, her body wound into a ball on her bed. She only offered a few words of greeting when Judith returned that night. But at least the act of speaking, of pretending to be normal, helped brush away some of the terror. She fell asleep, and woke to hear Judith's soft snoring in the dark. By dawn the next morning, Maria had molded her fear into something close to a story, a sequence of events she could follow, and by doing so, she tamed her terrors a little. The man came, he touched her, and he left. He was gone.

She stood and glanced over at Judith, still sleeping. Once, shortly after Judith had arrived at the De Grebber house, the two young girls faced down a small cluster of stone-throwing boys. Maria could not remember why the boys had started pursuing them, although in the tale she and Judith later recited, it was because the boys had called Maria, then fifteen, some names. Judith, only thirteen, tossed a rock at them, which unleashed a volley in return. But Judith was undeterred, and

Maria, girded by her young companion's courage, joined her in throwing rocks back at the boys. They, in turn, were so shocked to see their female targets return fire they scuttled away. When Maria exhaled and looked at her friend, Judith was beaming and reaching for her hand. For weeks, they retold the story of their joint bravery. Maria let Judith shape the tale, for she understood this recitation would form part of the bedrock of their friendship, and she never corrected Judith when the girl boasted about how bold Maria had been in repulsing the boys.

It was years now since they had reminisced about that early adventure. Maria wondered what Judith would make of yesterday's assault. She couldn't tell her, though. She couldn't tell anyone, especially not Samuel or her father. That she had experienced something so shameful made her want to dissolve into the muck of the street.

Now Maria needed these scarce, quiet minutes. She had little time before Shrovetide and Samuel's arrival, a week and a half away, and she knew she needed this painting to fortify herself before the debaucheries of the pre-Lenten excess. She silently picked up her package of azurite from her chest of clothes and tiptoed down to the workshop. There she ground the pigment, working her wrist and fingers until they ached, and blended it with linseed oil to make a paste. The work let her forget anything except the force in her hands.

The blue paint glowed like a piece of the Virgin's sacred gown snipped and placed upon her palette. She had done well in making a small amount, only what she would need to add a touch of luminescence to the space between the flame and the woman's head. Nothing a casual observer would ever identify as blue, but enough to hint the sapphire hope existed.

With her eyes squinting and her hand still and slow, Maria applied the tone. To her right, she heard a yawn. Judith had entered the workshop, but she said nothing to Maria. Careful to demonstrate she was not peeping, Judith walked in front of Maria's panel over to her small workspace, on Maria's left, where she tapped her small palette against the easel, as though considering what project to turn to.

"I didn't have a chance to tell you the other night," Maria said. "Your brother came by again. Two days ago, the day before I . . . got sick. He was looking for you."

"He was?" Judith pulled a dirty smock over her black, wool dress. It was chilly in the workshop, but neither woman bothered to light a fire; they were too anxious to seize the dim scrapings of light coming down from the high windows. Then Judith paused and smacked the heel of her hand against the easel. The panel rattled.

"What is it?" Maria took a step back from her painting.

"He was probably looking to pick up the money I promised him. Oh, Lord in Heaven." She rubbed her fists into her eyes. "I forgot about that. I need that money, though, now that I've signed a lease, and I have to pay a sitter's fee . . . I'm sure he was exaggerating about his landlord. Don't you think?"

"Wait, you've signed a lease agreement? You didn't tell me. And you're hiring a model?"

Judith quickly pressed her lips together and regarded Maria. Her brown eyes turned flat. "I shouldn't have said anything."

Maria tapped the wooden handle of her brush gently against her wrist, careful not to spatter any paint. "Please, tell me."

Judith exhaled. "I've earned a commission. It's an unconventional arrangement, but I'll be needing a model, a particular model, and I'll have to pay him. But since I've signed a rental agreement for the workshop and given my savings over in deposit, I can't spare the guilders." She shook her head.

"A commission, congratulations! Have you told my father?"

Judith's eyes flashed. "No. I can't tell him, Maria. It's bad enough I already . . ."

"You already what?" Maria's stomach sank.

Judith lifted her chin. "Already sold one painting to this man. One that I painted here. I can't mention this other piece to your father. Though," she hurried to add, "I'll be buying new supplies for my workshop, so this commission won't cost him anything. I can't share the profit with him."

"You sold a painting? One you did here? But Judith, that's stealing." A dark sensation washed over her, as if a cloud of bats had swooped over her head. Judith wouldn't steal, not from Maria's father.

"No, I'm entitled to sell my own labor."

"That's not what I'm talking about." Maria glanced at her own painting, at the ridge of blue that rose up over the black. "I mean the materials, the pigments. Even the brushes."

Judith picked up a long brush and started running the bristles over her lips, a habit that irritated Frans de Grebber.

"I didn't steal. Don't you see? I used materials given to me in the course of my responsibilities as an apprentice painter in this workshop. And I spent my pitiful savings on the rare colors and the wooden support. That work was mine, Maria. I had to sell it. I need the money for my workshop. And I'm still paying to live here. I'm being fair, Maria. But I need this commission. I don't want to hurt your father. But how else can I be independent?"

Maria scrutinized her painting and could not bring herself to look at her friend's face. Judith's ambition astonished her, though she had been hearing of it for years. No woman had her own workshop. No woman was a full member of the Guild. Maria nodded and returned to her painting, but her concentration had evaporated. After a few minutes, she covered the panel and left.

Chapter 9

JUDITH UNPINNED THE PAIR OF linen sleeves from the wind-chilled line in the rear courtyard and tossed them into the small basket, where the sleeves crossed over the pile of clothes like defiant arms. Appropriate enough. Earlier that afternoon she had told Frans de Grebber that she would have her own painting space soon, and would apply for master status whenever she could find the coins. She didn't mention the commission, though looking at his vein-crossed hands, she promised herself again she would pay for all the supplies herself. "Do you think you're ready?" he had said, his brush paused for a moment. Judith wanted to pinch her lips in irritation, but she kept her face still. The last two senior journeymen in his workshop had left at age twenty-two, off to set up their workshops in Amsterdam, and now Judith was well past twenty-three. "I hope so," was all she said.

Judith hefted the basket up and waddled into the house and up the two flights of stairs to her loft. And as she began to fold her meager set of clothes into her trunk, the furrow between her brows eased. No matter Frans de Grebber's concerns, there was an order to this world. Clean clothes belonged in a box, folded neatly. Painters, once their skills were sufficient, needed to work on their own.

Downstairs, someone knocked at the door. Judith stood, but crouched back down. She didn't need to answer every door, and the household would have to get used to her absence.

After a long silence, the knock sounded again, and finally she heard a pair of male voices. Judith pressed her hand to a brown linen bodice, her favorite one for painting in, and placed it on the top of the pile. Easily accessible. She closed the wooden lid just as footsteps clomped on the stairs outside her door.

"Judith, you in there?"

She raised her eyebrows in surprise. Abraham rarely visited her at the De Grebber house. She suspected he felt out of place, though she never asked, since she didn't want to embarrass him. She opened the door.

"Come in," she said. Elsewhere in the house a few voices joined in bawdy song. The boys must have started their evening early today.

Abraham came inside and ran his hand over his damp hair. He seemed too large for the space she shared with Maria, though Judith had never thought of her skinny younger brother as a big man. Perhaps he had grown.

"Very tidy," he said. Then he blushed, as if there were something indecent about commenting on a woman's room.

"We aren't here much," Judith said. "I wasn't expecting you. Should we go pour a little ale?"

He shook his head. "I'd rather talk up here, if you don't mind."

She sat on the flat top of the trunk, with her legs tucked under to stay warm, and pointed at Maria's. He hesitated, then sat. There was a small table to his left, which held their family Bible and a fist-sized box.

"What's in there?" he asked.

"You can look." She wondered if he had come to ask for more money. A few days earlier she had given him what coins she could, and as it was, she had to borrow from Maria to make her first rental payment. She had nothing left over to buy an easel, so would have to convince the linen-seller to lend her a table.

He opened the box and lifted out a small metal sphere hung on a chain. The jewelry was the size of a plum and made of curving openwork, like birds' wings punched into the silver.

"Maria gave me that pomander," she said. "Are the cloves still fresh? I put some in last month."

He held the orb to his nose and inhaled. He nodded, but seemed distracted.

"What is it, Abraham?" She probably didn't want to know, but she understood he needed her to ask.

"I'm not at the dock anymore. Hans had me unloading with Paulje, and we dropped a crate. Cinnamon."

"That doesn't sound horrible, dropping cinnamon," she said. She twisted a bit of her skirt in her finger, and the faded red threads strained, revealing darker ones below.

He shook his head. "Hans said it wasn't the crate, but that I was the youngest one at the dock, had been there the least time. So if someone had to go . . ."

She sighed. She couldn't tell if bad luck followed him from job to job, like one of the gulls that trailed the fishing ships pulling into the dock, or if he had earned his misfortune. She knew what the preacher would say.

"And then I ran into Bartol. You remember him? It's been years since I've seen him, and he didn't say much, just asked after me. But it had me thinking."

"Abraham, you can't be thinking about that. Bartol is only going to get his neck stretched one of these days, you know it. You promised me you wouldn't get involved with him again."

He nodded, his eyes on the floor. "I wanted to hear you say it."

"I'll say it any time you want," she said and smiled. "Come on. A bit of ale?"

He exhaled loudly and then stood. "No, I shouldn't. Thanks though, Judith. I'll let myself out." He stepped through the door and then turned back to face her.

"Have you ever painted a tulip, Judith?"

She laughed in surprise. "No, it's not what we do here. More like scenes, merrymaking and such. Others do flowers."

"But you'd be good at it, wouldn't you?"

"That's kind of you, Abraham. But I don't know. I suppose if I had a tulip to look at, it couldn't be that different from painting a tankard or a lute. A bit lovelier. Though ten times as expensive, Abraham, so I don't expect to have the chance to practice soon."

He nodded. "Maybe someday. You can paint anything, Judith. I know you can."

She walked over and kissed his cheek. "Thank you, brother."

He whispered something that she couldn't make out, and he walked down the steps before she could ask him to repeat it. She closed the door behind him. After listening to his footsteps disappear into the house, she opened her trunk and thought about refolding the last blouse, but closed the lid again. Then she glanced over to her small table. The pomander's box was still open, so she went to close it. But when she looked inside, the silver ball was gone. And then she figured out what it was he had whispered.

"I'm sorry."

Chapter 10

JUDITH RAN DOWN THE STAIRS from her room and out into the street without pausing to grab a cloak. But an icy rain cut down from the sky, and the street was filled with muck. She ran only the length of two houses calling Abraham's name before she gave up, damp and shivering. It was nearly dark, and she would be mad to run after him now.

She slammed the door to Frans de Grebber's house and stood in the entry hall shaking. Why would he take her pomander? It wasn't very valuable. The orb was small, and its openwork was so broad that there was hardly any silver gilding to it, and the chain it had hung from was clumsily made and short. Barely the length to tie to her belt, if she had been the sort to perfume herself. Maria had bought it for her when they were first becoming friends. Maria had saved her coins for months to buy the pomander, and for a girl of fifteen, it was an expensive luxury. Now, though, it would earn Abraham a couple of stuivers at most. She couldn't understand why he would steal it.

Tomorrow she would find him. If she had time in the evening, she realized. Tomorrow, her work began.

THE NEXT DAY, Judith opened the workshop door and invited the red-nosed man inside. Her workshop and her first model. She tried not to grin like some foolish milkmaid, but it was difficult. Gerard Snellings reached up to finger the white clay pipe tucked into his hatband. Then he stomped his boots, sprinkling Judith's bare, wheat-colored floor with raindrops and mud.

"Miserable as a fisherman's breeches out there," he said and shook his arms to spray the water from his linen sleeves. She suspected he might take his outer sleeves off, and wondered if she should invite him to do so. After a moment's thought, she handed him a clean rag to use to dry his face. When he finished, she held the damp cloth and looked around her empty space, wondering where she could put it. The room had only two tables and two stools, one each for her and the model. She had propped her wooden painting surface against two heavy jars and a broken piece of loom, all borrowed from the linen-seller. Her few surfaces were covered with painting materials or props, with no room for a dirty rag. When Gerard wasn't looking, she dropped the rag on the floor and kicked it under her table.

"I've only got a few hours," he said as he glanced around. "Sorry about that. But the rhetoricians are meeting tonight, and I've got to be there." He cleared his throat, as though he was going to say more, but instead folded his hands in front of his burgundy doublet and fell silent.

Judith frowned at the mention of the rhetoricians. It was a club for men, the elite painters like Frans Hals and Salomon de Bray. They met at the tavern De Pellicaen, where they claimed to pursue rarified heights of speech and art, but, in truth, they spent the evenings chasing the bottoms of their tankards. Or so people said. As a woman, she was forbidden from entering. A drunkard like Gerard, though, was not only welcomed but sought out for the entertainment he provided. Such uninhibited drinkers served as a polished measuring stick for respectable debauchery. Judith busied herself gathering her brushes for a moment. The crockery shard from Lachine rested next to the pewter plate holding her brushes, and she straightened it so the shadows turned the sharp edge dull.

"I'd like you to sit there, at that table. No, on the side closest to the window. Yes, thank you. Would you like some water?" She had filled a pitcher earlier in the day and gestured to it, a lovely cornflower-blue and white piece.

"Who was it you said requested my portrait? Or character, or however you call it." He flashed a jolly smile that Judith supposed was intended to represent Peecklhaering.

She hesitated a moment. He might balk if he knew, but she couldn't bring herself to lie.

"He called himself Lachine."

Gerard shrugged. "Don't know him. There must be plenty of people out there who want to be reminded of me. How I act, I mean. You want me to hold this tankard? Like this?"

He tilted it toward himself and popped the lid open, all while grinning jovially. It wasn't hard to imagine he would be a congenial drinking companion. His warm eyes crinkled at the corner and his brown custard lips had something of a woman's delicacy, curved as though he were about to laugh at someone else's joke.

"Yes, that's the pose. Let me frame out the general shape, and then we'll focus on your face. At that point you can rest your arm. No, not yet, wait until I've finished this first sketch. I'll get someone else to sit for the rest of the painting." She had no idea how she would find the time and money for another model, but she would have to.

She painted quietly for some half an hour in the gray scrim of light from the rain-damp window. This was the dead coloring phase, where she roughed in the oval shape of his head, the broad but soft shoulders, and the growing paunch, all on top of the oil-bound, umber-tinted grounding she had prepared earlier. She glanced back and forth between his jovial face and the simple lines taking shape on her panel. As she mirrored the rightward tilt of his head into a leftward pose on her painting support and channeled the warmth from his smile into a charming grin, the familiar intimacy and protectiveness began to grow inside her. By seeing this man in a way that few others had, she was creating him again. A soft smile wafted across her lips as she painted.

"Go ahead and take a break," she said.

Gerard stood and shook out his arms.

"That pipe of yours," she said. "I think we should add it to the painting. Yes, that's good, put it on the table there." She stood, and picked up a floppy cap adorned with a long feather from the table. She held it out. "Do you mind? The curve of this feather will frame your face."

"That's fine," he said, and replaced his worn black hat with her prop. He took a deep breath and looked at her. "I was only wondering. No, it's foolish. But . . .this man you're working for, he didn't have a French accent, did he? Hideous nose?"

Judith sat down and finished swabbing at a line along the figure's back before answering. The angle of his head was sharp, but otherwise she had a good outline. She wished she could talk about the beautiful painting she was going to make, not Lachine.

"He did. Do you know him?"

He froze. The color drained from his face, though his nose

stayed a wan shade of red.

"I don't think I can do this. I'm sorry, little lady."

He stumbled over the stool he had been sitting on and moved toward the door. Judith shot up from her stool.

"Wait! Gerard, wait." She touched a hand to his wrist. "Don't rush out. Please, talk to me for a minute. I'll stop the painting. But talk to me."

He hesitated at the door, and his eyes flicked between the handle and her face.

"You have some drink?"

Judith nodded. She had taken a cask, half full, from the De Grebber kitchen. She knew they wouldn't miss it, and she had suspected the drink would prove useful. She would pay Frans de Grebber back, someday, for all the kindnesses he had done to her, even those he didn't know about. She poured the crimson liquid into Gerard's tankard and held it near the stool he had sat on. He regarded her warily, then walked back to sit down again.

Gerard shook his head. "You don't understand."

"No, I don't." She sat on her stool, though she pulled it away from the panel so nothing stood in between them but the table. "What's the harm in giving him your portrait?"

"You don't understand," he repeated. "That man, Lachine, you call him. He wants me killed." His eyes widened in emphasis.

Judith blinked in surprise. "Killed?"

Gerard took a long sip. "It's ugly business, I shouldn't get into it with you. Though it's been so long since anyone . . ."

"You can tell me," she said softly.

Gerard puffed out his cheeks as he exhaled. "May as well, I guess. We work for the same man now. Maybe you know him, Paulus van Beresteyn? He's a magistrate. I didn't know Lachine worked for him when I signed on, and I wouldn't have agreed to the work if I had, but then I didn't want to do the work anyway. Paulus pressured me, you see. He knew things, er, about me, and I didn't have a choice. You know?"

Judith didn't see why a magistrate would stoop to blackmailing a drunkard, but she nodded in agreement anyway. She didn't want to hurt his feelings, and it would be better for him to keep talking.

"So now me and Lachine are competing, you see, only I never meant to be in that spot. So now he wants to kill me."

"Gerard, I can't imagine anyone wanting to kill you." Particularly not over some nonsense about working for the same prominent Haarlem gentleman.

He pressed his lips together and tapped his fingers on the tabletop. "I'm sure that's what he wants. It's the only thing that makes sense."

"Did anyone tell you this?"

He took another sip. "Well, no."

"Maybe he sees it differently than you do. And in any case, I don't understand how a portrait would help him kill you." She glanced at her own nascent portrait. It was going to be beautiful.

"Isn't it obvious? So he can show the killers what I look like."

"But you're famous. Everyone knows what you look like. I hadn't met you before last week, but I knew what you looked like. Or close enough. I don't even make it to many of the Shrovetide celebrations. And obviously I can't go into the rhetoricians' club."

She reached a hand toward him to close the distance between them. "I need this portrait. Please. It's my chance at getting into the Guild. No one else would pay me nearly enough."

He waved her plea away with a snap of the wrist, but he

stayed seated. Outside, the rain pattered against the window.

"Gerard. It's a portrait. A good one too. I promise. I can see that you're a gentle man, and I'll show that. Lachine will see it too." She didn't know what tension might run between the men, but surely that would dissipate when mediated by art.

He rubbed his chin with his hand, already spotted with age. "Hmm."

"You've already been painted. So what's one more? And then, there's the fee . . ." A feeling that might have been guilt crept up from her gut and into her throat and fingertips. She wasn't lying, but she was trying to convince him to stay. He would be glad to have the money, she told herself.

"Well, that's true. Even the great Frans Hals painted me once. When I was younger."

He rested his tankard on the pine table. "The Frenchman's a demon, I tell you. But I won't be the one to walk away from a lady in need."

Judith exhaled and closed her eyes a moment. "Thank you, Gerard." She smiled. "Let's make the most of our time. No need to hold the tankard. Tilt your head as you did before. A little that way. Yes. And could you smile, as if you're enjoying your wine?"

"I'd find that easier if you had some more wine to enjoy." He gave the innocent smile of a wicked child.

Judith laughed. "You drank that quickly. But yes, of course."

She poured him another cupful and set to painting rapidly, trying to catch the worn skin and lilting smile of her subject before the day faded. As her brush flew across the wood panel, her thoughts were consumed by color, shadow, and lines. She examined the arch of his eyebrows, like a bridge sweeping over a canal. But occasionally, when she paused, she wondered what Gerard had meant, and why Lachine would want to kill him. It could only be the fantasy of a drinker. Still, she wondered.

The light was dim when she stood back and regarded the completed first stage of the painting. On the panel, Gerard—no, Peeklhaering—cocked his head and grinned warmly at the viewer, his eyes crinkled in delight. He held a tankard, its lid flipped open to suggest he had taken a long pull, or was maybe contemplating its empty bottom. The setup was common enough, the merry drinker, but Judith was pleased with her execution, even in this early stage. Enough delight in his expression to suggest the joy of drink, enough wear in his face to remind one of the perils of overindulgence. The lightness of the feather in his hat contrasted with the weight of the metal tankard. It was all a pleasant balance. She would still need someone to sit and let her finish the body, but she could find someone. Lachine should have no difficulty selling the painting.

After Gerard left, Judith closed the door behind him and then leaned against the workshop's cool wall. The plaster seemed to infuse her thoughts with its blank white, and she exhaled. It was too late now to look for Abraham. Perhaps tomorrow. Though now, with the empty workshop surrounding her and begging to be filled with portraits and merrymaking scenes, she wasn't sure his theft mattered. Or was it her brother she was willing to give up on? No, that wasn't right. Everything mattered, she just needed the time for it all. She was tired, and she pushed herself away from the wall. Paint still clung to her brushes' bristles, and she needed to scrape the palate clean. All that before returning to her room in the De Grebber house before dark. She had better hurry.

Chapter 11

As soon as the chilled dawn broke on Shrove Tuesday, the chorus of merry crowds bubbled and swelled until, by midday, the drinking, music, and laughter seemed to paint every surface of the De Grebber workshop. Maria stayed inside. She had no interest in those carnal pre-Lenten revelries, and would not expose herself to the drunken men roving the streets. Every time she walked outside now, she found herself nervously scrutinizing the crowds in search of the rough hands she remembered in her nightmares. Though she had not seen him yet, she was certain each time she left the house that she would. Today would be the worst day to be reminded of her defilement. Today she had to prepare her sacrifice.

The household had already burned through much of their supply of wood for the season, and Maria did not want to ask the servants to buy more. The request would get back to her father. Instead, she resolved to make do with peat fire and the scraps she could scavenge unnoticed from the diminished woodpile.

After the midday meal, her father and the apprentices went out to have a drink at the Illumination, a high-end tavern favored by many of the St. Luke's Guild elite, in addition to a smattering of burgomeisters and wealthy merchants. Naturally, neither she nor Judith were invited. Judith had scurried off to her workshop. Maria had suggested they share some wine, but Judith said she was busy. Maria nodded and bit her lip. She would instead, in her friend's absence, make the most of the quiet house.

Outside, drunken men hollered off-key songs and children tittered at the antics of a rommelpot player, whose hideous instrument shrieked and groaned as he pulled the stick through the pig-bladder drum. Maria closed the shutters over the window of the front room, which served as her father's primary display space. The rain from the night before had now eased into an unseasonably clear day, and she was reluctant to shut out the precious sunlight. But she needed solitude in this room with the large fireplace.

She leaned her painting, with the cover still over it, against the wall, and then scattered a few sticks around the stack of peat disks glowing softly in the hearth. Even with the small peat fire, her breath fogged in the cold room. Maria paused, swallowed, and considered her next steps. She reached into the fireplace and tinkered with the position of a stick, moving it closer to the peat flame. She sat back on her heels, with her wool skirts pulled back from the hearth. After a minute, she got up to find more kindling.

When her nest of wood finally sparked into flame, Maria exhaled. This gift to God would be that much more meaningful for the effort entailed. She slid the cloth off her painting and held her work at arm's length. A feeling of pride surged inside her. Instead of quelling it, like she might ordinarily, she reveled in her accomplishment. The woman's nose still wasn't quite right, but her eyes glowed with real warmth, and they were fixed upon the candle in her hand. Maria imagined she could feel that little flame's burn, and she gave a strained smile.

The fireplace crackled and hissed, and Maria extended her painting into the flames. At first the flames seemed to hesitate, but after a moment they licked the corner of her wooden panel. The paint bubbled and smoked. An exploratory flame took root in the wood and flared with warmth. The impending destruction was agony. As if the flames were reaching into her chest to rip her pride from her heart and roast it alive. But she pushed her painting closer to the fire. More of it caught, and soon the entire upper edge of the panel hosted small, dancing lights. She released her hold.

Her heart contracted as she watched the consumption approach the woman's crown of brown hair. She wished she had shown the painting to her father. He would never believe she was capable of such work. But no, she had to keep this painting private. Anything else would have been succumbing to temptation.

As the fire lapped at her paint and crept across the panel, Maria stood. She wrung her hands and paced in the large room. She couldn't watch. A sharp scent, more pointed than the loamy smell of burning peat, filled the room. Maria tried to breathe through her mouth and looked around for distraction. A wooden chest holding dozens of her mother's napkins and tablecloths hulked under the front window. Otherwise the plank floor was bare, save for the dusting of sand meant to keep it clean. Maria had been urging her father to update to a more fashionable surface, marble or even ceramic, especially for this, his display room, but he always cited the expense and brushed the suggestion away. At that moment, ten paintings of various sizes filled the room's walls. She forgot herself and inhaled through the nose, and the painful smell of her disappearing art filled her nostrils. She lifted her hand to her nose and stared at one of her father's paintings, a variation of Daniel with the lions. Lacking lions to model from, her father had relied on a set of etchings, so the resulting beasts looked stylized. But Maria liked it even more for the acknowledgment of artificiality. The grace in Daniel's eyes and the confidence in his hands were palpable. Her brother Pieter, now in his thirties and running his own workshop, had served as a model for this one, and there was a freshness to his image that tugged at Maria's heart. Or perhaps it was her father's evident affection for the son he considered his artistic heir.

The fire popped behind her, but she forced herself to turn to the next piece, a commissioned portrait of a burgomeister that was already sold, obviously, but on display for a short time for advertising purposes. Her father had executed that piece quickly, for his subject had little time to sit for the portrait, but she thought it had come out well all the same. The lace around his neck glittered in an intricate pattern, and she could almost touch it.

A chill swirled around her ankles, and she shivered. She checked to ensure the window was tightly closed and turned to the fireplace. But the fire was extinguished. Using a stick, she poked at the embers, hoping to urge them back to life, but they glowed and then dulled to gray. Her painting was partially consumed, with only the crown of the woman's head lost to the fire.

Her fingers shook, and her head swam as she stood up and began searching the room for a way to relight the fireplace. She was about to go find a lamp from which to borrow a flame when a certainty settled upon her. Her sacrifice had been rejected. There was no reason for the fire to have gone out: no draft, no damp wind. She wrapped her arms around her waist in a protective self-embrace. No, it had been God's work. The fire's stillness was a message, an indication that her sacrifice was insufficient. Or tainted, perhaps. Vanity and pride infused her effort too deeply for it to be meaningful.

Maria snatched the painted panel from the hearth, shook it clean, kicked the remaining charred sticks to the back of the fireplace, and ran upstairs to her loft bedroom. She stowed the painting in the small space under her clothes chest and sat on the chest's polished top. Through the window she could see the striking celestial sky of the afternoon and hear the raucous celebrations below. Her throat tightened with shame and embarrassment, but she did not allow herself to cry. Instead, she bit her lip until it bled.

Later that afternoon, while the streets bubbled with the sound of good cheer, someone knocked at the door. Most of the house was empty, and Maria sat reciting her memorized prayers in her room. She would pray until the ache in her chest eased, however long that took, and she was willing to wear her fingertips bloody from the nubs on her rosary beads. The knock sounded again, so she closed her eyes, took a deep breath, and went to the door.

"Master De Grebber home?" asked the narrow-faced man. Maria recognized him as a messenger often used by Salomon de Bray, a painter and an officer in the St. Luke's Guild. It was an unusual day for Guild business, and Maria fumbled for the right words.

"I'm back here," her father called.

She escorted the man through the entry hall and up two steps into the room that served as her father's sleeping quarters and sitting room. Carved doors concealed his large sleeping cabinet, and a small peat fire burned in the fireplace. Frans sat in a straight-backed chair with his stockinged feet propped on a foot warmer, a small wooden box containing a clay bowl and hot embers. He had picked up the habit of relying upon foot warmers from his wife. Maria did not know of any other man who indulged himself with what was considered a woman's comfort, but her father was either oblivious or indifferent. He preferred being comfortable to correct, and sometimes she envied him.

"I'm sorry to interrupt, but Master Salomon de Bray wanted you to see the letter tonight. I understand you've already discussed it? He'd like your signature as soon as you can."

Intrigued, Maria lingered in the doorway, her hand on the cool wall. Her father usually had little use for the Guild and was often at odds with them for their efforts to restrict his painting sales to approved channels. He scoffed at their rules and sold his work as he pleased, for the prices he pleased. But now he sat reading with his fingers pinching the bridge of his nose in concentration. The room was silent as they waited, and Maria could once again hear the muffled noise of laughter from the streets.

"Wait a minute." Her father prodded at the paper with a finger. "This is not what we discussed. Salomon said this was the version I should sign? What a whore's son. Did he think I wouldn't notice?" Frans de Grebber snapped the paper in the air and folded it closed. "I see what they're doing," he continued. "Two birds with one stone. I'll be damned, though."

Maria sucked in a breath, surprised at the strong language. The messenger raised his eyebrows but said nothing.

"What is it, Father? What do they want?"

He shook his head, his eyes still on the letter.

"A silly thing. No, quite important. But not as important as this," he punched the paper again with his finger, "would suggest."

The messenger took a step back, as though to disassociate himself from the letter, and held his hands clasped in front of him, waiting.

"We were aiming," her father said, "to retrieve the Guild's holy relic of St. Luke. You wouldn't have seen it, Maria. It was gone before your time. An ornamented silver box holding sacred bone and a carved bronze reliquary." He paused, glanced at the messenger, and pursed his lips. "I had it in safekeeping some years back, during some tense times with the Calvinists, and I gave it to a priest headed for the southern Netherlands. The Catholic parts. For safekeeping! I knew the Church was strong there. Here, the Reformed Church might have destroyed the thing." He crossed himself. The messenger kept his expression still.

"Now a few of the other Catholic officers of the Guild want it back. I couldn't agree more. But this. This! They've written the letter to indicate I will be the one delivering this same letter to Bruges. That's where Father Cloribus is. Or he was. But no, we had not discussed any travel, not by me. It's absurd. They're only trying to take me out of the market for a while." He tapped his finger to his temple, a gesture that often left his curly gray hair tinted with paint.

"Take this back as it is. Salomon doesn't need an answer tonight, no matter how much he says he wants one. Yes, tell him that. We'll discuss how to proceed." Her father nodded, satisfied. "And Maria, this is for Judith." He held up a second letter, which she hadn't seen. He must have noticed the curiosity in her eyes, for he smiled. "That's right. They've approved her request to apply for master status. With my endorsement, of course." He waved the letter, and Maria took it. The wax seal made the paper sag, and she clutched it to her chest.

"Go on, then," her father said, his face serious again. Maria bowed her head and escorted the messenger out of the house. She ran upstairs to see if Judith had returned, but their room was still empty. Maria hesitated, then placed the letter on the blankets smoothed over Judith's tidy bed. Her friend would want to learn of the news as soon as she returned.

Maria tugged the linens on her own bed straight and then descended back to the first floor. Outside, voices jumbled into a drinking song and, nearby, a donkey brayed. She wanted to learn more about that relic, which seemed like a hint from God. Her sacrifice had failed, yet here was a hint of a real martyr. She went to her father's study, but his door was closed. She knew better than to knock.

Chapter 12

JUDITH PULLED THE DOOR OF the De Grebber house closed, and she rubbed her cheeks, stiff from the cold. She hung her cloak on a hook near the door. The streets outside were muddy from yesterday's crowds, and a few merrymakers still lingered today. She pulled the notice announcing her permission to apply to the Guild from inside her linen shift, where it nestled warm against her breast. She opened it again, but the thrill had soured. This morning, she had gone to share her excitement with Abraham. She had crossed town to the docks and then again to the poor district in the south.

"Judith," Maria called from the landing one flight up. "There you are!" She ran down the stairs. "I need—wait, what's wrong? You look pale."

"I think Abraham had some trouble. He's gone." She reached out to lay her fingers on Maria's wrist, as if the touch might bring her unmoored thoughts back to shore.

"What do you mean?"

"I'm not sure, but I think he's left the city. I went to that wretched manure pile of a boarding house of his, and the landlord said he packed a bag, paid up his bill. 'Actually paid,' he said, as if it were a miracle. Then Abraham ran right out of there. As quick as a mouse with a cat on its tail, is how he put it. Maria, how could he have left? Without telling me." She wasn't sure if she wanted to yell or cry.

Maria wrapped her friend in a quick, tight embrace, then held Judith at arm's length. Judith looked at her friend's feet, so small in her slippers.

"After our parents left," Judith continued, her voice hardening, "running away like they did, I never thought Abraham would do the same. He isn't like that."

"It must have been something serious, whatever happened. Maybe someone was trying to hurt him."

"I'm sure something happened." Judith picked at paint dried onto one of her knuckles.

"He would have told you if he could," Maria said. She brushed a strand of hair behind Judith's ear. "I know he would. I envied the two of you, you know that? How you held to each other like wreckage in a shipwreck when your parents left. You knew neither of you deserved that abandonment, and you clung to one another. When my mother died, my brothers stayed away from me. As if they could see her features in my face, and the pain at seeing her reflected would harm them."

Maria looked away, toward the floor, and seemed to hold her breath for a moment. Her words were like a blanket thrown over the embers of Judith's distress. He had broken the most important covenant between them, and he had taken her money as he did so. When she needed the coins most. But Maria was right, in a way. Surely something had happened. Abraham did love her, and he needed her, as Maria had said. Judith squeezed Maria's forearm, and then stepped away.

"You were about to say something, Maria, when I started

in on all that."

"Yes." She reached up to touch her dark hair. "Can you come with me? Now. I need your help."

Judith examined her friend, who was looking fixedly out the window behind her. "Of course. Are you going to tell me what it is?"

"As we walk. Come on."

Judith pulled on her cloak, still warm from her furious walk through town, and she waited for Maria to do the same.

Out in the street, a light mist fell, and Judith rearranged her white cap.

"Do you remember Samuel Ampzing? The poet?" Maria kept her voice low, and Judith thought she saw a hint of flush rise to her cheeks.

"How could I forget? He was so generous with his praise."

"Generous, yes," Maria said, and her whole neck grew pink. "He's expressed some interest in me, and he's back in town now. That's where we're going. But I can't tell Father." She bit her lip anxiously.

"Maria, really?" Judith grinned and nudged her friend's arm.

"No, it's not like that. I can't return his affection. I don't. He's not Catholic, and he wanders so much. I don't know how to tell him, but I have to make that clear."

"It's too bad, Maria. I think he'd be a good match. So what if he's not Catholic? Most people aren't." Judith smiled again, but it melted away when she saw how preoccupied Maria looked. They stepped out of the way to let a horse and cart pass, then continued walking. "I understand. I'm sure you can find a way to tell him gently."

Maria shook her head. "He's ill. I don't want to make it worse."

They said nothing else until they reached the door of the

house where Maria said Samuel was staying. The shutters were recently painted white, and a bunch of freshly cut rosemary hung upside down on the door.

Maria knocked, timidly at first, and then more loudly.

A round woman wearing an apron opened. "Yes?"

"We're here to visit Samuel Ampzing," Maria said. "At his request." She clasped her hands at her heart, as if in supplication.

The servant simply nodded. "I'll see if he's awake. Come in, it's damp out there."

"Awake?" Judith asked, when the servant walked away. Inside, the house smelled spicy and sweet, like cinnamon cookies, though it shouldn't have been the time of year for speculaas. Judith's mouth watered.

"He's ill. Perhaps it's worse than I thought," Maria said, her eyebrows raised in worry.

"Do you know whose house this is?"

"No. Only that it's a friend of his. He doesn't have the money to stay in his own house anymore."

They stood silently, and Judith's eye wandered to the walls. The house's owner had hung a few pictures, including one of a laughing boy that looked to be by Frans Hals, judging by the loose brushstrokes and bright expression. The other two paintings, still-life portraits of irises, roses, and carnations, she did not recognize. Perhaps he had purchased them in Amsterdam or Den Haag. A wooden shelf held a pewter pitcher with a graceful curved handle, and a row of hand-painted blue and white tiles ran around the edge of the floor. The owner had some interest in spending money, it seemed. Perhaps when she earned master status, such a man might look kindly upon her own colors and figures.

The servant returned, her face gray. "He isn't well," she said. "Are you sure you'd like to see him? I've asked the Overmerchant, Willem van Dielen that is, and he says if you wish to trouble yourselves, you're welcome to visit his friend."

Judith looked over at Maria, who was biting her fingernails, a gesture Judith had not seen since they were teenagers.

"I must," Maria said finally, though Judith could barely hear it. The servant raised her eyebrows in query, and Judith repeated Maria's decision.

"All right." The woman sounded doubtful, but she dipped her chin in acknowledgment and led them up the freshly polished stairs.

On the second floor, through an open door, Judith could see a small vase of fresh marigolds resting on a chest of drawers. Despite the thin rain clouds outside, the light from the window made the orange petals glow, and Judith wanted to enter and marvel at their beauty. It was rare to see cut flowers, especially at this time of year. But the servant moved briskly through the hallway, and Judith followed.

"Could he be dying?" Judith whispered to Maria as they stepped across the threshold of one room and the servant continued into another. The house was bigger than it looked from the outside.

Maria whispered something unintelligible, but from the pale cast of her face, Judith suspected he might be.

The servant knocked on a closed door and, without waiting, opened it. The young women approached the entrance. Inside the room, curtains were drawn back from a recessed bed compartment, and the small figure of a man reclined in the bed. The air was stale, and a timid peat fire burned in the fireplace. Curtains were drawn over the windows and two oil lamps were lit, an extravagant accommodation to the sick man, to keep out the damp air and any aggravating sunlight.

"He was up and speaking this morning," the servant said, her voice hushed. "But just now, he seemed . . . look for yourself."

Maria hesitated, so Judith approached first. Samuel was propped up against the pillows along the wall, but his head listed to the right, toward her. She had not seen him for some five years, though it seemed fifteen had passed for him. His cheeks were sunken into his face, and dark circles shadowed his eye sockets. He had been a handsome enough man, easy with a smile, yet now his beard seemed to pull his fragile skin downward like ballast.

His eyes were open, and he looked at Judith unseeingly. But when Maria neared, over Judith's shoulder, his expression lit up, as if someone had opened all the curtains in the room.

He moved his lips, and a hoarse scratching came out. His hand, resting on the coverlet, twitched.

"I think he would like you to take his hand," Judith said, though the words felt heavy in her mouth. She knew an embrace, even one as small as a handgrip, would make Maria uncomfortable.

Still, her friend stepped alongside the bed and laid her hand in the poet's. The green-striped coverlet stippled as Maria added her hand's weight to the bed, and Judith thought of the fields of hay bending in the wind that she had seen once while traveling to a countryside tavern. Someone had since harvested that hay, and what did the field look like now? Stubbled and sallow, most likely.

Samuel again tried to speak but was interrupted by a fit of coughing. Maria reflexively pulled away, then, blushing, stepped forward again to replace her hand in his. Samuel's eyes softened in apology, and he squeezed her finger.

"Would you like something to drink?" Maria asked.

"We have a very good small ale," the servant offered from the doorway. Judith had forgotten she still stood there.

Samuel shook his head slightly. "You came," he said finally, his voice as rough as a house painter's brush.

"Yes." Maria glanced at Judith, and her eyes were wide with panic. Judith stepped closer and pressed her hand, for a moment, against Maria's upper arm.

"I am gladdened," he said. "To see . . ." The words faded as if the bellows of his lungs sagged. He tried again. "Your kind face."

"We should speak more when you are well," Maria said.

He closed his eyes. The room around them was silent, and all Judith could hear was the rough progress of his breath. Maria withdrew her hand.

Samuel opened his eyes again. "We will speak. To arrange things. Later, then." It was more of a question than a statement.

"Yes, soon." Maria stepped away from the bed. She opened her mouth to say something else but then closed it. Then, quickly, she reached for Samuel again, gave his fingers a swift caress, and left the room. Judith nodded at the man, but his eyes followed Maria, and she departed.

At the bottom of the stairs, they thanked the servant and stepped out into the gentle rain, which seemed about to shift back into mist.

"That was terrible," Maria said and pressed her hands to her face. "I misled him. And yet what else could I say?"

Judith wrapped one arm around Maria's shoulders and eased her into a walk. "You did what you could."

They made their way home slowly and said nothing. Judith listened to the knocking of wagon wheels against the paving stones or the scolding of a mother, and she couldn't help but look around each street corner for Abraham. Haarlem had never felt more vast. She looked at Maria, who let the rain accumulate on her cheeks like tears.

The next day, Judith went to her workshop. She checked on the drying layer of varnish over her portrait of Peecklhaering, or Gerard, and his drunken grin radiating upon the panel made her smile. She dabbed a fingertip at a corner of the panel, and it came away dry. That was a relief. At the grinding table she spooned cubes of Cologne earth into the mortar for grinding. The exertion in her shoulders transformed the world into a rhythmic noise, like beautiful pebbles underfoot.

The door opened, and Maria stood at the threshold. She had never visited Judith's workshop, and Judith raised her eyebrows. The linen-seller must have admitted her downstairs, and it was strange that he didn't tell Judith first.

"Come in, please," she said.

Maria stepped inside but did not close the door behind her. The hallway at her back was dark, which had the effect of making her outline difficult to see clearly. Maria glanced around the room but made no reaction to the paintings or the light. Judith couldn't help but feel a twinge of disappointment.

"He's dead," Maria said. "The overmerchant's housekeeper sent me a message today."

"Oh, Maria."

Judith rested her pestle against the mortar and moved to give her friend an embrace. But Maria stepped back.

"I should not have deceived him," she said. "I feel wretched. And then I feel terrible for feeling terrible, all over a promise I shouldn't have made."

"You made no promise yesterday," Judith said.

Maria shook her head. "It's more complicated than that. I had prayed . . ." Her voice hitched, and she took a deep breath to control herself. "I had prayed for a resolution to my problem with him. I hadn't meant his death, though. I hadn't realized he was that ill." She rested her face in her hands and then looked up. "I'm sorry. I'm making a mess of everything, as usual." She turned and closed the door behind her.

Judith stood. She could follow Maria, and they could

talk about her prayers and the poor dead poet. She exhaled and pressed her lips together. Her eyes wandered to a canvas stretched upon her new easel, with only a dead coloring sketch laid in upon it, and no buyer for it yet. There was too much work to do here in her workshop for Judith to worry about excavating every guilty crevice of Maria's tortured conscience. That was Maria, always blaming herself for the slightest fault, imagined or otherwise. Judith shook her head. She would speak to her friend later. For now, she returned to the mortar.

Chapter 13

JUDITH CLUTCHED THE WRAPPED PANEL to her chest and pressed her back against the brick façade. A steady rain fell, and she hoped the sailcloth covering and the roof's overhang would protect her painting. Few pedestrians walked along Kleine Houtstraat that morning, and she strained her eyes for any glimpse of the Frenchman. He was late, and though she had expected he would be, she was still annoyed. He probably thought to pressure her to lower her fee by playing on her fears that he wouldn't come at all. Judith narrowed her eyes and squeezed the painting closer. He would not find her so pliable.

The rain hammered on the roof tiles above, and Judith wiped the splatter from her face. Just then, she saw the Frenchman appear around a bend at the other end of the street. He saw her, waved, and ran to meet her.

"There you are," he said.

"Yes, right where you told me." She gestured at the small brick house behind her.

"If by the compass emblem painted on a house on Gortestraat, I really meant the compass emblem painted on a house on Kleine Houtstraat, then yes, exactly." He squinted up at the raining sky. "Come on, follow me."

"No, this is . . ." Judith started to protest that she had not mistaken the street, but he had already turned and walked back in the direction he had come from, toward the market square and the canal. She stepped out into the street, which was as wet as her spot alongside the wall, and followed.

"I'm sorry to drag you through this," Lachine called over his shoulder. The apology surprised her, and Judith said nothing. She was slower and trailed a few feet behind him. That might have been how he wanted it, she realized.

He ran under the tiled awning of a bakery and entered. A row of round rye loaves were set out on display next to the door, and even in the damp they smelled delicious. Judith followed.

Inside, the bakery was spacious. A large fire swirled in an open hearth, and two men worked kneading dough at a counter alongside it. A woman was cutting a pan of the hard, twice-baked zotinnenkoeken into rectangles to set on a display plate. She looked up at Lachine, who waved a greeting, and she returned to her work.

"It's better to do business somewhere dry. And private," he said. "That's my piece?"

"I'm confident you'll be pleased," Judith said. "Shall I unwrap it?"

"No, I haven't the eye for that stuff. You used Gerard Snellings, right?"

"Yes. As promised. You don't want to see?" She hoped he would, so he could see what a likeness she had captured.

He shook his head. Then he pulled a pouch out from inside his doublet and fished out a few coins.

"Here. Pleasure doing business." He dropped the coins, the exact amount they had agreed to, into her palm. With the coins in one hand, she leaned the painting toward him. But as he was about to take the panel, a boy ran into the store.

He was dressed in a torn shirt soaked through with rain, and he looked to be about eight or nine years old. Panting, he grabbed the hem of Lachine's plain shirt. Judith hugged her painting against her chest again.

"The new boy," he said. "He was watching at the dock, and he must have said something, I don't know. But one of the men there, they've taken him, they're beating him. You have to—"

Before the boy could finish his sentence, Lachine ran out into the rain. Judith glanced bewildered around the bakery, where none of the workers looked up from their tasks. She still held the painting, as well as Lachine's coins. He might accuse her of swindling him, and she knew she did not want such a man as her enemy. She ran after him.

She stepped outside in time to see him turn up the street alongside the canal, toward the river. She paused and then followed. Her skirts pulled at her waist, and holding the painting gave her an uneven gait. Judith was glad, in a way, for the rain, which kept people out of the streets. Hopefully no one would notice her. And if the water damaged the painting, Lachine could only blame himself. But still she pressed it against her chest.

Exhausted, she slowed to a walk. Ahead, she could see him reach the Spaarne River and hurry north, toward the Weigh House. Judith wiped the rain from her brow and glanced at the sailcloth. Water still beaded on it as the raindrops fell, and she exhaled in relief.

When Judith reached the river, she heard a swell of men's voices yelling. She kept close to the tall, brick buildings with their tiered frontages along the waterway, and approached slowly.

Lachine faced two sailors dressed in loose linen shirts

turned brown by the rain. He pressed his finger into the chest of one. Both sailors and Lachine erupted into shouts. Behind them, a third sailor stood with his boot pressed on the chest of a boy splayed out on the ground. A small, masted ship was docked alongside the riverway, and about a dozen small barrels were stacked on the pavement. Further in the distance, Haarlem's large-wheeled wooden crane reached skyward, as if to turn its nose up at their indecent behavior.

One of the two nearest sailors pushed Lachine. Judith walked a little closer, and she saw the grimy messenger boy cringing at Lachine's side. The boy on the ground watched the argument with wide eyes. Judith couldn't tell if it was tears or rain that ran down his cheeks, but as she approached, she noticed a faint trickle of blood, diluted by the rain, winding its way along his face.

"You've no business," Lachine yelled.

"We've got all the right," responded a sailor in a floppy brown hat. "Just doing our work here, when we find this rat poking about." He gestured back behind him to the third sailor.

"And that's got nothing to do with you," added the second, this one with a day's worth of golden stubble on his round face. He again pushed Lachine, whose face grew red. The man by the boy gave the child a kick, and the boy moaned.

Lachine rocked back on his heels, as if he were calculating the situation. He clenched his fists, Judith saw.

"Excuse me," she called as she approached the group. All of them looked at her in surprise, except the man in the hat, who continued to glare at Lachine.

"I'm sorry to interrupt your conversation, but I couldn't help but notice the impressive casts to your expressions. I know, so like a woman to push her way in where she has no business. But I'm a painter, you see. I'm always searching for exemplary faces. And the . . ." She paused, and made as if to count the men. "Three of you, you're sailors, yes? I've never seen such perfect faces for showing life on the water. The sun, the honorable hard work, the waves. Have you ever sat for a painting?"

She took another step closer. "Not you, though. I'm sorry." She gestured at Lachine, who frowned for a moment before erasing his expression and moving away from the group. "That nose won't do you any favors. But the three of you, let me see . . . Well, yes, particularly you there—in the hat. Oh, and you've got a boy with you? Let him up, let me see his face."

The man with his foot over the boy glowered, but his companion gave him a nudge. Still, he refused to lift his foot.

"A lady painter, is that right?" He pressed a little harder on the boy's chest. "Never heard of such a thing."

Judith laughed, and the man's mouth twitched in surprise. "True, I'm something of a novelty. All the more reason to sit for me. Look, under this sailcloth I've got a painting I completed, on commission. I'll show you."

Her fingers trembled as she fussed at the twine knots, and she didn't dare look at Lachine. She prayed the rain would do no damage to her wood, and that Lachine would forgive the risk to the painting. He had already paid her, at least.

Clumsily, she dropped the sailcloth on the ground, and then turned the panel around to show the sailors. The two closest widened their eyes in surprise and approached to see the painting more closely.

"Now that's something," said the unshaven man.

"A lively picture, that," said the other. "Why, I'm sure I've seen the fellow."

"You probably have, if you've spent much time in Haarlem," Judith said. She hoped the tremors in her arms weren't making the painting shake.

The man standing over the boy grunted, and then he lifted his foot. "Let's have a look," he said and walked closer. The boy scrambled to his feet and ran over to Lachine.

"I've been wanting to do a sailing picture," Judith said. "Perhaps something like three sailors sitting on deck, passing the time."

"We don't do much sitting on this cursed river," the man in the hat laughed.

"But it's not a terrible idea," said the unshaven man.

"Come see me," Judith said. "I've got a workshop on Korte Barteljorisstraat, near the corner. And I pay my models, of course."

The third man's eyes lit up at the mention of payment. "You're there all the time? We haven't time this port call, have to hurry with the load of oil here, but next . . ." He kept his eyes fixed on the portrait of Gerard. Judith wished she could see her artwork too, as she held the panel in front of her like a shield. She wanted to see Gerard's warm eyes and laughing mouth. Surely, if nothing else, the painting would make the sailors yearn for a drink.

"I'm sorry again for interrupting," she said. In her peripheral vision, she couldn't see Lachine, but she didn't turn her head. "I know you're busy. I couldn't resist. Will you help me? Come sit for a painting?" Her heart skittered at the thought of sharing a room with these three rough-hewn men, if they did take her up on her offer.

The unshaven man ran a finger down his chin and looked at his companions. "I always knew I was a good-looking fellow," he said and laughed. The man in the hat patted him on the back.

"Look, the damn boy's gone," the third man growled. He glared at Judith, who tried to look alarmed.

"And I had wanted him to pose too. A boy always adds good balance. Though I could still do a fine work with three figures. If you can't bring him, that is." She was losing track of her argument.

"Jan, forget it," said the man in the hat. "He's a wharf rat. Next time we see him or that damned Frenchman, we'll take care of them. Sorry," he added to Judith.

"I only wish I could paint sailors' colorful language in addition to your faces," Judith said with a smile. The rain dripped in a rivulet down her temple. She stepped back. "Don't forget, will you? Korte Barteljorisstraat. Ask for Judith Leyster if you can't find me."

The man with the blond stubble nodded and clapped his hand on the other's shoulder. "Maybe if we hurry, we can be back in town in a week's time."

"That'd be perfect," Judith said. She picked up her sailcloth from the damp ground. Before they could say anything else, she turned and walked away.

Her heart pounded as she walked back toward the canal with the ship and the stone Weigh House behind her. But no footsteps followed her, and she heard only the chatter of the raindrops falling on the roof tiles above her head.

When she turned the corner, she leaned against the nearest building and hugged the painting to her chest. Lachine and the two boys stepped out from a doorway. The taller one held a rag to his forehead, and a rivulet of blood dripped out beneath it.

"This way," Lachine said, turning away.

Judith stared in astonishment before gritting her teeth and following. He couldn't even say a word of thanks? When she had intervened for no reason. And now she might have to pay three models, when she didn't have the funds for a single one.

She was fuming by the time they turned down a narrow street. Lachine and the boys entered a small inn pinched between two houses, and Judith stood outside glowering. The older boy opened the door and beckoned.

"Fine," she said, scowling, then entered.

Inside, the smell of stale beer and old sweat hit her, and her eyes blinked in the dim light. She saw no other patrons. The room had no fire lit, and it was cold. She shook the rain from her sailcloth and draped it again over her panel. She couldn't bear to look at it for damage.

Lachine sat down at one of the few tables. He gestured at the bench across from him. The boys slunk off to another table, where they spoke in low voices.

"That was clever work," he said. "My boy is grateful."

Judith nodded. She slid the painting across the table, but Lachine ignored it.

"He got here some months ago from Roermond, down south. After your prince kicked the Spanish out and orphaned hundreds in the process. Not that you'd care, but the boy's had a tough go of it."

"Why would you say I wouldn't care? I helped save the poor child." She glanced over at the boy, who seemed to be smiling at something his friend had said.

"Sorry. I'm used to no one caring about these orphans. I'm not used to polite conversation, either." He smiled, and Judith was surprised to notice that his eyes were gray, not dark brown as she had thought. She was dismayed that she had made such a mistake.

"And you do care about them?"

Lachine shrugged. "I know what it's like. I give them some work, pay them fair. Don't stop them from getting coins elsewhere, either. Which is more than others might say."

"Others?"

Lachine didn't answer.

"He was looking into that ship, wasn't he? Which was filled with barrels of oil. Linseed oil, judging by the markings. Do you sell linseed oil?"

Lachine laughed. "No. It's my business to know things,

and sometimes knowing things helps other men make their deals. That's all I'll say about that. Here are your coins to pay for those models, by the way." He slid a small pile, perhaps eight, of silver schellings across the table.

She pushed the painting toward him. "I hope it's not damaged," she said, and she couldn't keep the apology out of her voice.

He shook his head. "It couldn't be."

He rested a hand on the package but still didn't open it.

"I'm surprised you don't want to see it. Disappointed, even," Judith said, blushing with the confession.

His eyes widened. "I didn't mean to offend. I knew it would be a good likeness, and that's all that matters. The painting is a gift, in a way, but I don't care if it pleases. Wait, I'm not saying your skill doesn't matter. I knew from the other painting that you could do the work."

Judith fingered the edge of the cloth. She loved the portrait, she realized, and was a little sad to see it go. She picked up the coins and stood.

"Thank you for the commission."

"You know, lady painter, if there's anything you ever need, maybe a bit of information—that's about all we have. My boy Oloff would be glad to help."

Judith nodded and looked over at the boy, who gave her a faint smile.

"I can't think . . ." She paused. "There is one thing. My brother, Abraham. He left town in a hurry, and I don't know why. Or where he went. Anything would help." The room suddenly felt washed in cold, and she hugged her arms to herself to still her heart's tremors.

Lachine pressed his lips together. "I'll keep that in mind. Pleasure doing business with you, Judith."

She dropped the schellings into her hanging pocket

and left the dim tavern. Outside, the rain had abated. Still, she would have to change out of her soaked clothes when she returned, or she would catch a chill. She walked slowly along the canal and watched the ripples as well as the few remaining raindrops fracturing the reflected trees. Why was it so complicated, she wondered, to have what so many others had? A livelihood, a scrap of freedom to do as she pleased. The chance to paint whatever scenes and snatches of emotion she wanted. She shook her head. She was wrong, she knew, to think success came easily to others. She knew many journeymen painters had stumbled along the path to master. And they were men. Judith would simply have to work harder and try to put her worries about Abraham from her mind. He could make his way. She had to find hers.

Chapter 14

A WEEK PASSED, AND THE SAILORS did not come. Judith locked the door to her workshop and walked down the stairs and out of the linen-seller's house. She had only a few blocks to walk, a turn toward the cathedral, and then down the street to the right before continuing straight, but she still had to hurry. She had delayed her departure for so long that now she feared she might be late. Judith clutched the stretched canvas, still tied to its frame, against her chest as she walked, her palms damp with sweat, and her fingers cramped with the tension of her grip. Firm, but not too tight, like hands holding a sleeping baby. She was grateful the rain had eased up for the moment, for the light, misting damp was easy to fend off. Her boots tapped on the paving stones as she walked. She wished Abraham were here to accompany her, but she had heard nothing from him since she last saw him two weeks ago, nor had she heard anything from Lachine. After thinking about it, she wondered if her brother's landlord had been wrong. Perhaps Abraham had signed with a ship, as he always dreamed of doing, and set off to make his fortune in the Far East. That he had done so without telling her made her want to yell, or vomit, or write him a dozen letters that he would never receive. But she found herself hoping he had sailed away. It was better than imagining him joining a band of highwaymen or sleeping in a musty barn while hiding from whomever he was fleeing. Or worse. Judith gritted her teeth. She missed him. But it was no good thinking of him, especially not today.

She passed a seedy tavern as a peasant—identifiable by his short haircut—stumbled out. Judith angled the covered painting so it concealed the pouch hanging at her hip. She so rarely carried this much money with her.

She glanced around as she walked. She should focus, not thinking about Abraham but observing the details of the day—the way people moved and expressed their emotions. Such observation taught her to better capture moods when she picked up her brush. But her thoughts were drawn back to the painting in her hands and the four she had left behind. Had she chosen wisely? Was this a fitting "master piece"? A work sufficient to demonstrate her worth to the Guild leaders? Then, there was the healthy dose of daring involved in her choice. She walked past a flower stand selling a few early blooms, and Judith shook her head. No, she would not worry about the message. Her skill, yes, that still gave her concern. But that was different from her worth.

Guild meetings were, for the time being, held in the large, new house of Jan Bouchorst, deacon of the Guild this year. There was some talk of relocating to the Pand, a municipal building behind Town Hall, but Judith had heard nothing conclusive. Some leaders hoped for a dedicated building of their own now that the Guild was growing so large. Not too large for Haarlem's market, she hoped. But large enough to accommodate some new artists.

"Here we go," she said to herself, and she knocked on the large door.

One of Jan Bouchorst's apprentices opened the door, and the sound of animated conversation rolled out behind him. She smiled at the boy and then tried to sweep the pleasant expression from her face in favor of something more authoritative. She nodded at him and walked past. She could feel the sweat pearling up under her blouse.

The sound was coming from a large room off to the right of the entryway, and Judith lingered at the entrance. She did not want to hesitate, but anxiety swept over her. Frans Hals, Dirck Hals, Paulus van Beresteyn, and two others stood clustered in a group, their tall black hats bobbing as they encouraged one another. Paulus was a magistrate, not a painter, and she was surprised to see him there. He had a winged brown mustache, sprinkled with gray above his finely trimmed goatee, and he nodded as the other men spoke. Even Jan Miense Molenaer was there, talking to another of the younger masters as the soft daylight sprinkled down upon them from the window. His curled hair framed his round face, and his leather-brown eyes glowed, even from a distance.

Forbidding portraits of Haarlem's leading men from last century gazed into eternity, past the artists below, some of whom were probably the sons of the men who had painted and donated the portraits to the Guild. The paintings were as dark and dusted with age as many of the men in the room, layered in somber black and brown.

Judith took a deep breath and strode inside. Her heavy underskirts thumped against her legs as she walked up to Jan Bouchorst. He had lost weight recently, leaving his cheeks hollow beneath his cheekbones, and his fingertips palpitated against her shoulder when he bent to kiss her in greeting. He was not very old, maybe fifty, and Judith was surprised to see him in such low health.

"I'm honored to have the opportunity to present myself today," she said, more stiffly than she had imagined while practicing on her walk over. "Am I the only one?"

He looked over her head at the closed door.

"Michiel Jansen was supposed to be coming too. We'll wait a few more minutes for him."

Next to Jan Bouchorst was Hendrik Pot, a man with small, warm eyes and a pointed, fallow-colored beard. He tapped the deacon's elbow.

"I'm afraid," he said with a nervous cough, "that the other candidate had a conflict." He glanced at Judith.

"He didn't want to present at the same time as me, did he?" She stood up straight.

"I don't know," Hendrik said and looked away. He traced his lustrous mustache with his finger and thumb, and kept his eyes to the rest of the murmuring group. He was smaller than the rest, Judith noticed for the first time. It came to her suddenly that the painters had a ranking among themselves, unspoken perhaps, but consequential. There were not simply masters and apprentices, but rather masters with more commissions than others, masters with greater influence than the rest. The jostling was never finished. She squeezed her eyes shut then opened them. She would have to pay more attention.

Jan Bouchorst shook his head. "All men have their preferences. Understandable. In any case, we can begin." He cleared his throat and walked over to a long table. "Gentlemen!" He pounded the table with his fist, and grimaced at the pain. "Take your seats."

"Do we wait for her sponsor?" someone asked.

"No. Frans de Grebber sent word he could not come," Jan Bouchorst said in his soft voice, without looking at Judith.

Judith knew she was to remain standing in front of the

table, and she was glad to, since indignation now sent a righteous fire up her back. How could Frans have left her here alone, if tradition suggested otherwise? Chairs scraped and fabric rustled as the men settled into their seats, adjusting the pillows that propped them in the straight-backed chairs. Paulus van Beresteyn, the magistrate, departed. A row of beards faced her, and Judith, for a moment, felt soft and vulnerable, with her smooth cheeks and rounded chest, even if her body was concealed in four layers of clothing to ward off the cold. She straightened her starched collar and plucked at the matching lace adorning her cuffs. She lifted her chin and waited.

"Judith Leyster, you can rest your exemplar upon the display," the pale Jan Bouchorst said in a tone that suggested she should not have needed the instruction. She flushed and turned away from the men to face an easel that she had not seen earlier. Behind her, someone tried to suppress a coughing fit.

Judith propped the stretched canvas upon the display easel, then slowly unwrapped the painting. The dark background at the top showed first, nothing interesting, but then, as she continued, the portrait became visible. Her elbow, the back of the chair, the delicate lace of her wide, starched collar, and her face. The self-portrait exuded confidence, with her arm resting on the back of the chair and a brush in that same hand. In it, she wore her best clothes, the same garnet-hued sleeves with gold buttons, white collar, and fine, nearly transparent linen cuffs as today. Her figure sat in front of a painting in progress, as though she had lifted her brush from the scene of the smiling, cerulean-suited fiddle player. Her image regarded the viewer directly, with her lips slightly parted. As if to say, "I am worthy."

The room was silent as Judith worked. Up close, the painting's shading in the buttons on her sleeve and the graceful curve of her hand holding the brush pleased her. Judith stood straight, swept a hand over the canvas as if to give it one final gloss, and she turned to face the group.

At first, in her nervousness, the men only registered as a dark blur, but after a moment, their faces began to resolve into clarity. Jan Bouchorst squinted at the portrait as though he was trying to see it in the distance; Hendrik Pot looked instead at Judith and leaned forward on his elbows, his expression encouraging; and Frans Hals ran a finger down his sparse goatee—Judith had always thought his loose brushstrokes were an inspired extension of his unkempt appearance, with his brown hair falling to his shoulders in messy waves. Of the Guild leadership, only Outgert Aris von Akersloot was frowning. In his early fifties like the rest of them, Outgert had a bald pate beneath his hat and the remaining ring of blond hair well on its way to white. His pale face was pinched around a sharp nose, as though he had swallowed something sour. Judith reminded herself that he was a silversmith, a representative of one of the many less influential professions grouped under St. Luke's broad auspices. But still, he was an officer. And he leaned to whisper into Jan Bouchorst's ear. Beyond them all sat the rest of the artists.

"Would you like to speak about the work?" Hendrik Pot asked. His soft voice did not break the silence so much as ease it away. Yet Judith had not anticipated having to explain herself, and she felt her breath flutter in her chest. She had assumed the painting would speak for itself.

She coughed in an attempt to summon her voice and clenched her fists. "Starting with the pose of the subject, I chose a casual posture here, echoing a pose favored by both Frans and Dirck Hals, to evoke a lightness and familiarity. The positioning of the easel in the image, in turn—"

"No, Judith," Jan Bouchorst interrupted her. He sounded weary. "On more of a technical level please."

"Oh. I'm sorry." She thought of the absent Michiel and stood up straight. "Let's see. I started with a flesh-colored grounding, also similar to Frans Hals's work. Chalk and glue, of course, followed by a thin layer of lead white and umber. I chose that grounding to highlight the lighter tones."

She spoke for a few minutes. Once she lost herself in the recitation of her process, it was easy to speak about the painting. Easier, in fact, than trying to explain what it meant, as she had first thought she must.

When she finished, the room was quiet. Hendrik Pot wrote a note in the record book he regularly carried with him, and then gave her an encouraging half smile. No one said anything, and Judith opened her mouth to fill the silence. But she had no idea what the situation called for. In the street outside, someone walked past while delivering an angry tirade, and the barrage rumbled through the closed windows.

"That is sufficient, Judith," Jan Bouchorst said. He gingerly twisted himself in his chair to look behind him. "Does anyone have any questions?"

Frans Hals pulled at his hat and asked her a question about shading, which she answered easily.

Outgert van Akersloot coughed. "Judith Leyster, tell us, is it true you have your own workshop? Without having yet earned the title of Master?"

Judith sucked in a sharp breath. "I—Yes, I do have a workshop. But, wait, no, not like you mean. It's a little private space to paint. I have no students, and I don't sell paintings from there. I still live in Frans de Grebber's house, where I also work."

A low murmur of voices spread across the room.

"You don't sell them from there? But you are selling them, then. On your own?" Outgert arched one eyebrow.

"No, of course not." She tried not to think of the painting

of Peecklhaering, the one painting that made her a liar. Or two, if she counted the profits from the one Lachine had taken. He did pay her for that as well, albeit indirectly. She focused her thoughts on the portrait to her left and tried to keep from flushing. It was terrible, having to lie, but she couldn't confess what she had done. And she couldn't have done differently, not if she wanted to wrench herself into independence.

"You're certain?"

Judith looked at the men sitting at the table. A bored Frans Hals picked at his fingernail, and Jan Bouchorst looked at her without giving the impression that he saw her. But the others were listening.

"I'm certain. I've sold works through Master de Grebber's workshop, as is appropriate." She squeezed her hands together at her waist and gave a silent prayer that God would understand.

Outgert laughed. "That's reassuring. Our most flagrant violator can vouch for you. And he's not even here."

"Now, Outgert, I appreciate your concern for our sales controls," Jan Bouchorst said. "But Judith is not making silverworks. I think the painters in the room are satisfied with her behavior." His tone was neutral, but the insult was unmistakable. Van Akersloot's cheeks flamed scarlet, and he sunk back into his chair. The light sharpened in reflection off his forehead. He narrowed his eyes at Judith as though she had been the one to slight him.

"No further questions on my part then, Deacon." He emphasized the title and appeared to be suppressing a grimace.

"Very good. Judith, you have the requisite fee? Place it here, please." He tapped the table, and she dropped the coins onto the dark wood. She exhaled as she did and hoped he wouldn't notice the half-moons of sweat under her arms, surely visible even with all her layers. "Thank you. Now you may step out while the Guild considers the merits of your application."

Judith gave a quick nod and walked out. She waited in the hallway, first fidgeting then pacing. She was not sure if the deliberation was a formality. By allowing her to present her masterwork, as they called it, they had certainly implied she was worthy. But maybe anyone who had completed an apprenticeship was entitled to present a painting. Maybe the deliberation was when the true decision was made. Her lie about the sales weighed on her. But what could she have done? She repeated the question as she paced. After a few minutes, she paused in front of the closed door, but the muffled sound of her name made her stomach wrench, and she kept walking. She would identify the shades in the plaster along the walls to give her something to think about.

One of the younger masters opened the door and stepped out.

"You haven't seen the servants, have you?"

She exhaled and noticed her hands were trembling. "No, I haven't."

"If you do, could you send them inside? We could use some drink."

"Oh. Yes."

He nodded and shut the door before she could try to divine the tenor of the discussion from his expression. After he disappeared back into the room, she moved down the hallway, away from the door. She did not want to be caught eavesdropping.

Surely the Guild would not bring her here to scorn her. But then there was Daan Pietersz, an apprentice at Frans de Grebber's house some four years ago. He was more confident of his own talents than his master was. Still, he wasn't a bad painter, and Judith had admired his bold coloring, even if his forms needed refinement. When he brought his masterwork to the Guild, he chose a relatively subdued painting, an Old

Testament scene rendered in layers of olive, moss, and emerald greens. They rejected him. She never saw the young man again, though Frans de Grebber claimed the boy had merely moved to Den Haag to paint for the royal court and their rainbow of courtiers. She was not sure she believed him.

Still, rejection must be unlikely. It was more probable they would tell her she was not quite ready. That she needed to spend more time as an apprentice. She grew cold at the thought of extending her dependency upon the De Grebber house and workshop. The Guild would certainly scrutinize her sales and attempt to prevent her from making any independent money. She would be shackled.

A young woman with an apron covering her yellowed dress and a broom clasped in her hand stepped into the hallway from an adjacent room, and Judith relayed the request for ale. The woman nodded and swept half of the hallway before putting the broom down. She returned with a bucket of sand, accompanied by another servant carrying a small barrel of beer on his shoulder. When the door opened, a soft swell of voices spilled out. Judith wondered if they were still talking about her. Could the decision be that difficult? In spite of the chill, her sweat trickled down her ribs.

Outside, a group of boys enjoying the start of their midday break from school yelled and bantered between themselves as they ran by. In the distance, the clang of a blacksmith's workshop sounded.

The door opened again. The same young painter emerged, and this time he beckoned for Judith to enter. He held the door open for her, but his face was blank. Judith's stomach twisted, even though she told herself she had nothing to worry about. She was a competent painter no matter what these men said. She examined their faces for any hints. Most of their expressions were neutral, though she thought she detected a glimpse of a smile beneath Hendrik Pot's combed mustache. And Van Akersloot glowered. Her heart raced with hope.

Jan Bouchorst cleared his throat and tapped the table, as if to call them to attention, but no one was speaking. His fingers trembled like twigs against a windowpane.

"As many of you know, the work of painters, artists, has long been misunderstood. The ignorant have thought there was no difference between slapping paint upon the side of a house and capturing the image of a king. We know differently, however, and the craftsmen and artists in our guild deserve more recognition. Even those among us who do paint houses—none here today I assume? Even those deserve better than what they get now. So it's important we take care when considering who we allow to join our ranks and represent the Guild. We face the world united, as artists, and we must show we all, as artists, produce only the best.

"Judith Leyster." Jan Bouchorst paused and held her gaze. "The St. Luke's Guild has considered your application to be a master in said guild. In light of your apprenticeship and your work, we have decided to admit you. Your painting here will be hung, with those of the other masters, in the Guild Hall." He coughed with a deep, wrenching sound. "When we finalize the location. In any case, congratulations, Master Judith Leyster."

Judith pressed her palms to her chest and fought back her tears. She gave a short bow of thanks toward the seated men. Master Leyster. She was as good as they were.

After the meeting adjourned, Judith lingered, accepting the well-wishes of the friendlier Guild members. To her surprise, the older painters were more forthcoming than the younger ones. Jan Molenaer was the exception, congratulating her with a hearty smile and a warm kiss on the cheek. She squeezed his hand and wondered if he had advocated for her.

As she stood talking to Jan and Hendrik Pot about the

state of the art market and the best-selling subjects, three low voices behind her caught her attention.

"Frans de Grebber. How could he not come?" asked one. Judith guessed, without looking, that it was Dirck Hals, with his distinctive baritone voice.

"I'm certain he's avoiding us. No, scorning us."

"Do you think so? That seems cowardly. Not like him."

"Not cowardly. Manipulative. He wants to make us worry."

"Let him worry. And at least we have another one under our control now."

Judith shifted her stance a little so she could attempt a glance over her right shoulder at the speakers. A few paces away, in her peripheral vision, she saw Dirck Hals, as she had guessed, and with him was Pieter Molijn, judging by his English accent, and Salomon de Bray. As if sensing her attention, Salomon shrugged and turned his head of curled blond hair. He had a fine profile, almost Roman in the clarity of lines to his nose and jaw.

"No matter. I'll see you tonight, I imagine?"

"Yes, of course. What's the topic?"

"Theatre recitation, I believe."

Dirck groaned. "I hate those."

Judith kept her eyes focused on the diminutive Hendrik Pot, who was telling the story of his own induction into the Guild. She wondered, now that she had crossed this one bridge, if she might have a chance at others—like joining the rhetoricians' group Dirck and Salomon had mentioned. No. The Guild could not deny her skill, but ability had no meaning for those clubs. Entry was based on who you were, not what you could do. And even here, where only a few Guild members came to kiss her cheek in congratulations, she was no one important. Worse, she was a woman.

Chapter 15

APRIL

THREE WEEKS INTO LENT, WHICH was a timetable only Haarlem's Catholics kept, the Guild messenger returned to the De Grebber house. Again, Maria led him through the cool, dark house. She stood at the threshold of the workshop and did not conceal her interest when the messenger delivered the sealed letter. Her father had been examining the day's work in the workshop, the brightest room in the house, and now he gnawed at the end of a brush while he read the missive. When he finished, he groaned.

"What is it? Are they still asking about the relic?" Maria pinched the wool of her skirt between her fingers. The messenger crossed his arms and waited. De Grebber looked at him then stood and handed the man a coin.

"Salomon de Bray doesn't need his answer now. I'll be in touch."

The man shrugged and pocketed the coin. "I doubt he'll be happy about it. But that's your business. Until next time then."

Maria escorted him out then hurried back to talk to her father.

"Tell me. It's about the relic, isn't it?"

"Yes. You're interested in it?"

"Of course. A relic! Of St. Luke, even. Who wouldn't be interested?"

He nodded, though his expression was distracted. "The letter said that Father Cloribus isn't in Bruges; it says that they've traced him to Leiden. Leiden! Only, what, four hours away, and they are still insisting that I go. Bastards."

"But if you wouldn't be gone for long, what do they gain by sending you? Maybe they mean it. You would have a better chance of getting the relic back. You're of the true Church."

He snorted. "They're trying to save themselves from embarrassment. And there's no way I'm going on that hunt. It's absurd."

Maria glanced out the large casement window toward the silver sky that hugged the rooftops. "I could go. It's close; there's no harm. And then you don't have to leave. They couldn't object to your daughter going, right? You could say you were offended if they did." She smiled, and her father caught her eye and grinned back. Her heart raced at the suggestion, but she kept her smile in place. She had been hoping for an opportunity like this—a quest—and she had been prepared to send herself to Bruges. Leiden was a much less intimidating destination.

"There's something to that," he said. He stood and took his brush to a worktable, where he dipped it in a cleaning solution. "But I don't know. I'm not sure I want you traveling by yourself."

"I would be fine. The carriage is safe—people travel in them all the time. And Father Cloribus couldn't say no, not after I'd gone to that effort."

"I would enjoy setting Salomon back on his heels." He lifted his chin, giving his neck a stretch as he thought.

"Exactly." She was surprised at the stillness of her hands. If she left Haarlem, she would not have to dodge Judith's questions about her painting, and she would not have to glance around every street corner for fear of seeing a shadowy, blond head and an unshaven face.

"I'll think about it." He tapped the brush on the rim of the vessel and shook the cleaning solution off. "It might work."

She wanted to press her case further, plead with him even, but she knew that wouldn't help. She smiled, as if his decision was of little consequence to her, and left the workshop.

After their salted herring dinner that night, Judith, who still spent her nights in their house, pulled out her latest songbook and insisted the household join her in some singing. Frans de Grebber, as usual, declined, but he conceded to follow the group into the large entry hall, where the oldest apprentice brought his lute and Maria her cittern. They pulled chairs together and, after a few bad laughing starts, set into playing the first song in Judith's book, a sample of Jacob Cats's verse set to melody. Judith bobbed her hand in the air to set the time while she sang, and the boy strummed the melody from the curved belly of the lute. Maria liked playing the cittern, with the sharp tones produced by the wire strings and the resistance those strings gave her fingertips. Her notes pierced the others' music, and yet somehow made it all whole. They played long into the night, until the candles burned down, and no one could read the notes any more.

Maria and Judith hauled themselves up the steep staircase to their second-story bedroom and, by the dim light of the moon, dressed for bed. Maria pulled her dressing robe over her gown to keep out the chill. She was still as slender as a teenager and prone to shivering, and she was about to draw the curtains of her sleeping compartment closed when Judith whispered her name.

"Mmm." Maria rubbed her eyes and stifled a yawn.

"I want to ask you something, since you're a Catholic. I've been thinking about sin," Judith said, her voice level. "Because that's what people want to buy. Not sin, I mean. But reminders not to sin. The strange thing is, those reminders, our paintings, they make sin look rather nice. Delicious, even. Do you know what I mean? The idea has been gnawing at me. I know you think about sin, being a Catholic."

Maria sat up in her bed and leaned against the wall by her pillow. She stared at the ceiling of the small sleeping chamber, which was so dark that it grew deep in its blackness.

"Yes, I do."

"Is that why you did that? The burning. I figured it out, you know. I can't imagine doing that to my own painting. So much work . . . gone."

Maria blushed. "I needed to atone."

Judith gave a coarse laugh and stirred in her compartment, as though turning over. "Atone for what? You've always been harder on yourself than you deserve, Maria."

"No, I'm not. My sins . . . and after Samuel died, all I've felt is guilt. I was so wrong to speak as I did to him. To avoid telling him the truth, letting him believe something untrue."

Judith sighed. "Maria, you did nothing wrong. You must know that. Look, I'm sure my list of sins is longer, and I've lived a pretty dull life. Chastity intact here." She laughed, drily, again.

"You don't have to live an exciting life to sin. Come on, Judith, they tell you every Sunday, right? I know that much about the Reformed Church. The Devil is everywhere."

"Maybe. I still can't imagine that you need much atonement. Whatever sins you might think you have, it's not what art buyers are worried about. Your sins can't be what the merchants want me to paint about and warn them against."

Maria took a deep breath. It had been so long since she and Judith had talked like this, alone in the dark. She wrapped her fingers around her forearm and felt the scratchy wool of the robe. "I'll tell you. Something I've never told anyone." She paused.

"Yes?"

"It was some years ago, fifteen maybe. I must have been nine or ten. My mother was still alive. Our neighbor Floortje van Goyen, you know her, she had her brother visiting. He was younger than her, so about twenty-five, though his size made him seem older. He terrified me, and when he caught me alone he'd leer and say crude things. I tried to stay away from him. But then he fell sick. His body grew burning hot, and he got to where he couldn't lift himself from his bed. Poor Floortje was beside herself. Her first husband had died, and she kept coming to cry to my mother that she didn't want to be alone. Mother sent me to watch over him one afternoon when Floortje had to leave to sell her smallwork in the market. She'd gone two weeks without laying out her pieces for sale. Mother thought she needed the fresh air as much as the money. I didn't want to watch him, I'd have rather gone to the market, but Mother insisted." Maria paused and coughed.

"Maria, so far this is a story about you listening to your mother. Hardly sinful," Judith said.

"The moment I walked into the room, I gagged. There was an overflowing waste bucket by the pallet, which lay directly on the floor, and I don't know what else in his bedclothes. He tossed and turned, mumbling some insanity about worms and rats. He kept scratching at his clothes and trying to tear them off. I forced myself to put a hand to his forehead, and it was scorching. I thought I should help, but I hated being near him. A few times he seemed to come to his senses, and he looked at me. Once, he smiled. But it made me tremble, and I pulled my stool back against the wall.

"Then he started to moan. He begged me to help him. I filled a cup with water, but he batted it away. 'Let out the heat,' he said. 'It'll burn me up.' He moaned and pleaded, and I realized he meant for me to let his blood, as surgeons might. I didn't know what to do, so I went down to Floortje's kitchen. Partly to escape the room. Partly hoping she would return. And still I could hear him crying above me. I checked to see if she had a myrrh tincture or any of the usual ointments, but she didn't have a single small pot in the kitchen. So I took a paring knife and a bowl. I returned to the room and held the knife to his skin. But he shuddered, knocked my hand, and the knife dropped to the floor. And then something inside me changed.

"It was like I saw his suffering and, God help me, I enjoyed it. I pulled away from him, as far as I could. He was a bad man, I told myself, and I wouldn't help him. He deserved that pain. He thrashed and groaned. He asked for the knife himself, but I wouldn't give it to him. I didn't come any closer. And then, all of a sudden, he fell quiet. He had fallen asleep. I leaned my head against the wall and watched him. And I must have fallen asleep, because the next thing I knew, I heard Floortje running up the stairs. I stood up and watched as she ran to her brother. And then she screamed. Because he had died. Right there, as I slept. And I didn't do anything to help him. I chose to let him die."

The room was quiet, and Maria blinked back a few hot tears. She thought of the man in the street, with the blond hair and the unshaven face, and how much pain she wished upon him.

"That's awful," Judith said softly. "But you were a child. I don't see how that's a sin, Maria."

Maria shook her head. "No, it's the feeling inside that's the problem. Like I have a dark seashell, sealed shut inside my chest. It's evil, and I know I should bury it, heap sand over it like we would at the beach. But sometimes I don't. I yank it out and pry it open. To see what emerges. And so I watched him suffer. Because I wanted to listen to that darkness in me."

"You're being too hard on yourself. Is that what those priests teach you?"

"No! Judith, you're not listening. I wanted to tell you that story to show you. It's the temptation to sin that's inside me, like a stain. Others must have it too, but the worst part is that I succumb to it. No, the worst part is, I enjoy it. I enjoyed watching him suffer, Judith. All because he said some thoughtless things to me. Things any bored man might say." She pulled the quilt over her head, but then pushed it away. "I've never told anyone this. Not even the priest. I know I have to, to ask God's forgiveness. But I'm too scared to ask. He won't forgive me. That sealed-up shell is still inside me."

"Maria, it still sounds to me like the worst thing you did then was to do nothing. That's just like you, isn't it, to sin by doing nothing?" Judith gave a small laugh, and Maria's chest constricted.

"What does that mean?"

Judith was silent, and Maria waited. "Nothing."

"You think I don't ever do anything for myself."

"No, Maria. That's not what I meant." She paused again. "It's late, I'm tired. What I meant was that I find it hard to imagine you enjoying suffering."

Maria kept silent. She couldn't bear to convince her friend that it was true, and yet she knew it was. She was torn between the desire to expose herself, to be known, and the conviction that dwelling on this would only disgust Judith. They seemed to understand one another so little now, and she didn't know if it was better to repair the breach by saying more, or if she would risk even more damage by showing her sinful self.

"You could tell your priest, Maria."

Maria heard the distance in her friend's voice, and her stomach clenched in regret. "You're right. I should tell him. Contrition, reconciliation . . . they are important."

"You're lucky to have that, you Catholics."

Maria could not tell if Judith was trying to be jovial, and she was too tired to do anything but agree. "Yes."

They were silent. She shouldn't have told Judith. Though in a way, she was relieved that she had. She waited.

Judith yawned loudly. "Good night then, Maria."

"Yes. Good night."

But Maria lay in bed for hours, long after Judith's measured breathing fell into a light snore.

The next morning, Judith was gone when Maria awoke late, long after dawn. She pulled on her clothes, added a few extra sleeves and underskirts for the lingering cold, and rushed downstairs. Her father was finishing the last of his breakfast bread and washed it down with a draught of small beer. His gray curls were still flattened from sleep.

"Have you decided?" Maria asked. She pulled a chair up to the table and perched at the edge of the seat's pillows.

He blinked slowly, as if trying to assemble his thoughts. "Oh! The relic. Yes, I did think on it."

"And?"

He dabbed his finger at some crumbs on the table and lifted them to his tongue. "I don't see the harm in you going. I don't want to go; no, I can't be away from the workshop. There's a big auction soon."

"I'm ready to go. Today."

"Already? Hmm. That would catch Salomon off guard and

have the relic back before they know it."

Maria forced a smile. "That's right."

"Assuming that priest still has the thing. But he must. Such a holy item."

"Yes, he must." Her hands were cold, and she clutched them together.

"I'll give you some money for the trip. The Guild will reimburse me. When you're ready, come get the coins, and I'll tell you where to find Cloribus. There's no reason to wait for their permission, is there? Yes, I like this. Present them with everything already completed." He tipped the last bit of small beer down his throat. "You'll need this letter, with the details of his whereabouts."

That afternoon, wearing two additional bodices and carrying a bag with a change of clothes, Maria settled into her hard seat inside the passenger carriage that serviced the route to Leiden. The interior smelled of horse and close bodies. Across from her, an old woman wearing the thick, wide neck ruff of last decade's style did needlework in a hoop on her lap. Next to Maria sat an old man with rounded shoulders but sparkling, lively eyes and a doublet of fine black velvet. He called out the window to the driver, who yelled back in a sharp voice. The old man turned to the other two passengers and shook his head, though he smiled. "Impudent wretch. As usual."

The coach rocked into motion, and they made their slow way out of town. When the town wall had receded behind them, Maria stared out the window and tried not to think. She watched workers digging a long trench, which would someday be a canal connecting Haarlem and Leiden. Then travelers would be able to take a horse-drawn ferry, a smoother passage than the bumpy, bouncing carriage. She closed her eyes and tried to still her stomach. When she opened them again, she saw the low fields edged by rolling dunes across the wide panorama. Maria had been to the beach a number of times, and to a few country villages nearby, but not to another city, certainly not one as grand as Leiden. She imagined the very streets would be swollen with the learning that flowed from the renowned university.

The carriage jerked to a halt, and she could hear the driver clamber down from his perch. She glanced at the old man, who nodded.

"A toll," he said. "It'll take a few minutes to move the barrier."

"Ah."

"Hardly seems worth the trouble, this travel, doesn't it? We could walk. Though not, perhaps, a young woman like yourself."

"I suppose not."

"Unless it were for a good reason. I've heard some women have followed the Way of St. James, all the way down into Spain. But really, these roads can be dangerous." He paused, gauging her interest in conversation, and she gave a small, encouraging smile.

"When I was a young man—and it's true, I was once—I was riding to Frieslaand for business. Me and a partner. There's not much up that way—wasn't then at least—but we had some commerce. On our way, two highwaymen came galloping down the road. My friend wanted to run away, but I thought it would be easier to deal with them gently. Oh, now I don't know why I started telling this story. It's not fit for a lady." He looked away and drummed his fingers against the worn seat cushion.

"Go on, seigneur," she said, hoping the French-styled title might flatter him. "You can't stop there."

He drummed his fingers a moment more, then waved his hand, as though brushing away a fly. "The short of it is that my partner concealed a good number of florins. They found the coins and killed him. Hung his body from a tree. A lesson, they said, for those who resist. I've never traveled a road without hoping to see their rotten bodies strung up high, instead of remembering his. Goodness, I'm sorry. That's dreadful business."

"No, it's fine." She had not seen many decomposing bodies, but she had witnessed enough executions and enough dead dogs floating in the canals to guess about rotting humans. "And did you continue?"

"Continue?"

"On to Frieslaand."

"Yes, of course. Ah, there we go," he said as the carriage lurched forward. "On with our journey."

Maria gave a weak smile and turned to watch the countryside roll past the dirty window. Now she had to figure out how she was going to find her way in a new city. And what she would do if she didn't find the priest.

Chapter 16

The day Maria left, Judith had risen early, though it was not because she wanted to avoid her. True, Judith was not eager to have another private conversation with her friend. It had been easy to be friends when they could whisper about distant dreams, but now grinding those dreams into a messy daily reality had created wounds she neither wanted to share nor see. Judith spent nearly every waking minute now thinking of her work and how she might transform her love of painting into a livelihood. Painting was the only thing she knew how to do well, and she couldn't imagine giving herself over to anything less satisfying. Maria, on the other hand, seemed happy to go where life took her. Or, if not happy, resigned. Maybe that wasn't true, but there was never time anymore to find out. Judith always had too much work. And today, she had urgent business in her workshop. She loved the sound of it: her workshop. Now that she was a master, she could host apprentices. They were an important source of potential revenue and crucial to increasing her production. That morning, she had an interview with the first candidate and his mother. Judith had to ensure the workshop was spotless.

She arrived at the linen-seller's house as dawn was wrenching the night from the streets, and to her surprise, Chrispijn de Mildt called out to her from his bedchamber as she ascended the stairs to her room.

"Judith Leyster, a minute of your time please."

She paused and could hear him throw back his blankets and dress himself in a hurry. He emerged from the room with his nightcap still on, and his breeches untied at the calf.

"I'm glad to see you today. I've come to a decision recently, yesterday actually. I'm moving my shop to Amsterdam. It's where the work is now, where the customers are. But I'm going to keep the house, in case I decide to return to Haarlem. Which is why I'm glad to see you. Because of the house, that is. It makes the most sense for you to rent it, don't you think? You can have your quarters in the same spot as your work, which, let me tell you, is much more convenient. And you can hire a servant, bring on some apprentices. What do you think?"

She pretended to look around the large room so that she could gain a moment to think.

"And the price?"

"Reasonable, I promise. I would rather let it to you at a modest rate than deal with someone I don't know. I don't have a figure now. I wasn't expecting to see you. But I'll come up with something." He gave his shirt another quick tuck into his waistband.

"Let's talk more, when you're ready." Maybe she could trade him some paintings for the rent; she'd heard of such arrangements happening in Amsterdam. She turned away and then paused. "And I'm pleased you thought of me. Thank you."

Upstairs in the workshop, thoughts of coins and rent tumbled inside her head. But she didn't have time for that. She propped one of her recent paintings on an easel so it could be readily seen and its lustrous yellow could reflect more color into the room. She straightened each of the props: the floppy cerulean hat, the pewter flagon, the scuffed violin, and the others, all hung on nails along the wall. She swept the floor clean. But the boy, Davit de Burrij, and his mother arrived before she had time to throw down fresh sand. The boy, about twelve, was clean and simply dressed in a white shirt and brown breeches, and he sat quietly while his mother roamed the space. Judith tried not to cringe at the woman's careless handling of the prepared panels and canvasses, and she struggled to remember the questions Frans de Grebber had asked her father about her budding skills and discipline, some ten years ago.

At the end of the interview, the boy's mother paused to look out the window at the street below, and then turned around. She plucked at an indigo satin ribbon woven into her bodice.

"But where will my Davit sleep?"

Judith glanced at the boy, who kept his tawny head lowered. He struck her as a pliable youth.

"I forgot to mention. How careless of me. I will, by the time your son joins my workshop, be renting the entire house. So he can share a room with the other boys."

Davit's mother raised a thick eyebrow. "Will you apprentice girls too?"

Judith shrugged and lifted her chin. "If any skilled girls apply, I will consider them as I would the boys."

"But they would have separate quarters?"

"Of course." Judith suppressed a laugh.

"And the fee?"

Judith had spent much of the previous afternoon trying to come up with a fee. But she had not, then, planned on lodging the boy, as unrealistic as that seemed now. Of course an apprentice would be housed by his master, even if that master was a woman. She remembered what Dirck Hals had mentioned charging his youngest boys, and then took a few guilders off of that.

"Thirty-two guilders per year. Payable half now, half in six months."

"Paid in advance? That's unusual." The woman placed her hands on her broad hips and tipped her head to the side.

Judith swallowed. "I could make an exception for a boy as talented as your son."

She nodded. "It sounds reasonable. I was wary, I admit, about sending him to live with a woman. And a young one at that. But you've got a nice, clean space here, and your figure paintings are pleasing. I imagine they sell well. I'll speak to the boy's uncle. My husband is deceased, I suppose you should know. But I expect we will accept an apprenticeship, should you offer one. You will?"

"I would be glad to have such a fine boy." She looked at Davit, who gave her a shy smile. His sketches had been decent. But most importantly, she needed a student. Her workshop was nothing without the status granted by apprentice labor. And there was the fee.

As soon as the boy and his mother departed, Judith rushed downstairs to find Chrispijn de Mildt and accept his offer. She negotiated for the sake of negotiating, and she certainly needed whatever discount she could obtain, but she knew she would accept what he offered in the end. They agreed to sign a contract later. Judith stepped out into the damp, gray street, which glowed with promise and life. A puddle next to a tailor's shop transformed the white cloth hanging from his display into silver melted upon the earth. She grinned. Her own house, her own workshop. She held herself tall and plucked a new leaf from a bush extending its branches between the bars of a wrought iron fence. She caressed her palm with the soft edge of the leaf and smiled as she walked. She was not her father, coming home with his grand ideas for the brewery he had purchased, as everyone else was investing in Haarlem beer as well, building breweries by the handful. No, she had talent and conviction—she would succeed. An image of her father, ruddy with excitement, came to her. She closed the leaf in her palm and then dropped it into the street.

Chapter 17

When Maria stepped down out of the carriage in Leiden, her bottom ached from the few hours spent bouncing along the road. She had no idea where she was, but she declined the directional guidance of the older gentleman who had chatted with her during the ride. She was afraid of what accepting such help might cost her in this new place. Better to feign confidence.

They had disembarked from the carriage at the city gates, by a large canal which ran alongside the city walls and would, one day soon, the burgomeisters claimed, connect Leiden with Haarlem and Amsterdam beyond. The water in the canal reeked of excrement and rot, and she covered her nose with her sleeve while she stood considering the city that stretched in front of her. Leiden was larger than Haarlem, and the bustle of the city's university gave the air a complication that she had never felt in her native city. Or perhaps it was the foreignness of this city, its more numerous windmills perched high on their pyramid bases and the wide canal below, all overlooked by the De Burcht fortress. The hilltop fortress and the cathedral, which lacked Haarlem's Grote Kerk's broad presence, rose in the distance, barely visible over the rooftops. She knew that Father Cloribus was staying with a university professor named Jacob Golius, but she didn't know where Professor Golius's house was. She decided to walk to the cathedral and ask someone there. Surely the predicant inside could be trusted to help a woman on her own.

She followed one of the canals that cut through the city, a waterway that the surly carriage driver had told her was the Old Rijn. The linden trees lining the water were tipped in buds, but no leaves had emerged yet. A pack of boys careened toward her, throwing rocks at one another and into the water, loosing ripples and swirling sediment from the canal. She pressed herself against the brick frontage of a tall house, where the cold of the brick seeped into her shoulder, and she waited for the children to roar past. Those antics had never bothered her in Haarlem.

She reached the gothic Pieterskerk with its steeply gabled, narrow nave. The exterior was splashed with mud and had known better days. Inside, she tapped the shoulder of a sleeping prelate sagging in a pew. He shouted in surprise upon waking, but quickly calmed himself. To her relief, he directed her to the scholar Golius's house.

The sun was setting and taking its weak light from the overcast sky when Maria knocked on the green painted door that she hoped belonged to Jacob Golius. She clutched her small, rough cloth bag of clothes and fingered the drawstring while she waited. She had not found herself a place to sleep. And here she was, knocking on a strange man's door as night approached. Soon it would be too dark to venture out at all. Curfew would lock everyone in their homes, and she would have nowhere to rest, nowhere safe to scuttle away to. This was foolish, to press forward with her search at this late hour and place herself in danger. She turned to walk down the cramped lane of two-story brick houses, back toward the city center, where surely she would find an inn, but then the door opened.

"May I help you?" A round-faced woman a few years older than Maria opened the door. She wore a strange, brightly colored shawl over her blonde hair, and her cheeks were flushed.

Maria stood a few steps away from the door.

"I'm sorry. I must have the wrong house." She thought about leaving it at that, hoping she did have the wrong house, at least until tomorrow, but the woman's eyebrows raised in curiosity. "Well, I'm looking for Jacob Golius. Or Jacobus. The scholar." Maria stumbled over the Latinized name. Like most girls, she had never studied the language.

"Yes, that's us." The woman smiled. She gave a quick glance at Maria's mud-encrusted skirts and dusty sleeves. "Come in and tell us what this is about."

Maria gave one last look down the street before stepping into the entry hall. It was a small space but unusually lush with decoration. Shelves displaying plates and vases lined the walls, but instead of the usual pewter and blue and white pottery, they held enamelware resplendent with deep indigo, emerald, and eggshell-blue tones. Judith would have marveled. As Maria took off her dirty boots, she saw the floor was tiled in a bright geometric pattern, with yellow rays looping and embracing cerulean polygons, like dancers tangled in ritual motion.

"I'm Hendrikje Golius," the woman said. They gave a quick kiss in greeting. "You're here to see my husband? It's not about Tamer Lane, is it? You don't look the type. Though, I'll admit, one never knows who will be interested in that man."

Maria frowned and tried to surreptitiously brush the dust from her skirts. "No. I'm here to see Father Cloribus, actually. I was told he's staying with you."

"That old lout. Yes, he's here. I'm glad you're not another messenger coming to deliver a note on the Persian. Those always leave Jacob distracted."

"No. No notes."

"Very good. Come on in."

Hendrikje waved for Maria to follow her into the room to the right of the entry hall, up two steps from the main level. Inside, in the waning light, sat two men. One, the younger of the two, had a heart-shaped face and a long nose.

"Jacob, this is . . . Oh, I didn't get your name, did I?" Hendrikje put one arm on her hip and cocked her head.

"Maria de Grebber. Daughter of Frans de Grebber, of Haarlem. I'm here to see Father Cloribus."

Jacob smiled and indicated, with the pipe in his hand, the other man, stout with leathery skin, as if he worked outdoors.

"De Grebber? The painter?" The priest had a small dimple on his chin that emerged as he frowned in thought.

"Yes, that's right. The elder is my father. I mean, my brother's a painter too, if that's who you were thinking of. Or not." She clamped her jaw shut and blushed.

"Have a seat, Maria de Grebber. I'll get you a foot warmer."

As was customary, the men were seated closest to the fire, and although there was an empty chair beside Jacob, Hendrikje pulled a fifth chair next to the one she had obviously been occupying. They formed a semicircle around the hearth.

Maria set her bag on the floor and hoped someone would comment on it and suggest a solution, but no one noticed.

"We were doing a little dramatic reading," Jacob said and pointed at his wife's colorful head covering. She pulled it over her mouth and raised a coy eyebrow.

"I'm sorry to interrupt. You should go on." Even with the little foot warmer that Hendrikje slid under her feet, the room was cold, and Maria shivered.

"No, I think your arrival provides us with a nice excuse to stop," said Jacob. He inclined his head toward the empty chair. "Réne was getting bored, I'm certain. He practically leapt from his chair when Hendrikje left to answer the door."

"Or he had to piss from all that small beer and *jerez*," Father Cloribus said.

"Same thing." Jacob stretched his legs out, and Maria saw that the black robe she had mistaken for a dressing gown was rather something more formal, with fine stitching and ribbed trim. Perhaps it was a tabard, which only professors wore. She straightened her skirts and again tried to flick away some of the dirt accumulated during her journey.

"Would you like some?" Hendrikje held out a small pewter cup filled with light-colored beer. Maria nodded her thanks and drank it quickly.

"Well, since the reading is done, a little Pass Ten?" Father Cloribus reached into his doublet and held out a pair of dice.

"If you like. But I want to hear what our guest came for, don't you?" Jacob's face was serious, but Maria thought she detected mirth in his tone. "Ah, Réne! Took you long enough. May I introduce Maria de Grebber, from Haarlem?"

The bearded man who had entered gave a hesitant smile. "Réne Descartes. Also visiting." He had a strong accent; French, she guessed.

"Réne, some Pass Ten?" Father Cloribus rattled the dice in his open palm.

Réne shrugged. "If you like."

"Cloribus is only trying to distract us from conversation with the young lady, who has come here expressly to see him," Jacob said. "Go on if you want, but I want to hear what Maria has to say."

The priest grabbed a small cup from the sideboard hulking

along the wall, and he shook the dice inside it before tossing them at the Frenchman's feet. He groaned.

"It's about a relic that my father's guild gave to Father Cloribus for safekeeping. A relic of St. Luke."

"For St. Luke's Guild, of course. That makes sense." Jacob elbowed the priest, who ignored him. "What was the relic? I have some interest in ancient artifacts."

"Bone fragments. In a silver reliquary, which was itself inside a bronze reliquary." Maria paused and glanced at Father Cloribus, who looked up from the game and gave her a quick smile. His lips were feathered with fine lines. "The Guild gave it to the Father here, back when they were worried about the war and feared the city might get sacked. But it seems the Spanish aren't going to be retaking us, not Haarlem or anywhere, so I guess we're safe enough to want it back."

The Frenchman looked up from the clattering dice on the tile. "Oh? The war is over then?"

She was not sure if he was mocking her, and she frowned in confusion. "No. I mean, I don't know. I guess it's still going on. But the Spanish aren't likely to invade. Right?"

Jacob looked between his guests. "We had real trouble with them here, you know. Had to gather everyone into the citadel and flood the bastards."

Hendrikje looked up from the needlework that she had been doing. "Jacob, you ass. That was nearly sixty years ago. Well before you were born."

Jacob gave a half smile and shrugged. "It's no less true. But in any case, Haarlem feels safe now and that's that. So, Cloribus, are you going to give the painters their piece of dead saint? Funny, isn't it," he said to Maria, "that the Guild still cares about that bit of popery? Under the Reformed Church, I mean."

"A few of us are still Catholic. Myself included."

"Bah! Jacob, you stop insulting the girl." Father Cloribus picked up his dice. "He's trying to irritate me. I'm sure he didn't mean you any offense."

"Do you have it, Cloribus?"

The priest frowned. "I'll have to check."

"Come on now," said Jacob.

Réne leaned back in his chair. "Something sacred like that, you know whether you have it or not. Like my rosary, blessed by the Pope. I always know where it is. So, do you?"

"It's hard to explain."

"No it's not, Father." Réne rolled the dice on the floor. "Metaphysics is hard to explain. The location of a sacred object? *Non*, I think not."

Father Cloribus puffed out his cheeks and, for a moment, the wrinkles in his skin smoothed. "I have the silver reliquary, yes. The rest of it . . . Well, you see, I had a friend in Flanders, in Saint Rumboldt's Cathedral, whose parish was full of artists. No, really Jacob, I mean it! Not painters, but sculptors or some such trade. So I loaned a part of the relic to him. For intercession."

"You loaned it?" Jacob leaned forward and slapped his hands upon his knees.

"Can you get it back to us? All of it?" Maria did not want to ask what part the priest had loaned. She hoped he had not segmented the bone, which was already small. Her stomach turned at the idea of the precious saint's bone cracked and split, further injury to the blessed man.

He puffed out his cheeks again. "I'll try."

"Ah, but how hard to try?" Réne ran his thumb and forefinger over the pointed beard at his chin. "Now that is an interesting question, Father. How much do you owe this woman, whom you have never met, but who represents a group of men who once trusted you with something? Something precious.

And does the answer change depending upon how well you know those men?"

"Or you could look at it a different way," Jacob said. He tapped the bowl of his pipe to empty it and restuffed it with dried tobacco. "Is his obligation, in this case, to God, whom the sacred object represents, or to the martyred St. Luke? He was martyred, right? Or is the obligation to the painters?" He lit the pipe and sucked in a deep pull of smoke.

"No, no, Jacob; you're looking at it the wrong way. It's not interesting to consider what we owe God." René exhaled, exasperated. "We owe God everything, we should sacrifice everything for Him. Just as we owe the plants and animals very little; why would we sacrifice for them? No, it's the middle ground that we need to consider. What would we sacrifice for a friend? Should Father Cloribus inconvenience, or even, say, endanger himself for a friend? Or a stranger to whom he is obliged?"

Maria blinked and tried to follow the argument, while a wave of fatigue pushed at her senses. She stifled a yawn.

"All the way from Haarlem today," Hendrikje said in a low voice as the men continued talking. "You must be exhausted."

"It wasn't that long of a journey. Not too bad."

Hendrikje clicked her tongue. "You'll never get an answer out of them, now that they're off." She waved her hand toward the men. "You'd better spend the night here. Unless you had other arrangements? I didn't think so. We've got an extra room with a small sleeping space upstairs. It's where Cloribus was staying, but I'll put him in with Réne. We'll get Anneke to change the linens for you."

"Is it always this crowded?"

Hendrikje smiled. "Often. Jacob complains, of course, that he can't get his scholarship done with all these visitors tramping through, but look at him. He adores the interaction. So yes, we're used to guests. Don't worry."

She left the room and, a few minutes later, reappeared in the doorway, where she waved at Maria to come over. Maria picked up her bag, nodded a silent farewell to the arguing men, and left. In the entry hall, Hendrikje picked up a candle.

"I'm going to bed now, so I want to show you to your room. Don't worry, I'll break the news to Cloribus. He won't be barging in on you. Do you want to sleep now? Or maybe you want to compose a letter for your family? Tell them that you arrived."

"Please. I hadn't thought of that. I was so tired all I could think of was sleep."

"Let me show you up and get you settled in. I know Jacob has some paper he can give you."

Maria followed her hostess up the narrow, winding staircase. The upper level was completely dark, illuminated only by the flickering candle in Hendrikje's small hand. When they reached the tiny room where Maria would be staying, Hendrikje lit an oil lamp and placed it on a small table in the room. She left Maria in the room while she went to get writing supplies, which she returned with some minutes later.

"We can give it to the man who runs the regular Haarlem route in the morning. That line is typically reliable. Will you be going back downstairs tonight?"

Maria regretted missing the men's conversation, but she was too tired and, she suspected, not welcome among them now that Hendrikje was going to bed.

"No, that's all right. I'll see you in the morning. Thank you for letting me stay."

Hendrikje patted her shoulder. "Our pleasure."

That night, Maria dreamt of colorful scarves, and when she woke, she had forgotten where she was. She had never woken in a bed that was not her own, and it had been years since she had spent a night without hearing Judith's noisy breathing a few arm's lengths away, even if they spent the day without seeing one another.

The room was only a shade brighter than utter darkness, and outside her window, the sky was a felted gray. She regarded the view and tried to let the location settle in her mind. She could hear the rumble of voices below as the house roused itself for breakfast, so she pulled on her skirts, two shifts, and a quilted bodice for warmth. She hurried downstairs to join them, for she was famished.

The Frenchman, Hendrikje, Jacob, and Anneke all sat around a table crowded with bread, cheese, small beer, and butter. Maria slid into an empty seat and tore off a chunk of the crumbly black bread. Jacob regarded her with a wry smile, but everyone focused on their meal and kept silent.

When Anneke began to clear the serving dishes and leftovers from the heavy table, Jacob leaned back in his chair. He flicked a tongue over his teeth, and Hendrikje shook her head.

"Your friend has flown the coop, so to speak," he said. "Our good companion left this morning before sunrise, and without saying farewell. You must have scared him, Maria. We should have invited you sooner."

"He's gone?" She glanced at the letter she had written, which now lay in her lap. She had said that the priest had the relic and would return it. She had not mentioned his misgivings; she had assumed he would find a way to return everything. "Do you know where he went?"

Jacob shook his head. "No. Maybe he went home. Maybe not. He tends to wander. Are you thinking of pursuing him?"

Hendrikje sighed loudly and stood to help Anneke with the dishes.

"I don't know. Should I?" Maria glanced back and forth between the men. Réne gave her a weak smile and shrugged; Jacob looked up at the plastered ceiling.

"That's for you to decide. I guess it depends on how important this relic is. A bit of bone? Doesn't seem like much to me. But who am I to say? Cloribus might even be on his way to retrieve the thing and bring it back to you."

"Do you think? Did he leave a note?"

"No, no note." He pressed his shapely lips together. "Probably not. You're right, he would have left a note. But listen." His face grew serious. "The priest is a good man. I've known him since our travels in the Levant. I'm sure he'll be in touch."

Hendrikje poked her head in from the scullery. "You're welcome to stay here, if you want to wait. Or while you figure out what to do."

Réne extracted a small sheath of papers from his doublet pocket, flipped through them, and returned them to the pocket.

"I'll be here through tomorrow," he said. "I return to Deventer then, but I could show you around here if you like. I spent some months here last year and know a few places. Including a house for Mass, if you're interested."

Maria blinked in surprise to hear the forbidden Mass mentioned so openly. But then, the Frenchman had mentioned his rosary.

"That would be nice. A look around, I mean."

"And Réne, help her deliver a letter please. To Arend Wichart, at the Hound's Tavern," Hendrikje called from around the corner. "Assuming you wrote one, Maria?"

The courage to ask for yet another set of expensive writing supplies withered in her throat.

"Yes, I guess I should send it. Thank you."

After waiting for Réne an hour while he did some writing in his room, Maria joined him for a walk in the gray, but almost warm, April morning. He took her past the imposing brick buildings of Leiden University, where knots of men in black robes bustled past them. They walked along one of the city's large canals, and Réne pointed the other way, away from the city center. In the distance, the canal gave way to a quiet river.

"You said you're from a family of painters, yes? It's too bad your timing is off. You've missed the miller's son, a painter whom I've heard is quite good. Rembrandt van Rijn, his family name is for the river here, of course. He was here last year when I was, but now he's off to Amsterdam. That's where the future is for men of talent. Not this old dusty place." He kicked a stone into the canal.

"But I thought you were in Deventer now, not Amsterdam. Was I wrong?" Maria had no idea where Deventer was, but she wanted him to know she had been paying attention. It was the best she could do to solidify her presence. If Judith had been in her place, she would have reminded the scholar that she herself was a painter, not just from a family of painters.

A man poled a punt up the canal, and Réne ignored her question.

"Look," he said, "the fortress. That hill, obviously, is man-made. No such rises around here, in this flat place. Is Haarlem so flat?"

"Yes, I suppose so." She wondered what land could look like if not flat, without the horizon stretching from fingertip to fingertip. They fell quiet as they walked, and she took a deep breath.

"You didn't hear Father Cloribus as he left this morning? Since he was in your room, I mean."

Réne gave her a crosswise look with his sharp, brown eyes, but the face under his wide hat remained impassive.

"Certainly, I heard him moving around, if that's what you mean. But I didn't know he was leaving."

"Of course." She caught her reflection in the mullioned windows as she passed, and she was surprised by how fatigued she looked. Or perhaps that was her imagination working on her image as it flickered by.

"I would have said something." Réne lifted his nose and did not look at her.

When they arrived at Hooglandse Kerk, a large cathedral with a pair of narrow turrets rising up beside the glass windows, presumably once ornate and glowing with colors but now clear in the old gothic frames. Maria asked if they could step inside. She knew the building was no longer consecrated, not in any way that was meaningful to her, and it would have little holy feeling to it. The Reformed Church had done away with the comforts of a sanctified interior, as her mother used to put it. But she still enjoyed the sense of entering a space separate from the busy world. A house built to honor God.

"They dedicated this one to St. Pancras," Réne said when they were inside the cavernous, white space. His voice bounced from the bare floors to the ribbed ceiling, even though he spoke in a low tone. She wondered what the cathedral would have looked like with carved benches and rich tapestries. A painted altarpiece at the front.

"Pancras, the child martyr," she said.

"That's right. Maria, would you wish such a thing for your son, once you become a mother?"

The question startled her, and she looked over at him, but he must have meant it to be rhetorical, for he had stepped away.

"Réne," she called quietly. "I think I'll stay here for a while. I can find my way back to the house."

"Are you sure?"

"Yes."

He nodded, as if he understood the need for contemplation. "I can post your letter, if you like."

"Yes, please. I had forgotten." She inwardly grimaced at the lie; she had still been debating whether or not to revise the missive. But she wasn't sure what else she would say. She handed him the letter.

When he left, she sought out one of the chairs lined up along the side. The side chapels were empty, but the light filtering through the leaded windows gave the space a soft, quiet glow like the brush of feathers against her cheek. She sat and considered her hand, turning it one way and then the other as she imagined painting it in this gentle light.

"You are looking for something, aren't you?" asked a woman standing next to her. She had silver hair, which was wrapped in a long coil under her cambric cap, and a smooth, broad-cheeked face.

Maria placed her hand in her lap. "No, just looking."

"That's not what I meant." The woman closed her eyes briefly. "I mean inside. Inside you, you are searching for something." She paused and looked at Maria. Her eyes were clear and, Maria thought, kind. "You have a purity, yes, but also a darkness. A question. I'm right, aren't I?"

Maria frowned and said nothing.

"I'm in the business of helping people find what they want," the woman said. She stepped back to look up at the window. "To find God's wishes. I protect purity."

"What do you mean?"

She stepped closer again and picked up Maria's hand to cradle it between her own. "I think you know, my dear. Let's talk. But not here. Think about what you want, Maria. And meet me tomorrow morning by the Groenmarkt. Canal side. Don't worry, it's safe, there are people about. And we can talk. You'll see." She smiled, a soft, knowing smile that made Maria's chest constrict. "My name's Sara," she said before walking away. Maria stood and wanted to call out after her, to ask how Sara knew her name, but she didn't. She didn't dare make such a loud noise in the merciless space. She sat back down and watched the sunlight flash over the woman as she walked between the bright pools cast by the clear windows and then out the church's large door.

Chapter 18

MARIA APPROACHED THE MORNING MARKET at the convergence of Leiden's river and canals, and she didn't slow her pace. She walked past the peasant women crouching on the ground next to baskets of onions or leeks, and she wove her way through the knot of children laughing at a farmer doing an impromptu puppet show with his cabbages. A goat stood tethered to a small wagon, and a little boy fed the animal carrot tops. The market took up the open space along the quayside patio, but it wasn't as large as Haarlem's open central square. Maria knew it was folly to agree to meet the silver-haired woman, and she hadn't said a word about the meeting to her hosts. She was returning to Haarlem, she'd told them, and that was probably what she would do. But she had to walk through the market once, to satisfy her curiosity.

At the far end of the market, the Rijn River swept toward her and under a bridge to run through town, to her left. A five-story white building stood looming over the riverside, and a couple stood laughing in front of it. Maria was about to turn to the left, toward town and the gate where she would meet the carriage, when she noticed a white-haired woman lying on her stomach at the quay's edge. Her arms reached down into the river. With a snap of her wrists, the woman snatched up a basket that had been bobbing in the water. She placed the small basket up by her hips and slowly pulled herself up to sit.

Maria approached. Sara partially eased off the top of the basket, which was the width of a dinner plate. She glanced cautiously at Maria before craning her neck to look inside. Then Sara smiled and lifted away the top. She pulled out a tiny, sopping wet kitten.

Maria kneeled down beside Sara and raised a finger to touch the kitten's light brown fur. The creature gave a tiny mew and blinked its terrified eyes at her, but it held still in Sara's palms.

"What children will do for amusement," Sara said. She held the kitten to her breast and used the square of white apron cloth on her skirt to towel the animal dry. "I'm sorry I wasn't on the canal side, as I'd promised. But I saw the boy drop the basket in, and I had to catch it."

"What will you do with him?" The kitten seemed too small to survive in the streets.

Sara furrowed her eyebrows and regarded Maria with blue eyes the color of tile paintings. "He's coming with us." She stood. With one hand she held the kitten, now purring, close to her breast, and with the other, she took Maria's elbow and led her away from the market.

"I'll answer your questions," she said as they walked down a street lined with brick buildings. "First, I knew your name from the other man. I have a sense for people, and you have a glow to your expression that is rare. But I won't claim any witchery for knowing thoughts or the like. Second, you should come with me because there is nothing better you can do. I don't mean that you have nothing to do, I wouldn't presume to know that. But rather that I know that my work, our healing work, will bring you its own healing. Only giving of yourself can heal a wound. You have wounds—don't worry, I won't ask. I don't need to. Everyone does. But God has suggested to you a way to heal yours. Despite these wounds, you have a certain purity."

They crossed a cobblestone lane and passed under a brick archway. Around them, men in long black robes argued or rushed from building to building.

"The university?" Maria asked.

"Yes," Sara said. "I thought you should see this. What men's learning brings them to. And how it differs from our learning."

Maria raised an eyebrow but said nothing. Still, Sara must have noticed, for she stopped walking and held out the kitten.

"What is this?" Sara raised both eyebrows.

"A cat." Maria ran her finger down the kitten's nose and over the dome of his head. He closed his eyes in pleasure.

Sara shook her head. "That's what these men would say." Two young men with red pimples around their nascent beards walked past, and they laughed nervously at the women. "Try again."

"A baby cat? An animal?" Maria wanted to guess Sara's meaning, but she felt like she did when her father would call her to an easel to critique an apprentice's painting. She would look at the bend of an elbow or the shadow under an eye, and she'd know he sought a particular response, but her mind flailed in dark confusion. What seemed a flaw to her might be a strength to him, and she didn't want to disappoint.

"No. A life. A spark of life. Though these fools might argue that the kitten is an animated machine, and I've heard their natural philosophers say as much, you know better. Look at him." Sara held the pink nose and wide, golden eyes close to Maria's face. "This kitten is feeling something." She wrapped the animal back into the fold of her apron, against her chest. She resumed walking deeper into the university. From behind, the silver of her hair and the white of her cap seemed to melt into a single luminous halo.

Maria hurried after her.

"Is it animals you heal then? People?"

"I do what I can, where I am needed."

To be needed. The words settled into an opening in Maria's chest, and her shoulders melted down, away from her neck. Farther down the pathway, a woman in a simple brown dress stepped out of a building with a basket of laundry balanced at her hip. There were very few women around, Maria realized. She crossed her arms over her chest.

"How do you know where to go?" Maria asked.

Sara glanced at her as they walked. "I don't, my dear. We have to find where people are hurting. But in truth, it's usually not hard."

They walked in silence for a few minutes. They passed an open window, where a man's voice rolled through the round sounds of Latin while he lectured to the students seated around him.

"I wish I could attend classes here," Maria said. "They have a world to take apart, piece by piece, and see how it works."

Sara said nothing but nuzzled the kitten against her chin. The apron bib fell back down against her skirt.

"I'm leaving this afternoon before the town gates close. I would love to have you join me, Maria. But I recognize that I know nothing of what I'd be asking you to leave. Do you have a family here? You have a gift to share—you might not believe me, but I can see it. Still I don't want to ask you to sacrifice your care of your children."

Maria shook her head. "I have a father, but he's not here. He has his work, in any case."

"You do what seems best. All I can say is that I hope you will join me in easing the suffering of others. I'll be at the western gate, the wooden building before the marshes. A short walk north of here." She held the kitten in one hand and, with her free hand, cupped her palm against Maria's cheek. Her fingertips were soft and cool, and Maria wanted to lean her head into the gesture.

Sara took a step back. They had walked through the university grounds and reached a brick wall. A tall tree shaded an open gateway, and beyond it were rows of raised garden beds. Maria could see the fresh green of new spring plants reaching toward the timid sun.

"I'm off to do some botanical investigation," Sara said. "I hope to see you after the midday meal. I'll bring an extra loaf for you."

Maria hoped Sara would embrace her, and her hand fluttered at her side as she wondered if she should reach out. But the older woman simply smiled and turned into the garden with the kitten still clasped to her chest.

Chapter 19

JUDITH STOOD IN THE BACK of the large room and watched the auction. Her first Guild auction. At the front of the room stood the auctioneer, a stooped, gray-haired man who had once been a painter but could no longer manipulate a brush. His voice, though, still carried. Behind him, the walls were lined with nearly fifty paintings hung one on top of the other, such that almost none of the plaster behind was visible. Busy history scenes with shepherds and lush green trees looked down on peasants caught laughing outside a country tavern, which sidled up against still life paintings of sliced apples and cheeses or tulips or pheasants still dripping with blood. It had taken Judith a few anxious minutes to search out her three paintings: two merrymaking canvases and a smaller panel of a little girl laughing and holding a kitten. The merrymaking pictures were twinned pendants—each with young men dressed in vibrant suits, whose crimson and sapphire folds she had loved capturing, but one painting showed the men delighting in their drink and company, while the second added the dark skeleton of Death to their party. Don't have too much fun, she had whispered to her figures while she painted them. Judgment awaits.

In the crowd she spotted the candlemaker, Abraham Recht, and his wife Baefje Willems. Judith's hand fluttered to her mouth, and she tried to unclench the snake that wound its way around her gut. The candlemaker was known for being a lavish investor in painters, and he took particular delight in discovering new artists. That he shared a name with her brother could only be a good omen, she hoped. She whispered a prayer begging for the merchant's favor, and then a second one for Abraham, wherever he was. He would have marveled at the room, and yet he would never have let it intimidate him.

"Attention, gentlemen," called Franchoys, the auctioneer. "Painters, out with you. The auction shall commence."

Judith glanced around. She had not realized that she would not be permitted to stay for the sale. She knew there was no risk of theft, not like her illegal auction, but she was too anxious to do anything but watch and hope her paintings earned her the money she needed. The other painters standing at the back began to file out. She tugged at the sleeve of one of them, Floris van Dyck, an older man with an aristocratic nose and an elegant beard.

"We have to leave?"

He blinked in confusion, and then narrowed his eyes when he realized who she was.

"Painters with paintings for sale are always asked to leave once the bidding begins. It's been like that for decades." He turned toward his companion, Willem Heda, and shook his head. "Astonishing who they'll let in," he said, loud enough for Judith to hear.

She clenched her jaw shut and remained still while they filed out. She couldn't make a scene here, not with the buyers present. But she wanted to drag him up to the front and show him her three paintings. They had more energy and passion than any of his glossy still life paintings of pewter plates and cheese.

By the time she had collected herself enough to look around again, she saw that all the artists had left. She inched toward the back wall, in hopes that the shadows might hide her. But as she did, she saw the auctioneer looking at her with a raised eyebrow. She exhaled and went out to the street.

The other painters had dispersed, surely gone to De Basterdpijp, the Guild's preferred tavern, off Grote Markt square. Judith couldn't bear to beg for a seat at someone else's convivial table, so she went home. It was her own home, at least. For now.

In the three weeks since she had signed her lease with Chrispijn de Mildt, Judith had moved into the house, hired a servant, and taken on a second apprentice—a dark-haired fourteen-year-old named Hendrik Jacobsz. The money from Lachine had proven barely enough to cover the first month's rent and supplies, and she had convinced Hendrik's father to pay part of his fee up front, which provided for the household's food. Now, as she walked in the gray afternoon light, she tried not to think about how many days her workshop would last unless she sold more paintings. But of course she couldn't stop thinking about it. Ten more days before the money ran out.

She opened the door and entered the cold house. She skimped on everything, of course, and certainly could not buy firewood. Upstairs, she heard the boys talking quietly in the workshop. At least they were working. Carolein, the servant, walked past with an armload of clean linens that she was taking to hang from ropes along the stairwell. Judith lifted a hand, thinking to tell the woman to rest, to suggest they relax together in the kitchen. But the older woman's gaze was fixed on the pile in her arms, and she bit her lip as she tried not to topple it.

Judith walked back to the kitchen by herself. She sat on the bench by the main table and looked at the onions hung from the ceiling. The light, thin as it was, still made the brown onion skins glow. Had Maria been there, she would have seen it and nodded in appreciation. But it had been three weeks since her friend had left. Maria and Abraham had been a constant rhythm in her life, like a mule's hooves on the paving stones or the slow passage of water in the canals. Judith rested her head in her hands and tried to think of anything trivial, anything like the breath of the wind against the windowpanes or the cold feeling of the tile under her thin shoes. Anything but the tears that seemed always now to threaten at the corners of her eyes.

The next day, a porter came to the front door.

"Here are the coins for the one that sold, Mistress," he said. Judith's mouth fell open. Only one. She sucked in a half breath, but the porter had turned away to gesture at his companion, who had a small wagon of painted panels and stretched canvases tied to their supports. "Bring the two on top. Yes, those up there." By the time he faced her again, she had composed herself.

"The panel sold? With the little girl?"

"If that's the one that's missing, I suppose so. I don't have the records; sorry, Mistress. I deliver what's left over. I'm surprised you had two left behind—I heard there were good sales. And yours look nice. Maybe I'll buy one next time," he said and gave her a smile with both eyebrows raised.

"Yes, thank you," she said, embarrassed that he had seen her need to be comforted. "I'll take those. Oh, here's a penning, and another for your friend, for the trouble." She shut the door before he could say anything else.

With the paintings nestled under each arm, Judith leaned

against the wall. She took a deep breath and lifted her gaze to the ceiling, where she could see, among the deep shadows, some gradients of gray where the uneven plaster caught the light. She took another deep breath and carried the paintings back up to the workshop. She propped them against the wall, image side facing the plaster. There, while the boys sketched quietly, she took out her ledger notebook and recorded the amount she had earned. Six guilders. Her vision blurred for a moment while the tears welled up, but she blinked them away before anyone could notice.

The next day Judith went to the De Grebber house to collect the last of her belongings: a few stray linen shifts that had been hanging on the laundry line and a copybook. Frans de Grebber looked at her with dark, sad eyes when she walked into his workspace, but she said nothing. What could she say? In the weeks since Maria had departed for Leiden, no one had heard anything more than her one cryptic letter. After four days, Maria's brother Pieter had gone to look for her, but no one in Leiden knew where she was. She had delivered the Guild's message and then disappeared. Judith walked through the workspace and up to her old loft bedroom. She couldn't bear another agonizing conversation with the despondent Frans. And she could not escape the sense that Maria's disappearance was somehow a reflection of her own inadequacy. She closed her eyes and took a deep draught of the house's familiar smells: the rich, mineral smell of paint, the warm aroma of simmering stew, and the earthy undertones of the peat fire. She wished she could send those scents to Maria, to somehow remind her how much she had loved her home. Or so Judith thought. But then, how much about her friend did she know? Judith was failing as an artist, and perhaps that was the latest failure in a long string of disasters that she was only now seeing. Judith tucked the book under her arm and descended from the loft. She walked, head down, through the workshop, left her key to the De Grebber house on a table in the entry hall, and quietly closed the door behind her.

Chapter 20

May

JUDITH HELD OUT HER PALETTE, a small paddle about the width of her outstretched fingers, and the apprentice Hendrik smeared onto it the ochre and yellow paints he had prepared. She was teaching him how to grind pigments and blend them with linseed oil to make paints. The boys were learning how to heat the oil to thicken it when necessary and how to sun-bleach it in shallow dishes to bind the lightest colors. Hendrik was proving reasonably able. The younger boy, Davit, crouched on a stool in a corner, sketching an arm from a book showing a series of disembodied arms onto a tafelet, a reusable notebook with pages that could be scrubbed out. The tafelet Judith had lent the boy was not as nice as her leather-bound one, with its ornate clasps that held the metalpoint stylus. That one she used for her own sketches. Still, Davit would cradle his and wrap it in a length of ivory linen whenever he put it away. He was a gentle boy. Nothing like her own brother had been at the same age, eight years ago. Judith sighed. Davit bit his lip as he worried with his charcoal stick at the knob of a sketched elbow.

Judith dabbed some of Hendrik's paint onto the prepared panel. She would have liked to ground the panels here in the workshop, but with such a small workshop she did not have enough hands to do all the work, so she bought the prepared wood and strips of canvas from a specialty store supplied by a newly accredited primuerder. With so many workshops, a man could apparently make his living selling primed supports. She tensed her jaw. The reddish-brown paint clumped to her brush and stuck unevenly when she wiped it across the surface.

"You've done a good job with the pigment size," she told him. "But this needs more oil. See?"

The boy furrowed his brow, drawing his dark, nervous eyebrows together. He was fifteen and hardly ever stopped moving. She doubted he had the patience for the minutiae of painting.

"It's . . . that we're nearly out. I didn't want to use it up." He held up the cork-stoppered jug.

Judith frowned. The price of linseed oil had been creeping up recently, and with her budget stretched as tight as it was, she could barely afford to buy more. She had tried buying walnut oil, which didn't work quite as well as a binding agent and was always expensive. Recently, both oils had become nearly impossible to find.

"That was good of you to try to conserve. But the paint does us no benefit if it doesn't flow properly. Here. See if you can redeem these."

Hendrik scraped the two colors back into their respective pots, each tone scrupulously separate, and returned to his blending.

Carolein stood on the workshop threshold and dried her hands on her faded gray skirt. She was so industrious in her enthusiasm to clean that Judith had banned her from the workshop. Carolein's energies might otherwise reorganize the carefully placed brushes or disassemble a set of props jumbled on a tabletop.

"Mistress Judith, there's someone to see you. A young fellow." Carolein's flat, plain face sparkled with unusual curiosity. Judith wondered what about the unexpected visitor had caught the woman's attention. She took a sharp breath, and her heart pounded. Abraham.

She wiped her hands on her smock, took it off, and hung it on a hook in the wall.

"Continue at your tasks, boys. I'll be right back." Davit looked up and smiled; Hendrik nodded and tested a little paint on the scrap of wood by his side. His foot tapped an irregular, unceasing beat that faded as Judith descended to the entry hall.

She had hung two of her finished pictures flanking the door but had otherwise neglected to decorate the wide space. She tucked a few stray strands of brown hair under her linen cap and cleared her throat. The young man standing by the door looked away from the painting he had been considering, a small, energetic piece portraying two children playing with a ball and stick, and he gave her a reserved smile. Not Abraham. Judith's shoulders sagged for an instant, until she straightened her back. He had large eyes the color of soft leather and a fine mustache curving over his mouth. He looked to be about eighteen.

"Can I help you?"

"Forgive me for interrupting you. You were painting?"

She nodded. His eyes brightened.

"Of course, that's wonderful. I mean, obviously you're painting, but it's wonderful work. That's what I'm here about.

Painting. I'd like to apprentice myself to your workshop."

Judith cocked her head to the right. "Aren't you a little old?" She was only five years or so older than him, but she had begun her apprenticeship much younger—at thirteen. As most aspiring painters did. By now, this young man should be approaching independence.

"You're right, but I do have some experience. I worked with Jacques de Gheyn for a few years."

"But he died, what, two years ago?"

"That's right." He gave a weak laugh. "That's why I left. I thought I'd try something else. But I want to come back to painting." His hands were clasped together. Outside, a vender down the street was selling his produce in time for the midday meal.

She didn't ask why he had chosen her workshop for his re-entry into painting. The answer was too embarrassing to them both. Who else would take an aged apprentice but the disreputable, even desperate, workshop of the new lady painter?

"Jacob de Gheyn was a strange one, no? Those drawings of witches and bizarre creatures. And his habits . . ." Judith had heard the old artist had regularly wandered alone after curfew—titillating, but not damning behavior—and she wanted to see how the young man reacted.

He shrugged and said nothing.

"And your name?"

"Willem Willmsooz."

"Your parents approve? And are you prepared to pay the fee?"

"Of course." He kept his eyes to a painting hung behind her.

Judith tapped a finger against her chin. "I don't think that's the truth. I'm sorry, but I can't—"

"You're right, my parents don't know yet. But they support

my interest in painting. They will pay the fees."

Judith pressed her lips together and looked at him, waiting.

"I'm reliable. I promise." He gave her a confident grin.

She exhaled. "Why don't you come up and do some sketches? Show me your training." She did not want to seem too eager. But the funds provided by another apprentice, even after subtracting the costs, would be a boon. As would be the extra help.

He looked her in the eye and held her gaze. "I'd be happy to."

She turned away to walk upstairs and tried to convince herself the warmth she felt creeping up her neck was the heat from the small peat fire or the contact of her rough collar. Something other than a flush.

Without so much as glancing at a copybook, Willem drew finely detailed images of flowers with silverpoint on a tafelet borrowed from a worried Davit. They were the sort of thing Jacob de Gheyn specialized in. The flowers were technically sound, but not consistent with Judith's more energetic style, and not really useful to her figure paintings. Still, she wanted a third apprentice.

"You never had any problems with Jacob? Anything I should know about?"

"No." His voice was steady.

"Well." She wiped the tafelet clean and returned it to Davit, who flickered his eyes up toward Willem before returning to his exercises. Willem was examining the small, bright workshop and did not seem to notice.

"Well," Judith said again. "If your family is prepared to pay the fee, I suppose we could find a place for you."

Willem's face glowed with a wide grin, and he grabbed her hand. "Thank you, that's wonderful. May I bring my belongings by today?"

Her eyes widened at the touch. Still, she left her hand in

his palm for a moment before withdrawing it. "Yes, that would be fine."

"Would you look at that?" he murmured. He had stepped closer to Davit by the window and leaned down to look at the boy's drawings. "That's quite good. See the shading at the arm?"

Judith joined them, while Hendrik stood by his mixing station and held a mortar suspended in the air as he stared.

"Yes, it's nicely done, Davit," she said. "But don't let this young man's praise get to you. Keep practicing. Willem, I'll tell Carolein to air out the loft for you. It's all we have left. These two share a room as it is." She knew he was avoiding something, but he was old enough to make his own decisions. As long as he paid. And maybe soon he would trust her enough to reveal what the problem was. She would enjoy having someone to talk to.

"That's perfect. Thank you. I'll be back soon."

That afternoon, following the midday meal, Judith walked over to the De Grebber house. The city's streets were damp and slick from intermittent rain, and a few buds were beginning to swell on the tree branches. She saw a new apothecary had opened, as indicated by the addition of a stuffed green crocodile to one row of shop fronts and signs. She would have to stop in and see how the proprietor had priced his linseed oil. Typically she bought the oil from a man by the lake who sold to all the city's artists, but with his prices skipping upwards, she wanted to inquire elsewhere. The stuffed crocodile, a twisted creature, swung in the breeze on new chains that did not yet creak.

As she waited for someone to answer her knock at the De Grebber house, she hoped, against her instincts, that Maria had returned. Judith needed to tell someone about the new apprentice, and she needed Maria's advice. But only Frans and his boys were home. His skin looked pale and fragile.

"I'm not worried about Maria," he said as they stood in

the entry hall. The familiar smells of baking bread and acrid paint tinted the air. "She's surely on her way with the priest to his home to collect the relic, and letter delivery isn't reliable in those parts." He paused, and Judith nodded as if she shared his judgment. "My daughter is very dutiful. She'll feel obliged to see her task through to completion."

Judith nodded again. There was no point in belaboring their fears. "And no word from Abraham, I assume."

"No. You'll hear immediately if anything arrives. I know what it means to you."

Judith already knew as much, and she grasped his hand in brief gratitude. She had already known Frans would share any message, but she still needed to ask. Without a spoken farewell, she left.

She missed both of them. Now, when she noticed how the light fell on a spring leaf, or that the timbre of a young man's voice was deeper than his smooth face would suggest, she had no one to confide in but her art. She walked home through the damp streets, her boots quiet upon the paving stones, and she wondered how it was she had become the one left behind.

Willem moved in with his single pine trunk that evening, and in the morning, he was waiting at the breakfast table before the rest of the household arrived. Hendrik rubbed his eyes, making his pimple-afflicted skin even redder, and Davit coughed, trying to disguise his newly changing voice. Judith noticed mold on the cheese Carolein had placed on the table, and she grabbed the plate so she could slice off the green smudge. She hoped Willem had not seen.

After the meal, she led the three apprentices to her workshop. She stood at the threshold watching the morning's haze illuminate her tools, like a curtain had lifted. The easels, gray grinding stone, brushes, and props were so beautiful in repose. She ought to paint a workshop scene, she thought. She would love to capture the tender detail hidden in her well-loved tools. But no, those scenes weren't what sold. Not for her, at least.

"Let's get started."

She let Willem spend the day refreshing his sketching; tomorrow she would task him with working through the copybook of essential body parts. She suspected his focus on naturalist work with Jacob de Gheyn had been at the expense of human anatomy. She would fix that. In the meantime, she needed to focus on getting a few of her own paintings ready for sale, and maybe she would paint one more revelry piece. She should find Gerard Snellings, now that Shrovetide was past. He might have more time to sit with her. She had enjoyed painting him, enjoyed replicating the spirit in his eyes and the lines alongside his mouth, his combination of joy and wear. Every time she painted, she fell a little in love with her subject, snared by the crevices and shadows and twitches that made the person. Painting meant focusing on the details, much like love. So each of her paintings became, in a way, an act of adoration. She would send Hendrik out later to find Gerard.

Two days later, Judith stepped out of the doorway to her bedchamber and collided with Willem. She stumbled back and brushed at her skirts. Crimson paint had spattered right next to her hip; she placed her hand over it. He hardly noticed he had run into her.

"Gerard Snellings is dead," he said. He looked stricken, his eyes grown larger with the news. His expression alarmed Judith even more than the message.

"What do you mean?"

"Hendrik couldn't find him yesterday, so I did some

looking. I knew the man, a little. He used to come by my father's banquets. I found his old neighbor, who told me Gerard died two weeks ago. No, not died. Was killed."

Judith took a step back and leaned against the wall. The cold plaster chilled her shoulders, even through her layers. She had painted his portrait only two months earlier.

"How was he killed?" Her voice was so quiet that she was not sure Willem could hear her.

He took a step closer. "A man beat him. Until he died." He shook his head.

Judith cradled her face in her hands. She thought of her deal with Lachine, and her stomach twisted. He had never explained why he was so set on a likeness of Gerard.

"I can't believe it," she said. She looked up at Willem, whose face was pale. "I painted him."

"I knew him, a little," Willem said again.

"He was kind. Don't you think?"

"It's awful," Willem said, his voice trembling. Then he leaned into her, his arms wrapped around himself but pressing against her breasts and shoulders. "What an awful way to die."

Her heart pounded. Her face was pressed into Willem's shoulder, and she could smell the sweet, earthy smell of him. Some of the threads in his white shirt still had a flaxen tint.

He pulled back.

"I'm sorry. I wasn't thinking." His cheeks flushed pink.

"It's fine," she said quickly. But it was not fine, she should not ever touch an apprentice. She had heard of such things between other masters and their boys, but not her, not in her workshop. She could not afford it.

But he reached out and grasped her hand, for a moment. Then he pulled away, whispered another apology, and hurried upstairs. Judith closed her eyes and pressed her knuckles against her eyes. She returned to her room and shut the door.

Chapter 21

SHE DECIDED TO PRETEND THE encounter had never happened. When she saw Willem in the workshop an hour later, he smiled neutrally and went back to helping Hendrik pull a canvas over a large stretcher. The younger boy's face was pink with effort as his thin arms strained at the ropes woven into the prepared linen.

"Mistress, we're out of oil," Davit said. He sat at a chair by the window, and the sunlight behind him gave his fine brown hair the radiance of a minor halo. He seemed so much more innocent than twelve years would suggest, and she wanted to kiss his forehead.

"Out already?" She exhaled and tried to focus her thoughts on the oil, away from the boys. She smoothed her countenance. The apprentices could not learn how tight her finances were. She knew how young painters could gossip between workshops.

"That's fine. I have a few errands to run anyway. I'll buy some more from the supply merchant." Without making eye contact with Willem, she turned and left.

But before buying the oil, she had a more important errand. Judith walked down her street away from the bustling Grote Markt square and the din of vendors moving their crates and wives talking to one another as they compared purchases of dusty turnips or onions. She nodded at a neighbor, who gave a hesitant smile, and she walked toward the canal. Away from the painting supply merchant. Below her, the murky water looked almost solid, and she kept her eyes on it as she followed the walkway toward the bridge. A gull with a black face like a masked bandit dove toward the water to snatch up something, and another one arrived to tussle with the first.

Bakenesserkerk, Haarlem's smaller church, was only a short walk past the canal. After a brief conversation with the prelate, she found Gerard Snelling's grave, or so he assured her. The rectangular paving stone along the wall had been replaced, and no one had paid for an inscription. The roof must have had a leak, for a puddle of water collected in the adjacent stone. Judith wished she had made another painting of the dead man, one for herself—an image that would allow him to endure. Her portrait of him existed somewhere else, and at least his face still grinned and radiated life wherever that painting hung. She remembered the pleasure she had taken in rendering the lines around his eyes and that distinctive mole. Now he was dead, and the portrait represented a dead man, and she wondered if she could still consider the painting as holding a scrap of Gerard, the man, the way it had reflected him when he lived. She shook her head. Surely that was a blasphemous thought. His soul was gone, and any image was illusion. But still, the details that had been him would persist in her painting, while below her was soil and bone. She exhaled deeply and murmured a farewell to the lost man. His soul's fate was set, and she could only hope for the best. Faced with the proof of Willem's story, there was nothing else for her to see. As she walked back through the heart of the city, she noticed the water from the leak had dampened her boots, and her toes grew cold.

The apothecary shop did sell linseed oil, but in bottles too small for her purposes, and the collective price of a sufficient quantity would have been five times what she ordinarily paid. There was no walnut oil available at all. She asked the shopkeeper if he had noticed an increase in the price of linseed oil, but he blew a puff of air into his orange mustache and said nothing. She glanced at the cherry and apple tarts lining the counter, standard fare for an apothecary, and left without buying anything. Outside the shop, the stuffed crocodile swung in the air above her head.

Judith pressed her hand to her hair to straighten it, and she turned to walk across town to the painting supply store. She walked through Grote Markt, where some peasants were already packing their wagons to return to their homes outside the city. She cut through the cavernous Grote Kerk, and while she walked down an alley she had to threaten a kick to ward off a begging dog.

The supply store was close to the docks and stocked prepared wood panels, long stretches of sailcloth usable as canvas, ropes for tying the canvases to the stretchers, and some whole pigments: lead white stored in water, ochre, malachite in little pots. Judith asked the young boy standing at the back of the cluttered room about linseed oil, and he pointed her to an adjacent, open door leading deeper into the house. She rested a hand on the doorframe, craned her neck inside, and called into the dark.

A scowling old man trudged into the light and waved a hand to silence her.

"Linseed oil? We have it. Though why a lady like yourself needs it is beyond me. Shouldn't the apothecary have enough for your poultices?"

She gritted her teeth. Judith had shopped at this store half a dozen times in the past year, and most of those times, she'd turned her money over to the same man. Generally she ignored his insults, but today she had no patience.

"As you know, sir, I am a painter. Maybe you are aware painters use linseed oil to bind their paints? Though maybe you're not. I would not want to tax you with such calculation." He was wearing a puce-colored dressing gown, as if he were not expecting to deal with customers today.

"Dabbling, are you?" He said it loudly, as if to suggest he had not heard what she had said. "A lady of your means deserves only the best. We do have some jugs of the oil, though not many."

"Don't play games with me. I've bought here before and know what you sell. Tell me what's on hand. If you please."

He raised a lip to show startlingly bright teeth, and he named his price. Judith gasped. One jug was nearly the cost of two of her completed paintings—the price had doubled since she last purchased oil.

"That's absurd. You're trying to take advantage of me." She hoped she was right.

He shrugged and turned away. "I don't have to sell it to you. We have three jugs left, and someone else will buy them within a day or two, I'm certain. Did I mention there's no more coming in? If you don't need the stuff, that's your business."

Judith tried to quell the sick feeling that surged inside her stomach. The price would account for almost all her guilders. Though there would be the fee Willem promised. The thought of his name made her blush, and she looked down to reach into the purse tied to her waist and extract a handful of lustrous guilders.

"That'll do," she said. It was only a little less than he had asked for, and when he counted the coins in his palm, he scowled again.

"Fine. But let no one accuse me of lacking generosity." He called out to the boy in the store and ordered him to deliver one of the jugs to the mistress's home.

"Or is your 'workshop' in another location?"

"I'll make sure your boy finds us," she said, turning away and leaving the man to his dark room.

Judith spent the afternoon sitting in her bedchamber going over her accounting books. She needed to find a way to cut costs or to sell more paintings. She had recently made a few sales, but she knew she was nothing close to the city's favorite artist. Little could unseat the vivacious Frans Hals from that position. It wouldn't even do her any good if he tumbled down a few notches, as far toward the bottom as she was. But her paintings were worthy, she knew. They had passion and heart. And she had been the first person in the city, as far as she knew, to paint a visible light source into nighttime scenes. Not that any of the other Guild members would ever credit her for it when they copied her and painted glowing candles and golden oil lamp flames onto their tables, but she knew she had been the first to try it. She ran the numbers again and dropped her head to the table. She skipped supper that night, and when Carolein came to ask after her, she assured the young woman she simply had an upset stomach. It was true enough.

When she extinguished her candle and climbed into her bed compartment, the room felt unseasonably cold. She shivered under the quilts and tried to will the oblivion of sleep to sweep over her.

The door clicked open, and her body snapped rigid.

"Who's there?" she whispered, though she already knew.

"Judith, oh Judith, I'm sorry." Willem threw himself to his knees beside the bed. "Please don't hide from me."

She sat up and swung her bare legs over the bed. Her

nightdress hitched up, and she squirmed to pull it over her calves.

"Willem, don't be dramatic. It wasn't that. I'm not hiding from you."

He grasped her hands, and she cringed in embarrassment. Her hands were dry and chapped from all the washing she did to scrub the paint from her skin, and she hadn't applied any salve recently.

"I'm sorry to trouble you; I was sick with worry. You won't be afraid of me?" He stood, still holding her hands, and now he looked down at her, his face invisible in the room lit only by the embers of the hearth.

"I'm not afraid of you, Willem," she said. It wasn't a lie, though her words felt false. She didn't fear him, but she feared the seams of heat he created in her veins, more intense than anything she had felt before, even around Jan Miense Molenaer. Worse, this man was her student.

He exhaled and gripped her hands even more tightly. She felt him bending down toward her, drawing her hand closer to his chest, and she pulled away.

"Willem. Go back upstairs. Go to bed."

He paused, took a step back, and then left without saying a word. She sat frozen, listening to the settling sounds of the house and his quiet footsteps creaking up the stairs. It must have been hours before she fell asleep.

And then she overslept. The window glowed brightly behind the latched shutters when Carolein banged on her door.

"Mistress Judith, are you alright?" she called in her rough voice. Carolein could be mistaken for a man when she spoke, if no one saw her small figure.

"Yes, all's well. Please come in." Judith climbed down from her bed and, once the door was closed again, began dressing herself.

"Judith, didn't you hear it?" Carolein said. "Willem's father was here."

"What?" She paused, leaving her unbuttoned skirt loose at her waist.

"He said he would never concede to his son working for a woman. And some other unpleasant things. About Willem being untrustworthy, and . . . and some women taking advantage of that." Carolein turned away to poke at the cold ashes in the fireplace. "He dragged Willem out from here, and his man brought Willem's trunk away with him. The boy looked, well, shocked."

Judith forced her fingers to continue their work on the buttons.

"They're gone now?"

"Yes."

"And the other boys?"

"In the workshop. Confused."

She had to make sure she did not lose the other apprentices as well. Without them, her workshop was a farce. A room with some paintings and a woman who fancied herself an artist. She could do no business without having workers. Her throat tightened, but she fought it off.

"I'll manage this. We'll have to respond quickly."

"He's not coming back. I can tell you that."

There was an edge to her voice that made Judith look up. But Carolein's pale blue eyes were blank.

"That's fine. I don't need him, not him specifically. But I can't let them treat me like this. We had an agreement." And as she spoke, a plan began to form in her mind. Yes, she would protect herself. As any man would.

Chapter 22

June

Maria awoke, but after blinking her dry eyes at the light tinting the sky above, she squeezed them shut again and gathered the blankets around her. She shifted, and the wagon creaked, but Sara slept on next to her. Maria buried her face into the warm wool and tried to recapture the sweet feeling of the dream she'd had. The details were lost, but she remembered Judith's face. And the comforting touch of her hands. Maria squeezed, pulled every muscle in her body tight toward her middle, as if she could keep the sensation deep inside.

She must have drifted back to sleep because when she opened her eyes again, Sara was sitting at the edge of the wagon brushing her long white hair. With a deft twist, she wrapped it up and tucked the coil under her cap. She cleared her throat.

"It's an important day for us," Sara said without turning

around. "Are you ready?"

Maria pulled herself into a seated position and stretched her arms toward the sky.

"Yes. I want to help." She did. Now, it was all she wanted. More than nourishment, more than comfort.

"Good. We have to be careful. Especially you." Sara turned around and reached out to brush the back of her thumb against Maria's knee. "A city like that begs to consume you." She waved her hand toward the city on the horizon, with its stone wall and the tufts of its early green trees.

"Then why are we going?"

Sara leaned forward. "Because it's there that they need us the most."

When Sara climbed down, Maria hurried to pull her clothes on before anyone from the surrounding wagons started walking around. Then she and Sara ate a quick meal before stepping back up into the wagon. The kermis—the festival—started in Den Haag at half an hour past midday today. And they had to get there quickly to secure a spot for Sara's small stand. But before spurring the mule into motion, both women prayed a single decade of the rosary with their lips moving silently in the hazy light and the beads clicking through their fingers. Sara was Catholic too, or at least that was how she labeled herself. They had only attended one Mass in the weeks since Maria left Leiden with her. Maria hoped to find a Mass and confession in Den Haag, but she suspected that, for Sara, such ceremony was missing the point.

When she first joined Sara, she had hopes of finding Father Cloribus and the artifact. Sara knew the hidden eddies of Catholicism in Holland, she had told Maria as they pulled away from Leiden. And they had searched for a week. But each village turned up nothing more than its own concealed priest or crumbling monastery, and Maria told Sara not to trouble herself. She would find the relic in God's time. That night, Maria cast into the campfire a letter she had written to her father to explain her prolonged absence. There was nothing, now, to say. With Sara, she had found the sacrifice God had been asking of her.

They finished their prayers and snapped the mule into motion, joining the stream of wagons and people on foot, mostly peasants from nearby villages entering the royal city of Den Haag for the week's festivities. Maria wondered if any of the nobility from the court would wander through the kermis. She and Sara had attended another, surely much smaller, kermis the week prior, and it was so raucous and chaotic that she had a difficult time imagining someone of noble blood deigning to participate. But Sara had assured her when the kermis arrived, no one was immune to the celebration's siren song.

"I'd like to attend Mass while we're here," Maria said with a quick glance at her companion, who was sitting next to her on the high bench. "It's been so long."

"Has it?" Sara's voice was distant as if she weren't paying attention. The cart hit a bump, and they jostled into one another. Sara glanced back at the wagon's contents. Maria turned around too and saw the tawny kitten still tucked neatly into the nest of blankets Sara had made for him. The mule twisted her head as she worked against the bit in her mouth, and Sara tugged the reins.

"Yes. Too long."

"This matters to you?" Now Sara was certainly paying attention, and her sharp gaze made Maria wrap her arms around herself as if that were an explanation.

"It does matter. It's what we do, right? We need to go to Mass to stay in the Lord's good graces. Or to show we are good."

"That seems weak proof of goodness to me. But if it's

important to you, I'll help you find one. Unless attending the Reformed service is good enough?"

Maria furrowed her brow and looked at Sara, who kept her eyes on the mule. She wondered if Sara was posing some sort of test to her.

"We are Catholic. That service is a parody." She tried not to sound petulant.

Sara's full lips curved in a soft smile. "If you say so. I wonder why the name of a thing is so important."

"It's not simply a name." Maria strained to keep her tone even. "It's who we are."

"And without these names and traditions, we wouldn't know how to be?"

"Probably." Maria clenched her jaw in frustration. She had not expected her request to prompt so much conversation, and she felt unable to explain herself. The Church's traditions were braided into her being, deep inside her chest, and she needed to honor those traditions to be herself. But she could not find the words. "I need to go to Mass. That's all there is to it."

"Yes, yes." Sara patted Maria's hand with her long, soft fingers. The gesture reminded Maria of her dream, and she wrapped her arms more tightly around herself and turned to watch the crowd as it accumulated along the road. She searched for any ragged children bearing the tell-tale signs of leprosy. Lepers were the only children Maria had ever seen Sara offer her services to for free, though the woman had certainly dropped a coin or two in a shivering hand. Maria was not sure if she wanted to see any of the bandaged children, but there were none along the crowded road. The royal town authorities would have rounded up any strays before the kermis. Presumably, people could not enjoy themselves when faced with the disease.

Sara found a space for their stand along one of the roads

leading away from Den Haag's central square and its small, still lake. Pond, really. Nothing like the wind-stirred sea at Haarlem's shores, certainly only a fraction of the size. Den Haag in general was more composed than any city she had been to, few that they were, and the buildings around Sara's wooden stall were freshly painted and ornamented with green plants cascading from their window planters. The canals she saw had little odor, though Sara assured her the kermis would soon change that.

While Sara began arranging her bottles, small pots, and other wares, Maria sat back and tried to clear her thoughts. She needed confession. She felt the weight of her sins like a grime crusting her chest, but Sara had insisted it would have to wait. Until after the kermis was over. For now, she would have to do the purification herself. It was necessary, Sara had emphasized from the outset, that Maria be as pure as possible for their work together. For her part, Maria could be confident only of her virginity. No other cleanliness was certain to her, but she would not admit that to Sara. She had wanted so badly to leave her shameful failure in Leiden, and she wanted even more to be the pure soul Sara took her for. So she tried.

She closed her eyes and listened to the clink of the glass bottles as Sara arrayed them in a row at the top of her shelf, and the gentle shivering sound of glass against glass when the woman removed a stopper to sniff the contents. Only once did Sara snort and splash the remedy out upon the ground. Maria opened her eyes and wanted to ask what had soured, but the forbidding expression on Sara's face as she hurried to pour new tinctures into the empty bottle silenced her. Sara moved too quickly for Maria to learn the recipes, except for one Sara had made a point to teach her, but she knew a few of the common ingredients: oil of olives, white lead, aniseed water, rainwater collected in a hollow stone, and others. And of course she knew a few of the more precious ingredients as well.

The bells tolled half an hour past midday, and the streets came to life, filling with animated revelers. Sara did brisk business selling her mixtures and charms, like a hollow walnut shell holding the head of a spider, intended to be worn close to the chest, or the small bones of a stranded whale tied together with a ribbon and infused in cinnamon water. People in fine clothes and those in tattered, dusty skirts came to whisper their ills in Sara's ear. She would nod, think, and point them to the solution. Some customers she obviously recognized from previous visits, and they greeted her warmly. A few glanced Maria's way and, when they did, she lowered her gaze to her hands.

The day wound on, and the sounds of the kermis wafted through the streets. In the distance, one man was touting the ferocity of his caged wolf, and another was advertising for a group of glassblowers who traveled all the way from Bohemia. The men and women jostling by were cheerful and jubilant in the early stages of their drink. Someone closer to the center square was whistling a lively tune on a wooden flute, and a stringed hurdy-gurdy soon added its energetic accompaniment.

A woman with fine, spotless lace ornamenting her green silk sleeves approached the stand. She had a thin face, and Maria could see the azure veins running under the skin at the bridge of her nose, although she could not have been more than thirty. She laid a trembling hand upon Sara's wrist and whispered into her ear. Sara nodded, whispered back, and nodded again. Then she looked at Maria.

Maria didn't know what ailment her special customers might have, but she knew what was needed to cure them. Sara and the frail woman whispered for another moment, and then they took a step back, as if offering Maria her stage. She stepped to the center of the stall. In a box on one of the side tables was a small glass bowl and a plain dagger. Its blade reflected the filtered light in the stall, covered by Sara's crimson linen tent. Sara had insisted Maria wipe the blade with a wet cloth until it gave the light back to her.

Maria rolled up her sleeve to expose her forearm. Three scabbed and puffy lines marked her right arm, below the valley at the bend in her elbow. There were four, still covered, on her left arm.

Her hand trembled as she drew the blade across her flesh, but she managed the cut. It was smoother than the second time she had offered herself; then, she had known how it hurt but was not yet accustomed to the pain. Now, the little line of agony in her arm drew in the turmoil of the world around her, like a river's wild waters finding boundary and calm in the carved earth of a canal. She sighed, and her breath came out softly scalloped along the edges. Blood rushed up and dripped down into the bowl. The cut was not deep, of course, and Sara only needed a small amount of virgin's blood. Maria held her arm out and waited.

A small crowd had gathered to watch the spectacle, and when Maria eased the edge of the bowl along her skin to collect the last bit before bandaging herself, she looked out at them. She scanned their faces in a daze, only half wondering if her demonstration had moved anyone. Perhaps someone out there knew what it was to need to sacrifice, or someone else might recognize the deep sincerity of her penance.

There, among the curious heads bobbing about and trying to get a better look, was a young man with a full, oval face and curly dark blond hair. The bowl nearly dropped from her fingers. She set it on the table and stepped back to wrap up her arm and wipe the blade down. As she did, she snuck another glance. The man still stood there, a half smile below his elegant mustache, and Maria knew she was right in thinking she recognized him. It was Jan Miense Molenaer, a member of the

Haarlem Guild. Maria had seen him at the workshop a few times when he had come to visit either her father or Judith. She hoped he had not recognized her—they had never exchanged a word. Surely he would not expect to find her here. But she could feel the pressure of his gaze.

The crowd dissipated, though one or two bought a few of the cheaper, bottled remedies, and Jan stayed. He smiled at Sara, who gave him a wary look, and he approached Maria.

"This is quite the surprise, Maria de Grebber."

She gingerly pulled her blouse sleeve down over her arm.

"For both of us. Have you moved to Den Haag? Trying to be a court painter?" Maria had no idea if the stadtholder, Prince of Orange, was interested in court painters, but she had heard her father refer to such men elsewhere. She wanted this conversation to be about Jan.

He straightened his collar, buttoned at his throat, and gave another half smile.

"You're flattering me. No, nothing so lofty. Don't tell, but I'm hoping a dealer here will sell a few of my paintings during the kermis. And I wanted to see what there was to see. More than I had reckoned for, as it turns out." He nodded his head toward her.

"Selling a painting here, and with a dealer no less, that's asking to get caught. I know enough about Guild rules to know that."

"And you know enough about your father's notorious habit of scoffing those rules to know I'm not worried." He shrugged. "We're all trying to get by."

Maria nodded, and they fell silent. She took a step back and thought he would leave. Instead, he suggested they visit the dances later.

"When you're done, I mean."

She blushed and looked over at Sara, who was staring

vacantly out into the crowd but certainly listening.

"I can't. Dances, that sort of merriment . . . It's not appropriate. For this, I mean." She blushed and wished she had not said anything.

"I didn't mean anything by it. Nothing inappropriate. Don't you want to see the sights?"

She did want to, but she shook her head.

"Very well. I'll give your best to Judith."

"No! I mean, I do wish her the best. But please, don't mention to anyone that you've seen me. I—how do I put this—I want to be alone for a while."

He brushed his sleeves down as if tidying himself for presentation. "This is a strange way of going about it. But that's not my business. I'll see you around, I suppose. Goodbye." He gave her a farewell kiss on the cheek and disappeared back into the crowd flowing past.

No one else needed or met the threshold for Maria's salve that day, so she sat quietly at the back of the stall and watched the kermis. A group of four girls, all likely on the cusp of courtship and marriage, walked from stall to stall. Two of them were engaged in animated, intense conversation, and the other two walked behind, keeping close with eager smiles on their faces, attentive to their ebullient friends. Maria watched the two following girls closely. She knew about that, smiling and waiting hopefully for the world to notice. That had been her life in her father's house, she thought now. She looked at Sara, who had her eyes closed and her face upturned toward the tent ceiling. On their journey to Den Haag, she and Sara had passed a dog lying injured in the road. The creature could not get up, not even to get out of the way of the wagon, but still it wagged its tail hopefully, waiting for a rescue. Sara steered the mule around the dog without stopping. Neither of them said anything, but the dog's pain pressed down upon them both.

The girls meandered into the distance, and Maria watched Sara sell her wares. She said little as she worked, merely listening to her customers, laying the occasional sympathetic hand on their wrists and forearms, and offering the necessary remedy. She must have had a reputation, for some customers sought out the stall, and their faces brightened with relief when they saw the white-haired Sara. Maria's arm throbbed a little with warm pain.

That night they slept in the wagon alongside Sara's most precious bottles and wares, which she had packaged up to protect from any revelers who would try to violate the curfew, which was in effect regardless of the kermis. Maria slept fitfully in the tepid air, her sleep punctuated by the voices of roving drunkards or the admonishments of the town guards. When dawn came, her head felt dipped in wax, heavy and obscured.

After the midday meal, which was a briny pickled herring purchased from another vendor, an old man with a slight stoop whispered to Sara, who soon nodded toward Maria. Her right arm was still tender, so she performed the ritual on her left. The man watched in grateful awe, and Maria smiled at him when she handed Sara the bowl.

Maria saw nothing of the kermis beyond the vicinity of Sara's stall over the next two days. On the dawn of her fourth day there, her right arm woke her with a throbbing pain. Her forearm was suffused with warmth, and her sleeves felt shrunken and tight. She drank her small beer and ate her cheese, and she wondered if she should tell Sara. The heat grew, spreading from her arm over the rest of her body like dye running up fresh cloth. She stood up from her seat at the back of the stand and wobbled as the world filtered slowly by.

"You're not well," Sara said. She pressed her soft hand to Maria's forehead. "An excess of heat."

"I'm fine. It's the weather."

Sara clucked her tongue and pulled up Maria's sleeves to examine her forearm. Small red lines shot away from the scarlet wound, like spider's legs. Maria wondered if a spider salve would counteract the manifestation. Or perhaps something that would be the opposite of a spider. A fly or something else, like a gust of wind. No. Her head swam.

Sara led her back behind the stall to the cart.

"Rest here for a bit. I'll get you something."

"No. I can't. They need me." Maria tried to keep her voice from cracking. Sara patted her hand and walked away.

Maria laid back in the cart. Her arm was tender and taut, and she tried not to let anything touch it. Her vision throbbed in pace with her heart.

Somehow, this sacrifice was being rejected too. She opened her eyes and tried to make sense of the veil of white clouds above, and then she closed her eyes to hear the wash of the kermis crowds. She was doing something wrong. A deep sense of defect, like two pigments refusing to blend into one color in a paint, suffused her. Wrong. She had done something wrong.

Someone laughed in the distance, or perhaps very close, and Maria was conscious of her solitude. She felt caught behind a pane of glass alone to watch the kermis crowds delight in one another. She closed her eyes.

She must have slept, for when she opened her eyes again the sky had the savory hue of late afternoon. A poultice was wrapped to her arm and moving was agony. Every bit of her body ached. Slowly, she rolled over onto her side and pushed herself up. She could feel the blemish in her soul, the dark guilt that sucked in the light. Deeper than any black background she had painted and without the relief of an illuminated figure inside. She slid down from the wagon and winced when her feet hit the ground. She needed to find a priest. To beg God to forgive her for leaving her family and failing to find the relic, and to cleanse her soul of the grasping hands of that man in the Haarlem alley. And to forgive her for missing her friend so deeply when she knew her friend didn't miss her. She needed the understanding granted by a solemn nodding head. God's messenger.

Maria skirted the edge of the stall, walking in the constricted space between their wooden shelves and the next vendor. Sara was talking with a young, blond man, her head leaned in close to his. Maria moved her aching body with deliberation, careful not to jostle any of the racks of bottles or tables of herbs. Her breath was shallow; the air skimmed across her mouth. She maneuvered past the tables and plunged into the crowd. Four days of kermis had littered the ground with an ankle-deep sludge of refuse, mud, vomit, and loss. She labored to trudge through it, and around her the drunk, merry voices bubbled. A hand clutched at her skirt and then her breast, but she pushed the man away. She walked toward the square. A priest. She needed to find a priest.

Chapter 23

JUDITH WALKED THROUGH THE CENTRAL square with her tafelet in one arm. She tried to move with confidence and hold her head high, but the muscles between her shoulders quaked with tension. She wondered, for a moment, how she might depict this sensation, this mask of self-possession. She thought of the painting now resting on her easel. The young woman at the panel's center stared, fixed in concentration, at the needlework in her hands while over her shoulder a man bid for her attention. In one of his hands, a pile of coins. His other hand pulled at her arm. Pay attention to me, give up your work and your honor for me, he said. Or so Judith hoped. The oil lamp on the table illuminated both their faces as well as the white of the woman's shawl. Stay fixed on your purpose, Judith told the young woman. But she wondered, as she walked, if she could show the tremors of fear beneath the woman's concentration. Showing what lay beneath the surface was always hardest.

Today was her hearing. Judith approached Jan Bouchorst's house, lined with black trim and shutters, the same place she had entered to bid for Guild membership. Now she would defend her rights.

The house was quiet when the servant let her in, though she heard the muffled murmur of conversation coming from elsewhere in the building. The black and white floor tiles gleamed from a wash. They ascended to the second floor, where a window in the passageway offered an unusually ample panorama of the city, looking out over a neighboring yard and the slate roof tiles of the nearby streets. In the distance, the inland Haarlem sea languished like an empty pewter plate.

The small room held only a few spectators, hardly any she recognized. They must have been associates of Willem's father, also named Willem, or maybe they were non-painter members of the Guild. She thought again of that painting in her workshop. These men and their families were the proper, comfortable customers she was selling her paintings to. Would they buy anything like her proposition painting? Or would they consider it subversive or, worse, unrealistic? The woman, after all, ignores the man's attempts.

The voices around Judith receded and then swelled once everyone had registered her entrance. She held her head high and walked to a long, empty table facing another table populated by Guild leaders. She assumed those were the judges, and she did not want to have to ask. The more it looked like she knew what she was doing, the better. She imagined she had a sort of invisible callous, a protective layer all around her body that divided her outer appearance from her inner and walled her off from any sally these men might make. She took a deep breath but exhaled quietly.

No one objected when she took her seat, and she busied herself flipping through the heavy pages of her tafelet. It usually held her drawings, sketches of paintings used to help her determine how to structure a scene. But for the purposes of the hearing, she had wiped a few pages clean and filled them with her notes. Observations of fees paid to other masters (hers were modest in comparison), quotes from the recently rewritten Guild bylaws, a few formulated sentences for her to fall back upon if she got nervous, and a breakdown of her stretched budget. The last she had no intention of sharing, for to do so would be embarrassing. But it was there to steady her resolve. She had to retain part of Willem's fees. She had made purchases—primarily the jug of linseed oil, exorbitantly priced—based on the assumption of that income. Without the fees, she, Carolein, and the other two boys would have even less firewood when winter came and very little food. Certainly no more fine pigments.

A matronly woman with smooth skin entered the room and stopped at the threshold. She looked around, her eyes open in question, and Judith wondered which of the men here she had come to fetch. She made eye contact with one of the seated men, smiled, and then walked to the head table. After a few whispers with Hendrik Pot, the woman nodded and took her seat beside Judith. She glanced at Judith and then scooted her chair a little farther away. Judith cringed at the noise.

"With the arrival of Freija Woutersooz, we can begin," said Pieter Molijn, recently elected dean, in his voice still resonant with the native English of his childhood. Other than him, most of the officers were the same group of men who had judged her master piece, except for the missing Jan Bouchorst, who was ill and said to be on his deathbed. In this very house. Pieter, she did not know well. He dabbled in a few different styles, but he was mostly a landscape painter. He had a square face with a prim mouth and storm-cloud eyes. Not yet forty, he was reputed to be stern but fair. She hoped so.

Judith looked over at Freija Woutersooz. She wore dove-gray sleeves and rested her forearms on the oak table. She introduced herself to the group. As she spoke, her mouth was tremendously expressive, twitching and curling, but the rest of her expression was calm. There was something about the dichotomy that made Judith shiver. She had no idea how she would paint that woman.

Judith introduced her case and explained her demands. Willem had paid nothing up front; he owed her a quarter of his yearly dues. She had made arrangements for him and needed compensation. He was welcome to go to Frans Hals's workshop if he wanted, but she still had her right to proper compensation. She used a few of the prepared sentences from her tafelet.

The room was dark, though it was a bright day, and she imagined she was illuminated by a single flame, with the rest of the murmuring faces cast in shadows or darkness. Much like one of her paintings. Salomon de Bray leaned forward and placed one elbow onto the table; beneath it, she could see a leg extended out straight, the other bent under him. The classic pose of Gluttony. The allegory anchored her, and she took a deep breath.

"You are claiming one quarter of the thirty-two guilders? A quarter of the annual rate, for a handful of days?" Hendrik Pot's tone lacked its usual warmth. For the first time, Judith could see why the soft-faced man enjoyed painting militias and guardrooms.

"Yes. We had a contract, an oral one, and—"

"In which I had no part." Freija Woutersooz knitted her hands together above her belly.

"But you and your husband—you're the ones who broke the agreement. How can I keep students if I can't rely upon them?"

"Judith, how can you keep students if you don't register them with the Guild?" Salomon de Bray shook his head in disappointment, though certainly he knew less than half of the Guild's artists paid to register their pupils. The boys were invisible labor, usually, and registering them only invited scrutiny and more fees. As it was, almost every workshop had more than the supposed limit of two students.

"I'll be glad to register my students. I'll do so upon the completion of this meeting. But that's not the issue at hand." She drew her lips together. Repeating her arguments would only make her sound plaintive.

"The inspectors will consult," Pieter Molijn said.

The three men at the head table leaned toward one another and whispered. Salomon rapped a finger against the taupe cloth that ran the length of the table. Judith glanced over at Freija Woutersooz. That expressive mouth, now still, had some of the full ripeness of her son's lips. Judith looked away.

Some men outside in the hallway raised their voices, seemingly in anger. She closed her eyes and tried to listen. How much better to be concerned with whatever they were discussing than to be here, facing this shame. If she lost, she might never be able to sign another student again. What family would want to be with a master whose own Guild had sanctioned her? Judith pinched her eyes even tighter. Outside, one of the men cursed.

"Judith Leyster." Hendrik Pot tapped his fingernail on the table. "We have come to a decision. We agree with Freija Woutersooz. Eight guilders is excessive."

Judith opened her mouth to object, but Salomon de Bray silenced her with a raised hand.

"He's not done."

Hendrik cleared his throat and glanced uncertainly at his colleague before continuing.

"But we agree you are owed something. Four guilders should be sufficient. And fair. But. We assess you a fine of twelve stuivers for not registering the boy in the first place."

"I won't pay this woman anything," said Freija Woutersooz, her smooth cheeks tinged pink.

"Oh, you will," said Pieter Molijn, and his fine lips lifted into a genteel smirk. "If you want your son to have any role in the art market here, you will pay."

She huffed. Then she dug into her hanging pocket, slapped two silver rijksdaaler on the table and stood up. She nearly knocked her carved chair over in her haste to leave.

Judith dropped the coins into her brown embroidered pocket and pulled out two small schellings. The United Provinces coat of arms glittered, and she walked over to place them in Pieter Molijn's hand.

"Is there a registry for me to fill out?"

"Of course. Let me go get it, after I finish these notes. You wait here," Hendrik said. The warmth had returned to his voice.

Salomon de Bray and Pieter nodded at her and left without another word. The few men sitting and watching followed him, except Hendrik, who sat writing something. In the quiet of the room, Judith could hear them all greet the men waiting outside. Maybe the men watching her had not been present for her hearing, but for whatever was coming next. The voices outside were hushed and urgent. Hendrik Pots finished making his notes in his ledger then stepped outside to get the registry. Judith sat alone in the room and noticed her bodice was damp with sweat. She closed her eyes and leaned her head back.

"Here you go. Put the boys' names here. Now you realize the Guild limit is two students, yes?" Hendrik looked down at her, and she could see a few strands of gray in the pointed beard at his chin.

"Yes, I know." She wanted to object that no workshop producing enough art to make money could get by with only two pupils. But she took the quill pen and filled in the two names alongside her own.

When she left the room, the men were still gathered with

Salomon de Bray and Pieter Molijn, apparently arguing about something. Salomon shot her a narrow look as she passed, but otherwise they paid her no attention. One man said something about the damned warehouse, or so she thought, but her interest would have been obvious if she had stopped to listen.

Outside, sunshine glittered between the puffs of cloud, and Judith straightened her starched collar. The lace was becoming more and more difficult to maintain stiff and radiating from her neck. She ought to buy a new one—it was important to look prosperous—but she could not afford it. Not yet. She hurried back to the workshop. She needed to paint.

Chapter 24

That night, she dreamt of Gerard Snellings. He wept from bloodshot eyes, and he held an outstretched palm toward her. Judith awoke nearly in tears herself. If Maria had been there, Judith might have been able to ask what the dream meant. Though the answer was probably simple enough. She tried to go back to sleep, but instead her mind retraced her conversations with Lachine and Gerard himself. Over and over, like paint layered upon the initial dead coloring sketch of a scene, her thoughts took shape. When dawn broke, her head swam with fatigue and misgiving, but she pulled herself from bed to dress and set the boys to work. They needed to know that nothing in her small workshop had changed since Willem's departure.

After breakfast, where Carolein was unusually quiet and preoccupied, Judith led Davit and Hendrik to the workshop and gave them their tasks—beginning a copy of her successful "Merry Company" for Hendrik, who still struggled with fine details but could manage the dead coloring and underpainting first stages, and brush cleaning for Davit. Hendrik kept his eyes to the floor and said nothing. When Judith told Davit his task, he exhaled.

"I don't want to do that."

"You what?" She turned to face him and propped her hands on her hips.

"Cleaning brushes. It's not important." His voice was soft and quiet, but he held her gaze. "If we're going to have to find new workshops, I want to be able to show I can do things. Draw, paint. Not just clean brushes."

"What are you talking about?" Her heart pounded, and she struggled to keep her face composed. "You aren't going anywhere. And brushes are the painter's tool. We're nowhere without clean ones."

"But people are talking now, after Willem," began Hendrik.

"No. Nothing has changed. You hear me? You both have a lot to do. Get to work."

She turned her easel, where she was adding texture and shine to the body of a fiddle held by a jovial young man. Her hand trembled, and she tried to focus on the instrument's wood grain, but she could only envision the merry eyes she had painted for Gerard. She took a deep breath, closed her eyes, and opened them to look again at the fiddle, now resting on a table in front of her. Its body bore the wear of many hands and songs. She swept her brush along the curve of her painted fiddle, but the effect was too bright. Too slick. She tried again, more gently this time, dabbing the brush against the painted image of wood. Tiny brushstrokes that would, at the right distance, coalesce and resolve into an image. An illusion. Maybe that was how God made sense of this world that so baffled her. From a distance, patterns emerge. But He must know the details first. She put the brush down, untied the smock from behind her neck, and hung it on a hook. Without saying a word, she walked out of the workshop, though she felt the boys' gaze on her back as she did. She hoped they had not noticed the unsteadiness in her hand. Her brush hand.

Judith went to her room, where she pulled her second-best lace collar from her bedroom cupboard. She buttoned it around her neck but then, while running her fingers along the outstretched lace, reconsidered. More humble would be better. She had one other, more worn, and she put that collar on instead.

She did not like leaving the house when the boys were in a sullen mood or maybe even thinking of moving to better pastures, but she needed answers. The sooner she could rid herself of her guilt, the sooner she could ensure her focus was where it needed to be. Gerard Snellings's disappearance was her doing, and she would do what she could to learn how he died. As if the details might lay her guilt to rest. Gerard had been a regular with the rhetoricians. She could start there.

She crossed over Haarlem's smaller, tree-lined canal and then turned east, toward the branch of the Sparen River coursing alongside the streets. She walked along the path that had been host to her childhood games, as her father's failed brewery was along the river. The side of that brick building came into view as she rounded the river's bend, and she turned away from the brewery to cross the bridge into the newer part of town.

The rhetoricians of De Pellicaen met in the broad house of Hans van den Velde, a successful art dealer who had died over a decade earlier, and whose son, in addition to dabbling in etching and draughting, made a good parcel of money by renting the ample lower floor as a club. Judith had never been inside; women were not allowed. Except, she imagined, as entertainment.

An elegantly painted pelican adorned the small sign nailed to the right of the door, which was set up a few steps from the ground. Judith hiked up her skirts to climb the stairs. It was late morning, an unlikely hour for any convivial meetings, but she hoped someone would be around. She knocked on the door.

A rheumy-eyed old man cracked open the door and squinted as he regarded her. He gave no greeting, and Judith swallowed nervously.

"I'm sorry to bother you." She paused, and still he said nothing. "I'm a painter, looking for a model who worked for me once. To hire him again. He works here, I think. Gerard Snellings. Do you know him?" She had to make an effort to speak in the present tense.

The man's wrinkled features collapsed.

"Gerard. The best Peecklhaering we ever saw. Oh yes, I knew him. Come on in, you'll need to sit down."

He ushered her through a dark entryway abundantly lined with paintings. A quick glance identified a few of the artworks: loose radiant portraits in the signature style of Frans Hals, the dark shadows of Hendrik Goltzius's prints, a small guardroom painting by Hendrik Pots. She looked away, ashamed to be faced with evidence of the men who were ostensibly her peers and, yet, were not. Her paintings would never hang on that wall.

The old man walked her up a step into a sparkling kitchen and then continued out the back door, down a few steps into a small walled garden. He indicated a chair on the patio and took the one next to her. Nearby, the splashing of laundry being washed in someone else's walled yard sounded, and birds flitted from branch to branch in the poplar tree that rose in the corner.

"Gerard. He was a fine fellow. Was, you see? Because he's dead now."

The old man paused, and Judith realized he waited for her

reaction.

"Oh!"

"Yes, that's right. What a waste. Dead from a knock on the head."

Judith sat up straight. "He was murdered, then?"

"No, no. Not like a real murder, like you mean. Killed in a brawl. Of course, he gave almost as good as he got. It started with a dispute over a who—I mean, a woman. Or so I heard."

"Was it a Frenchman? A Frenchman who killed him?"

The old man cocked his head. "Now, that's a funny question. You said you're a lady painter? Must give you funny ideas. No, it was some idiot from the weaving district. Or at least that's what I heard." He pressed his lips together.

"Poor Gerard." Judith bit her lip as she tried to think what question she ought to be asking. "I was so hoping he would pose for me again. Did he do much work for other painters?"

"Sure, some of them. Those in for that kind of work. Merry pictures, drinking. That's what you do?"

"In part. Any of them that he worked for, maybe they could recommend someone else? If there's a new Peecklhaering."

The man's eyes narrowed, and he stood up. "There is no replacement for Gerard here. Not so long as I'm around. But certainly you can ask the masters yourself. In a place where women are welcome, that is. Here, let me show you out."

Judith stood and hurried after him. "Yes, of course. That's not what I meant. Gerard was a tremendous man." She had hoped to learn who else Gerard had worked for.

On their way out, they nearly collided with Pieter Molijn. His gray eyes narrowed in suspicion.

"You too? What are you doing here?" Pieter said.

"I'm sorry, what? I was looking for Gerard Snellings."

The cloud darkening Pieter's face lifted, and his eyebrows

flickered in confusion. "Who? The fool? He's not been around for a while."

The old man shook his head and opened the door for Judith.

"Have a nice day, young lady."

She looked at Pieter Molijn, but he turned and disappeared into one of the side rooms. She walked outside, and the door slammed behind her.

She was walking through the square, nearly at her house, when she heard her name called. She turned around to see Jan Miense Molenaer running toward her, waving his hand above his head.

"Judith! Judith, I'm glad I caught you," he said, panting. She smiled to see him and reached out a hand in greeting, but he only grasped it briefly. Sweat ran down the temples of his reddened face. "You have to come help. Bring a spare blouse and skirt."

"What?" She clutched her hand, the one he had touched.

Jan shook his head as if he could not believe Judith's confusion. "It's Maria. She's sick, dreadfully sick, but she won't leave. In Den Haag." He groaned. "It's a lot to explain, but she needs your help. And I couldn't stay. I have a customer, a commission." His voice trailed off, and, blushing, he looked at her. Judith could not tell if he was embarrassed at his relative good fortune or at his abandonment of Maria.

"But shouldn't you ask her father?"

"No," he said, his voice soft. He pressed his hand against her forearm. "She asked for you, and the mention of her father makes her blanch and vomit. I'm afraid his appearance would be the death of her. Though she may find her way down that road in any case."

Judith raised her hand to her throat. "Is it that bad?"

Jan looked at the ground. "I've done what I can. I'll take

you back to her if you hurry, but I have only a day. I can't put this appointment off any longer. I came back today to hold on to him, and still the man is threatening to go to another artist. You know how it is. We have to leave soon. Before the last carriage departs. Can you meet me at the south gate in, say, half an hour?"

"I don't know, Jan, I have so much work, and . . ."

"Judith, Maria needs your help."

Judith bit her lip. She was scared, though of what she couldn't say, not yet. Next to them, a woman with a faded blue cloth tied around her hair tipped a bucket into the drain running along the side of the street.

"Of course I'll go. Let me tell Carolein, my housekeeper, and get some coins. I'll meet you there."

Jan laid a hand on her forearm, and under her sleeve, her skin shivered with a lacework of pleasure.

"I've got to do the same. I'll see you soon," he said.

Judith watched him turn down the nearest street and hurry to his workshop. And as she did, she wondered if God would judge her for wanting to share a carriage ride with Jan as much as she wanted to save her friend. She deserved it, certainly.

Chapter 25

JUDITH STEPPED OUT HER DOOR with a small pouch of bread and cheese that Carolein had insisted she take, and she nearly collided with Lachine.

"This way," he said. "You have to come with me."

She stuttered in confusion for a moment. "To the south gate? You're coming too?"

"The what? No, to Paulus van Beresteyn's house. Now, before they get there."

He grabbed her arm and pulled her along. Judith forced herself from his grip.

"No, Lachine, I'm not going anywhere with you. I have urgent business in Den Haag, and I'm leaving now."

"That carriage doesn't leave for nearly another hour. You've got the time, and you'll be glad you spent it with me. It has to do with your workshop. Something your fellow painters are scheming, though I don't know exactly what."

"Scheming against me?" Her heart clenched.

He shook his head, and she thought she noticed a new scar

running down the side of his forehead, where his dull brown hair met his rough skin. "Not exactly. I don't know. That's why I need your help. I need a painter. Oh, and I'll tell you what I heard about your brother."

He started walking, and Judith ran after him.

"Abraham? You know what happened to him, and you didn't tell me?" She grabbed at his sleeve, but he shook her off.

"Calm yourself. I only heard a little, and I didn't think it was news you wanted to hear. No, don't get that look, he's not dead, not that I know of. I would have told you, in repayment of that favor. But come on, the market square isn't the place for such talk. This way."

She followed him as he wound his way through the market stands and past the wooden stalls holding cages of resigned chickens or piles of woven straw mats. They emerged from the market and continued down smaller side streets, until Lachine turned onto a shadowed cobbled street. The neighborhood was quiet, with freshly painted doors and window boxes overflowing with thyme and marjoram. The sky was overcast, and the filtered light made the doorknobs and white window shutters look fragile, like colored glass.

"That house, the one with the square box next to the door, do you see? It's a poor box or some such thing. Most people keep those inside their houses, but not Paulus van Beresteyn. He's the one I gave your painting to, did I tell you that?"

They slowed their walk, and Judith frowned in confusion. "To the magistrate? Why?"

"I thought it would be amusing. A clever way to tell him I knew he'd pressed that drunkard Gerard into doing the work that I used to do for him." Lachine nudged her into the doorframe of a neighboring house. He stood uncomfortably close. "It was the last time I spoke with Paulus, when I gave him your painting. Maybe it was stupid of me to lose the job, but I think he was finished with me anyway. Now he'd like to throw me away. Get rid of me completely." His eyes narrowed, and he glanced away from her to look at the magistrate's house.

"What happened to Gerard?" Judith asked in a low voice.

He grabbed her arm and squeezed. "None of your business. I've no time for nosy women. And if you want to make that carriage in time, you'd better listen to me. There's a meeting in Paulus's house, and I need you to go. Other painters are attending. Demand to be let in."

A shiver ran through her, but still she laughed. "Are you mad? They'll never let me in to a private meeting."

He squeezed tighter. "They have to! I need to know what they're talking about."

"Simply because you want a thing, doesn't make it so."

"He's after me," Lachine said, and his eyes sparked. "And if you don't go, I'll tell them about our deal. Do you think the St. Luke's Guild will look kindly on a woman who's already been sanctioned once for breaking the rules?"

"How did you know?"

"It's my business to know. Go on." He nudged her toward the street.

A man in a deep black doublet strode up the street from the other end. Judith cowered back in the doorway and pushed Lachine back with her. The man didn't seem to see her. A middle-aged servant answered Paulus van Beresteyn's door, and with a nod, he let the visitor enter. When the man removed his broad hat before the door closed, Judith gasped. Lachine had told the truth, at least in part. Outgert van Akersloot, the silversmith, was a leader in the St. Luke's Guild, and there he was, meeting with one of Haarlem's leading magistrates. Judith paid little attention to town politics, but she knew that Outgert's brother was a member of the exalted governing council, the Vroedschap. She had heard that Paulus had similar ambitions, though she thought Outgert himself would hold little interest for the lawyer.

"See?" Lachine said.

"That doesn't change anything. If I go knocking on the door, they'll turn me away. I can't force them to do a single thing."

Lachine growled in frustration. "Then we'll try something else. If those men are going to talk about me, I'm going to know what is said."

He grabbed her wrist and pulled her around the block to a narrow alley that ran behind the row of houses. There, Lachine crouched under a window and yanked her down beside him. He held a finger to his lips, and she kept quiet.

Above them voices drifted out an open window.

"That's the good news," she heard. The voice sounded familiar, but Judith could not place it. She raised her eyebrows at Lachine, who shook his head.

"And commissions are holding steady," another voice said. He, too, sounded familiar.

The first man snorted. "At a mere thirty commissions in this whole town for the year, I would hope so."

There was some shuffling above, and Judith couldn't make sense of the conversation. If only she could hear a bit more, she thought, she would place the voices, neither of which belonged to Outgert. Then someone must have moved closer to the window.

"We can't give up yet," said the voice she had heard first. "And there's a shipment coming in. The last one of the season."

Someone deeper in the room objected, and the voices overlapped in conversation, drowning out the details.

"We'll give one to sailmakers as another gesture of good will. The rest are for you to sell," the man by the window said. "Say, mind if I close this? It's getting drafty."

The window snapped shut, and Judith heard the turning of the latch above her head.

Lachine glowered, and his skin burned with a crimson anger. "Let's walk," he said. He crouched along the wall until he reached the adjacent house, then he stood and walked away.

"Damn their whores of mothers," he said.

"I don't understand. Why would they be talking about you?"

"I told you—I had a fight with Gerard. He knew what was going on with the painters and their business, and I wanted in on it. That should have been my business."

"How would he know? He was a drunkard. A kind man. But not a schemer."

Lachine spit. "Shows what you know. Paulus had him reporting on what the Guild was doing. Gerard could listen to their conversations while they drank, don't you see?"

"And you killed him for it."

"No!" Lachine grabbed her again. "I fought with him, yes. My temper . . ." He released his grip. "He was bleeding but alive."

"But he died."

"That's how Paulus sees it. The magistrate has been sniffing around, trying to find someone to testify in a trial against me. It's only a matter of time. I was hoping to find out his plan, but . . ." He released her arm and pressed his fingers over the bridge of his crooked nose. "Whore's blood. I'll have to leave, which means I'll need money. That bastard Frans Hals owes me a crateful of guilders, and it's his fault I fell into this cursed linseed oil business in the first place. He'll pay. I'm willing to bet you'd like to see him pay too, after he snatched that apprentice of yours."

Judith shook her head. "That's done with. What do you mean, linseed oil?"

"I'm not done." His eyes brightened. "You know Frans. You find me a way into his workshop when no one is around. Ask your handsome apprentice friend, I don't care. But you get me a key or plan for the workshop to be empty some time. I don't care how you do it. And you have two days, or I'm telling our Guild friends about your little business with me."

She blushed at his mention of Willem but refused to satisfy the Frenchman by asking how he knew. "You can't do that. How can I find a way into Frans Hals's workshop?"

"Not my problem. I need to get out of Haarlem, and I need my money back to do it. You have to go to Den Haag? Fine, go. Look how generous I am. But you get back tomorrow, and you tell me how to find that workshop empty." He reached over and flicked a speck of dust from her dark green sleeve. "You'd better hurry if you're going to catch that carriage."

Her stomach twisted, but he was right. She turned to run off, then remembered. "You still haven't told me about Abraham."

"I don't know much. I never know as much as I'd like, it seems." He started walking. "I heard he was spotted in a burglary. Carrying off a basket of tulip bulbs."

Judith grabbed his sleeve. "Abraham isn't a thief."

Lachine shrugged and tapped his knuckles against a brick wall as he passed. "I heard it straight from the man who was there with him. Admitted he talked Abraham into it, that they'd been friends as children. That's what I heard. That he was spotted, and the tailor who'd invested the money in the bulbs knew Abraham on account of having worked with your father. I imagine Abraham fled town."

"It can't be true," she said, shaking her head. But Abraham had spent time with some rough boys when he was younger, before their parents had left, and he'd vowed to make his own way. And then she felt as if a black shadow passed through her gut. Abraham had asked her about his old friend Bartol.

The church bells tolled.

"You'd better get running," he said. "I know I sound cruel, but remember. I'm not stopping you from helping your friend. I need you to help me too. That's how the world works. That way." He pointed down a winding street. "The canal's around the bend, and then you'll be able to see the windmill and guide yourself."

Judith clenched her jaw, but she could think of nothing else to say. She ran.

Chapter 26

HER BREATH BURNED IN HER lungs as she reached the south gate and ran across the bridge spanning the boundary canal, her footsteps booming on the wood. On the other side of the bridge lay the small grove of trees where carriages waited before departing. There were a few skinny horses tied to tree trunks as they cropped the damp grass, but no carriages in the park. Not even a wagon.

"Judith!"

In the distance, nearly around a bend, a carriage jolted to a stop and Jan jumped out. He waved for her to hurry. Judith mustered enough energy to run the last few roedes. She arrived, sweating and panting, and Jan gave her an elbow up into the carriage. A matronly woman with a basket of yarn huffed but moved over to make space on the bench. There was no one else in the carriage.

"They waited as long as they could," he said, his voice reproachful. "I've already paid your fare."

"Thank you," she said. Her ragged breath could barely

shape the words. "I'm sorry."

He shook his head but smiled. "It's a long ride, nearly the rest of the day. If we're lucky, we'll get there by dark. You'll have plenty of time to catch your breath."

"It's been a long day," she said. His sympathetic eyes regarded her, and the urge to cry welled up. But Judith clenched her jaw. "I'll tell you about it later. Plenty of time." She needed to gather her thoughts before she tried to share them with anyone else. Particularly at the risk of weeping in front of Jan Miense Molenaer. He laid his hand over hers, and her lips melted into a smile. The older woman coughed, and he withdrew his grasp.

The carriage bumped along. Judith's empty stomach grew unsettled at the motion, and she chewed a bit of bread crust before wrapping the meal back up. They passed the small village which lay to Haarlem's south and then rolling fields spattered with twisted chestnut trees and mud-colored farm buildings. She had rarely traveled outside of Haarlem, and never as far as Den Haag.

"Tell me again how she looked," Judith said. Her knee bumped against his, and a shiver of pleasure ran up her thigh. She pulled her legs toward herself. She needed to be careful. Judith wouldn't let a man seduce her to a life away from her workshop, and she could not afford to fall into a compromising situation. Her family's reputation was bad enough.

"Poorly. Her face as glossy as a glazed tile." He shook his head.

Judith bit her lip and returned to looking out the window. An hour ago, she was eager to spend the time talking to Jan and asking about his art. But now, she willed the carriage to go more quickly. Away from Lachine. And away from the thoughts that begged her to ask Jan about his time in Frans Hals's workshop. At least when she reached Maria she could do some good.

But it was dark when they arrived in Den Haag, just before the town watch closed the gates for the evening. Judith ached from the hours spent cramped in the carriage, despite two brief breaks at roadside inns to water the horses and relieve themselves. The town watch escorted the two of them to the only inn still accepting guests that night, and the middle-aged woman hurried off on her own without another word.

"Two rooms," Jan told the skeptical innkeeper, a round man with a wide mouth crowded by yellowed teeth. Judith was grateful neither man made a joke about sharing a room for the sake of costs or some such thing. She was too tired to banter.

"We'll go to Maria first thing in the morning," Jan said at the threshold of her room. "Sleep well." He grasped her hand lightly, the second time he had touched her bare skin that day. Judith smiled and, for a moment, thought it wouldn't have been terrible if there had been only one room available. She pulled her hand away.

"You as well." She shut the door behind her and, after a moment listening to Jan's steps fade down the hallway, she collapsed, still wearing all her clothes, onto the hard straw mattress. She had one and a half days left.

The next morning, Judith and Jan stepped outside the inn shortly after dawn. The air was still cool and smelled damp. Along the street, men were hauling heavy bags out of wagons and piling them around wooden stalls. Each time a worker dropped a bag, a white cloud of dust rose up.

"Must be the lime market," Judith said.

"They make good use of it here." Jan gestured at the elegant buildings they passed. They walked along the canal and crossed a larger, intersecting canal, where the finely ornamented building frontages looked as if they had been carved in marble. Far more refined than most of Haarlem's brick homes and shops. What kind of paintings did the merchants of Den Haag buy?

"How long was it you worked with Frans Hals?" The words came out before she had decided to say them, and she pressed her lips together.

"Funny thing to ask. I started about the same time as you, and stayed on another year and a half. So nearly two years total. Why?"

"I . . . I was wondering about how he ran his workshop. If one of my students left me for him, maybe there's something I should know. About how he's better." Her chest constricted at the lie and the reminder of Willem's abandonment. He hadn't left because Frans Hals ran a more organized workshop. He had left because his parents were ashamed that he apprenticed himself to a woman.

Jan shrugged, then he gave her a warm smile. "You shouldn't worry about it, Judith. But if you want to know, the workshop was pretty disorganized. You remember. Students coming and going at all hours, even past curfew."

"I was thinking of his records. I try so hard with mine, but maybe he has a better manner."

Jan gave her a queer look, and her stomach twisted. "You're more organized than any painter I know, certainly Frans Hals. I doubt half of them can read, and Frans probably doesn't even keep a ledger book. His writing table was covered in notices, and he seemed to lose the key to his lockbox nearly every other day."

"Where did he usually keep the key?"

"What, are you planning on breaking in?"

Judith blushed, and Jan laughed.

"It was a joke," he said. "I had to borrow a prop from him recently, and I'll be returning it when we get back. Do you want me to ask him anything?"

Judith shook her head.

Jan held her gaze for another moment, until Judith looked down at her brown boots.

"Now, where are we exactly?" he wondered out loud.

They followed another narrow canal past more homes and some open garden plots. A hanging sign for a tavern showed a jovial man lifting a tankard.

"Have you ever had a buyer request a particular model?" she asked Jan, who was frowning as he looked over the streets.

"Other than himself or his wife? No. Not that I've had many commissions at all. Now, I'm sure the place she was staying was past this smithy. Or was it to the right?"

"I had one who demanded I use a certain man, and then it turned out the man was terrified of the same fellow who had commissioned the painting. And some months later, my model disappears. Dead, I mean. In a fight. Don't you think that's strange?"

Jan glanced at her. "Maybe. Seems more likely a coincidence. The people we hire to model for us aren't usually the most respectable."

A boy ran by with a basket of eggs on his arm.

"But the man who paid for the commission, now he tells me he was involved in some linseed oil business. Or he's trying to figure it out."

"Linseed oil?" Jan stopped walking and faced Judith directly. "The price is outrageous now."

"I know. There's to be a sale soon, I think, and that should help. What if my model died in relation to that sale?" Her shoulders trembled with a wave of nerves, and she squeezed her arms around her chest.

Jan shook his head. "How could that be? People die. All the time. Though I'm glad to hear of a sale, very glad." He ran his fingers down his mustache. "Ah, there's the main market. Just past that."

They walked through the central market square, noisy with the stomping of horses and the clatter of peasants still assembling their wooden stands. The town's kermis had only finished three days earlier, but already Den Haag's citizens needed fresh produce and meat. They passed the brick Grote Kerk, with its peaked roofs and belltower. Two blocks later, they came to a street packed with houses. The low morning sun couldn't reach into the narrow street, and all the darkened windows looked the same.

"The papists' district," Jan said. He knocked on a door.

A hunched old man opened it.

"Eh?" he said. Then, before Jan could speak, he recognized him. "Come on in. None too soon."

He led them into the house and to a back room. Even before they crossed the threshold, the stench of excrement overwhelmed her. Judith held her sleeve to her nose and blinked in the low light.

"My wife has tried to keep her clean, but she has fouled herself so much, we struggle . . ."

He approached Maria, who lay silently on a straw pallet on the floor. He crouched down and laid a hand gently on her head.

"You have friends here," he said in a soft voice.

Judith took another step forward. Maria glanced wildly around and cringed as Judith approached. Then she pinched her eyes shut.

"She hasn't spoken since she arrived. I'm not sure if she sees this world or the next," the old man said. He stood slowly, using the wall for balance, and shook his head. "We pray for her every night. There is no priest in town, but if there were, I would have asked for unction. The poor thing."

"Is it that bad?" Judith asked quietly. She glanced at Maria, who seemed to have fallen asleep, and in the low light, Judith could barely make out the slow rise and fall of her chest.

He pressed his lips together. "Only God knows. And I'm sorry, but we couldn't afford a doctor, so she's had no letting. Not even a purgative. Please forgive us."

Jan pressed the old man's hands between his. "You have been generous to host a stranger. We're grateful."

"Thank you," Judith whispered before getting down on her knees. She laid a hand to Maria's forehead, but then pulled her fingers back as if she had touched a flame. Maria's skin burned with heat, yet she looked pale. She was on her back, with her face turned toward the center of the small room, and her eyes were closed. Judith wriggled her fingers into Maria's clenched palm.

"I'd like to bathe her," Judith said. "We need to remove this filth."

The old man nodded. "I'll fetch Betje."

The men left the room, and Judith wished she had asked for a candle, even before a bath. Here in this dark room, Maria's colors faded toward black, as if death were claiming her by first leeching out the luster from her hair and the blush of her cheeks. Even her once-blue skirt looked somber.

Together, Judith and Betje, the old man's small but determined wife, stripped Maria of her sleeves, bodice, tunic, and skirts. Layer by layer, her friend seemed to shrink before their eyes until nothing was left but the linen underclothes, heavy with black filth.

"We should burn these," Judith said without moving to take them off.

"You'll want to take them off first to do that." Betje stood back, her arms crossed.

Judith nodded. She closed her eyes and pulled the shift

down Maria's shoulders, then untied the knot at her waist and stripped the sodden skirt from her hips.

"Do you have another bucket?"

Betje left the room.

Judith let her eyes flit up to look at Maria, but only in fractured glimpses. A ridge of pale ribs, or a scrim of downy hair along her thighs. Without the clothes, her body seemed to reclaim its light, at least a little.

Maria had stirred occasionally in the process, but as Judith began to draw a wet cloth across her body, she whimpered.

"I'm sorry, I'm sure it's cold. But it's for the best. I'll be quick."

Betje came back, and Judith pressed the fouled underclothes into the bucket.

"We should get rid of these, quickly. The stench will drive you mad otherwise. The rest, perhaps we can wash? I can pay if you know a washerwoman."

"She's a sweet girl, your friend," Betje said with the bucket in her hand. "She was only trying to help, you know."

"How?"

"Listen to her name. Maria. She wanted to give the world something to heal, to cleanse our sins. Waste of time, most likely. But she was trying."

The old woman left, and Judith returned to wiping the cloth across Maria's skin.

"We'll get you through this," Judith whispered. "You're strong, Maria. You're not ready to surrender your soul yet." She wanted to say more, to say how if Maria died, Judith would have no one left. No one that she trusted with her heart and soul, no one who could understand her without explanation. But it was selfish to think of what she would lose. How typical of her. Judith rocked back on her heels, away from Maria, and wiped away a tear. Then she pressed her eyes together, tried to steady her breathing, and went back to her work.

Betje returned with a pile of clothes in her arms.

"This was my daughter's. The skirt might be a little short, but it's clean. She never wore the bodice. I'd be glad for Maria to have the whole thing."

Judith stood. "You are a kind woman." She took the clothes into her arms. The fabric was rough-woven but smelled of lavender.

By the time she eased Maria into the clean skirts and bodice, the room had grown warm, and faint sun fell through a high window in the back wall. Judith mixed some ale and water that Betje had given her and dribbled it over Maria's lips. She groaned as Judith lifted her head, but she opened her mouth as if to take the liquid. Judith poured a bit more, swallow by swallow, before lowering the other woman's head to the mattress again.

"Judith."

Jan stood in the doorway. "Betje told me she was dressed. I have to go now; the return carriage leaves soon. Can we bring her? I'm sure you'll want to get back."

Judith stood and pressed her hands against her aching back. Her head swam, and she closed her eyes to steady herself. At home, she had painting to do. There was another auction in two weeks, and she hoped to ready three more works. Large ones this time, to better capture the eye. Even better, a tailor had expressed interest in one of her merrymaking pictures. She needed to talk to him again and see if she could broker a sale on her own before he turned to one of the other artists in town. And Lachine was waiting for her.

"She'll be better at home. If something happens," Jan added.

Behind him, Betje stepped into the doorway.

"You're thinking of taking her?" the old woman asked.

Judith looked at Maria. "Do you want to come with us? Back to Haarlem?"

"You shouldn't move her," Betje said.

Maria was silent, though her eyes moved from one woman to the other. Judith sat down next to her.

"I'm sure your father misses you," she said.

Maria drew in a rasped breath and shook her head. She forced out a brittle moan.

"Not him," she managed to say. She closed her eyes. Maria made no further noise, but her fingers trembled against the rough skirt.

"You shouldn't move her," Betje repeated.

"What choice do we have? I can't stay here. My workshop . . . and Jan too." Judith shook her head. "I don't know if we can move her, but we should try." Judith wished she could be the friend who stayed, who worked by Maria's bedside for nights on end. But she knew she couldn't. Already she could feel the pull of her workshop and the weight of Lachine's threat. As much as she hated herself for it, she couldn't resist. The best she could do for Maria was to take her back. Betje turned and disappeared back into the dark house without another word. Judith pressed her fingers to her temples and closed her eyes.

After a moment, she poured a little more of the diluted ale against Maria's lips, then helped maneuver her arms so Jan could hoist her up.

"She's lighter than I thought," Jan said. "She must have lost a lot of weight."

They passed carefully through the dim house, which Judith now saw was modestly appointed but clean. The old man held open the door, and Judith saw a porter with a small cart waiting out front.

"May God bless you," the old man said to her as she passed. "You are a good woman."

The praise made Judith's throat tighten. She was anything but. She pressed his hand in a silent farewell.

In the daylight, she could see Maria's pale skin. Her long cheeks had grown sunken, and there was a pink rash over her hand and up part of her neck. Maria's eyelids fluttered as the cart bounced over the cobblestone streets, and Judith gritted her teeth at every bump.

"Should we take her back?" Jan whispered. "What if she dies on the way?"

Judith shook her head. "Then she should be home. In either case."

At the eastern gate, they found their carriage alongside a tree-lined canal. It was not yet midday, and a few vendors selling cakes and cured sausages wandered the quay. Jan bought three cakes and two sausages, and then paid for all their tickets. The driver looked askew at Maria and tried to negotiate a higher price, but there were no other travelers that day. Jan prevailed.

As the carriage trundled along, Maria began to moan and turn. Judith's heart stuttered, and she offered her friend a bit of bread. Maria only moaned louder, until her cries became discernible.

"No, no. Father, no," she repeated, interspersed with fearful groans.

Judith smoothed her hair back and tried to console her. She pressed a little bread between Maria's lips as her head bobbed according to the carriage's movement. Maria let the crumbs fall from her mouth and only cried louder.

"I think she's worried about her father," Jan said. "That we'll take her there."

"Is that it? Maria, I won't. Not if you don't want." She ran her hand down Maria's hair. "I'll keep you at my house. Care for you there." Judith whispered her promises a few more times, and finally Maria grew still.

Her face had reddened during her fit, but as she calmed, her skin grew pale. Heat seemed to waft off of her. Suddenly, Maria belched, and a rivulet of yellow vomit hung from her lips. Judith gasped and dabbed at it with her sleeve. Maria slumped to the side, onto Judith's lap.

Judith hugged Maria to her chest to keep her from pitching onto the floor.

"Christ's blood," Jan said. "Is . . . is she alive?"

Judith held her breath and tried to loosen her grasp a bit. The moment lengthened. Finally, she could perceive a light rise and fall in Maria's chest.

"Yes. But barely, I think. She was fiendishly hot, but now she feels cold." She lowered her head to Maria's. "Stay here, Maria. Stay here."

Chapter 27

WHEN THEY TOOK HER FROM the carriage after traveling all day, Maria was barely breathing. Her body seemed even lighter than hours earlier, as if her soul had already departed. Jan carried her in his arms through Haarlem's darkening streets, and he arrived at Judith's house dripping with sweat.

Without a word, Carolein helped them carry her up two flights of stairs to the loft, where she hastily arranged spare blankets into a sort of bed.

"I hadn't expected this. I'll find a straw mattress tomorrow."

"Thank you for your help," Judith said. "See if the cloth merchant will sell us the length on credit, and I can help you sew it up."

"Judith, I can't stay any longer," Jan said, his eyes dark with worry. "I have that sitting to conduct. The man won't forgive me a second time."

"Jan, I can't thank you enough." Judith took his hand

briefly in hers. It was warm and still damp with sweat.

"I'll check with you later. To see how she's doing," he said quietly. He glanced at Maria, who lay still on the floor.

"She'll do well here," Judith said. She wished she could believe it.

That night Judith could not fall asleep. Her ears strained to hear the house's noises and conjured Maria's voice from them. And as her eyes tried to pull shapes from the heavy darkness, she thought of Lachine. She had only half a day more, and still no idea what she would tell him. After hours of tossing and turning, she gave up. She got out of bed, lit a candle, and started sketching in her tafelet by candlelight. From memory, she roughed out Lachine's face, Frans Hals's workshop, and her own front door. As her hand moved, her mind calmed. And a plan began to form.

She slept a few hours before dawn, until the waking city's noises began to shiver through the walls. After a quiet breakfast and a quick visit to Maria, who slept fitfully on her blankets in the loft, Judith left the house.

When she had nearly reached Frans Hals's house on Jacobijnestraat, a few doors before the street ended at the elegant old canal, she took a deep breath. This house, yet another rental, was new to her. Frans had probably moved at least twice since she had sat in his workshop, eight or so years ago, and though rumor claimed his debts chased him, he always managed to find a well-lit home on a pretty street. This house had two large windows facing the street, and two dormer windows in the roof.

A small boy in worn pants, which ended in a fray around his calves, ran past.

"Boy!" she called. He stopped. "Come here. Take this letter and deliver it to that house. If you do, and I'll be watching, I'll give you two pennings. Only don't say it was from me. Understand?"

The boy narrowed his eyes as he looked at her, but he took the letter and scampered off. Judith walked around the corner of a nearby alley, where she watched.

The boy knocked, and when a woman with a white cap and brown skirts opened the door, he handed over the note and ran. Judith bit her lip as the woman considered the folded paper, then shrugged and closed the door.

Fingers grazed the back of her arm, and she jumped.

"It's only me," said the boy. "You should have told me where you were hiding. I had to run around the block." He held out his palm. Judith dropped two coins into it, and he ran off.

She walked to the canal, which was lined by houses with tiered brick frontages. She kicked a stone into the water, where the brown ripples flickered with white light. The air was dense with the smell of stagnant water, and she tapped another pebble over the quay, just to watch the reflection again. Her pulse fluttered with nervous energy while she waited.

After a quarter of an hour, footsteps ran up behind her.

"I got away as quickly as I could," Willem said.

She turned to face him and, after a quick breath, pressed her lips closed.

"Thank you. I know this is strange, but I didn't know who else to ask."

"I'm always glad to help you. Always." He took a step closer.

Short blond stubble grew in faint patches across his chin and cheeks. To her surprise, her breathing grew easy. He was so young.

"It's awkward between me and your master, as you can imagine," she said. "But I need to drop something off for him. Without him knowing. Is there any day soon when he'd be away from the workshop for a few hours?"

"Couldn't I just give it to him for you?"

"This is between me and Frans. I won't get you involved."

Willem's shoulders sagged, and then his eyes brightened. "He doesn't usually leave, there's so much painting to do. But tomorrow, he's taking his sister and her children for a boat ride on the sea. In the afternoon."

"You're sure?"

"Absolutely. He's already told Harmen, his oldest, to oversee the workshop. You should have seen Harmen preening."

"Thank you, Willem." Judith reached out to clasp his hand. Willem took her fingers between his palms and then pulled her into an embrace. He rested his lips upon her cheek, where they left a shiver of saliva. Judith frowned and stepped away.

"That's enough," she said. But as she did, over his shoulder, she saw Jan Miense Molenaer approaching. He was frowning.

Willem brushed his fingers against her arm, but she stepped back.

"Have I interrupted anything?" Jan said.

"Not at all. Willem forgot a few things in his mother's haste to move him out."

Jan made a show of looking around. In his hands was an earthenware jug with a pewter top, and he waved it toward the younger man. "It must have been small, whatever he forgot."

Judith shook her head. "I didn't bring the trunk. He'll have to come get it. And you've brought your drinking vessel out this early in the morning?"

"It's Frans's, the prop I mentioned. Mine broke in the middle of a sitting, and I knew he had a similar one."

"Well, send him my regards," Judith said. "Willem, tomorrow it is then, in the afternoon?" The deceit felt like ash on her tongue, but she couldn't let Jan find out.

Willem gave a proprietary smile. "That's right, Judith. I'll see you then. Jan, shall I walk you to the workshop?"

"If that's where you're going," Jan said.

Judith waved a weak farewell and left the men to their silence. Lachine would be looking for her soon, and she needed to be easy to find. She turned toward home.

Even before she reached her workshop, he fell in step with her.

"What's it to be?" He lifted his chin as if to stretch his neck.

"Tomorrow. After the midday meal." Judith kept her eyes on the paving stones. A dusting of brown dirt turned the gray stone almost iridescent. Without another word, he walked away. Judith unlocked her door, stepped inside, and locked it behind her. She leaned against the bare plaster wall and closed her eyes. The sound of her blood pounded in her ear. When it faded, she went to the kitchen to get some bone broth for Maria.

Judith spent the rest of the morning trying to feed Maria, who let the amber liquid dribble from her slack lips. Spoonful by spoonful, she tried to ladle the broth into her friend's mouth, but most of it glazed her cheek. Judith pressed her palms against her eyes.

That afternoon, she left the boys practicing sketching the shine of a pewter pitcher, and walked to the shadowed cobbled street with the verdant window boxes. She knocked on Paulus van Beresteyn's door.

The same middle-aged servant whom she had seen when she spied on the door with Lachine answered.

"I'm here to see the magistrate," Judith said. Her mind rattled with the sentences she had memorized, but she pressed her lips closed. Not yet.

"And you are?"

"He won't know my name. But tell him it's about Lachine."

The servant nodded then invited her into the entry hall. He shut the door behind her and walked into an adjacent room. Judith pressed at the skin around her thumbnail. The walls here were naked, except for a single shelf which held two books. *The Familiar Epistles of Bishop Anthony of Guevara* read the spine of one, and the other had only an embellished design.

"It's an impressive family, isn't it?"

She turned around to see the magistrate standing in the doorway. "What?"

Paulus shook his head and approached. He was only a little taller than she was. "My grandfather wrote the translation. A true scholar."

"That's admirable," Judith said.

"But not what you're here for."

She waited for him to invite her further into the house, but he simply stood with a polite smile on his face.

"I'm the artist who painted your portrait of Gerard Snellings," she said.

His eyebrows jumped up, and his mouth opened before he composed himself quickly.

"I see."

"I wanted to tell you that I knew nothing of the business between the three of you. Lachine commissioned the painting from me. I needed the work."

"And the money."

"Of course." Below her dusty boots, the floor was tiled in black and white, alternating on a diagonal.

"Why are you telling me this?"

"So we understand one another. Gerard Snellings was a good man, and I'm saddened by his death. Tomorrow afternoon, Lachine plans to break into Frans Hals's house. Frans won't be home, and Lachine is trying to get money so he can flee you." She paused and held his gaze. "I'm telling this for your own purposes, not for Frans's sake. I'm not particularly interested in his well-being. You can't say anything to him, though. I wasn't allowed to sell that painting of Gerard. But I thought if you caught Lachine, you might be glad of it."

"I should believe you?"

"I painted that portrait. I can describe every detail of it if you like, from the white highlighting along the carmine-colored feather to the black shadows under the scalloped trim of his coat. And why should I expose my secret, unless it was to some gain?"

"You want to see Lachine caught?"

Her stomach tightened. "Not really. But he threatened to expose me."

Paulus laughed. "And somehow you think I will not?"

"You'll have to explain why Lachine gave you such a gift. If you reveal that I painted the portrait in your possession."

Paulus crossed his arms. "I'm fed up with painters and their games. But Lachine is dangerous. You're right, he should be punished."

Judith took a step closer to the shelf and examined the fine leather spines. She wanted to touch them, but didn't have the courage. And she wanted to throw the books to the floor and curse simply for the pleasure of not maintaining appearances, but she couldn't do that either.

"You've done the right thing," Paulus said. "Gerard would be grateful."

Judith nodded. She took one last look at the magistrate, whose face was as blank as a river stone, and she let herself out the front door. When she shut the door behind her, the wooden poor box rattled on its hook, and she thought she heard the echo of a coin inside.

Chapter 28

When she returned home, Judith went upstairs, where she sat by her friend's new straw-stuffed mattress. Carolein had spent the morning sewing the rough cloth together, and the fresh smell of hay filled the attic. Maria regularly murmured words Judith couldn't hear, and every so often she would open her eyes and seem to plead with Judith. Or someone just over Judith's shoulder. Judith stood. She was doing little good here.

"You're going to get better," she told Maria in a soft voice. And when she did, she would need to eat. Judith might ask Maria's father for help, but anytime she mentioned Frans de Grebber, Maria groaned and tried to swat her hands, as if pushing someone away. No, she would need to care for Maria herself, at least for a time. Which meant she needed to paint.

"I'm sorry to leave you," Judith whispered, and it was true. But it had been too long since she held a brush, and her emotions twitched like the lid of a simmering pot. She needed to release them into paint and color.

Over the next two days, Judith painted. She tried not to imagine the scenes at Frans Hals's workshop and in her own, where Maria lingered at the edge of death. Judith wished she could find Jan and explain to him what she had seen. But she didn't know how she could explain her connection with the Frenchman without losing Jan's esteem. She alternated her time between daubing Maria's forehead with a damp cloth and coercing the boys to sit still so she could use them as models. The experience would be good for their timing, she told them. They'd need to learn how to capture a model before fatigue consumed him.

On the third day, Maria finally drank a little more watered ale, and Judith was desperate for the feeling of the sunlight on her cheek. She offered to buy the day's beans and cabbages, and Carolein readily agreed. With the shopping bucket slung over her arm, Judith stepped outside, where she breathed in the heavy summer air and the mixed aroma of the horses, baked bread, and light sea breeze. In the market, a table laden with purple plums made her mouth water, but she knew she didn't have enough coins for the fruit. She hadn't had time to find that tailor who wanted a painting, and she had sold nothing since before leaving for Den Haag. Instead, she went to the few sellers she knew would offer her credit. She could pay them back soon. And what coins she had went to buying juice of ivy and a draught of cinnamon water from the apothecary, at Carolein's instruction, to help Maria's fever.

Just as she was walking back toward the square, a boy's voice called her name. Judith looked up to see a thin boy in rags.

"Mistress Judith," he said, wiping an arm across his nose. "I'm here from the prison. They sent me to find you, right? I asked for you at the house, and your girl said you were at market."

He gestured for her to follow, then he led her around the corner to the area in front of the municipal building. A curious crowd of market-goers gathered around the scaffold that stood near the adjacent prison. A crier continued calling for attention, and Judith tried to elbow her way through the crowd. The crier yelled, "Abraham Leyster."

She pushed her way toward the front, leaving the protests of the boy behind. The executioner, the same skinny, balding man with gaping teeth and ice for eyes Judith had seen so many times before, stood in his usual place beside a stained chopping block. The scaffold loomed behind him. She saw no prisoners, and she was about to ask the grinning gray-haired man next to her if she had heard correctly, when the prison guard led out two men. One was young, nearly a boy. The other was Abraham.

He was thin, and the shackles on his wrists seemed absurdly large. He blinked and bent his head away from the sunlight. Judith gasped and nearly ran to embrace him, but she stopped herself. Such unrestrained behavior would horrify the onlookers and might worsen Abraham's punishment. She held out a hand, low, but he didn't seem to see her.

The crier explained that the younger boy, whose name Judith missed, had sold dog meat and passed it off as lamb. The guard unlocked his shackles and marched him to the executioner. The executioner, wearing a long black robe, pushed the boy to his knees, pulled his arm over the chopping block, and, before the boy could move, swung down an axe. The hand fell twitching to the ground and, when the boy howled and grabbed at his maimed arm, blood sprayed across the paving stones. The crowd tittered and shifted.

"Heaven's mercy." The words escaped Judith before she could think. "For selling dog meat?"

The gray-haired man next to her hissed for her to be quiet.

The crier repeated Abraham's name. "For the crime of burglary and theft of very valuable investment items from the household of citizen Arnold Luik."

The guard unlocked him and yanked him toward the executioner. The thin man lifted one lip to expose a few snaggled teeth and then slammed Abraham's right hand to the block. Judith covered her eyes. But instead of the slam of the axe, she heard a singe. She opened her eyes and saw Abraham clutching his hand to his chest. His eyes were wide with pain and confusion as he stood cringing before the executioner. The crowd moaned in disappointment, though a few started chanting, "D for dief!" Thief.

The executioner hauled him to his feet and then said something to Abraham, who nodded. Using his uninjured left hand, he fumbled with the hem of his shirt, presumably trying to lift it over his head. Finally, the executioner sighed and pushed Abraham back on his knees. His face was away from the crowd, and Judith hugged her arms tightly over her chest. The bucket pinched the sinews of her wrist.

The executioner sliced his whip through the air. After half a dozen lash strokes, Judith lost track. Blood spattered out from the wounds on Abraham's back, and its crimson brilliance was horrifying.

Finally, the executioner stepped back, panting. The guard pulled Abraham to his feet and gave him a nudge.

"Go on, thief," the guard said.

Clutching his right hand against his chest, Abraham stumbled toward the edge of the crowd. Judith pushed her way past a few townspeople and ran toward him. He needed to get home before anyone might try to shove him around or throw refuse at him.

She pressed both palms against his cheeks.

"Abraham, come with me, quickly."

"Judith?" he asked, his voice confused. But when she took his left arm in her hand, he followed. They skirted the front of the crowd until she found a place where it had thinned and she pulled him through. Her cheeks burned with embarrassment. So many people had seen her.

They had woven their way out of the densest part of the crowd, and the crier announced another name.

"Pierre Keroy," the crier said. "Known as Lachine."

Judith spun around. She could see little over the heads of the onlookers except the scaffold beckoning above them.

"For the crime of murder," the crier added, at which the crowd bubbled over with murmurs and exclamation. No one was paying attention to Abraham now. Judith squeezed his arm tightly.

The crier waited until the noise died down before continuing.

"He is convicted of the murder of our beloved townsman Gerard Snellings," he continued with a flourish.

The guard led Lachine up the scaffold steps. The Frenchman's face was crusted with grime, but he had the same haughty lift to his chin. His hands were tied in front of him. He looked over the crowd, then raised his bound hands into the air.

"I'm innocent!" he yelled. "It was no murder!"

The executioner slapped Lachine on the side of his head. In a quick series of deft movements, he slipped the noose over the Frenchman's head, pushed him over the trapdoor, and stepped back to release the lever.

Judith turned away.

"We shouldn't see this." Her head swam as if she had been the one to receive the slap, and she struggled to find her breath. Beside her, Abraham was crying softly at her side and oblivious to the final proceedings. He wiped his eyes and looked at her.

"Judith."

"Let's go," she said. Behind her she could almost hear Lachine's legs kicking at the air. This wasn't what she had intended. "We have to go."

"Wait." He groped with his left hand at the pocket sewn to the front of his shirt. The angle gave him some difficulty, but after a moment he pulled a small chain and orb from the pocket. "I won't have this on me another minute." He handed the pomander to her. "I wouldn't sell it. Even when I had nothing, Judith. I'm so sorry I took it."

She wrapped her fingers around the jewelry and then brushed his chin with her knuckles. "Thank you," she said, and tears welled up in her eyes. Behind them, the crowd cheered at something. "It's time to go."

She took his arm again, and they wove through the crowd until they reached the edge, where the bystanders were fewer. A few roedes away, Paulus van Beresteyn was leaning against a stone wall and watching the execution. His lips were pressed together in grim determination, and his small eyes glittered with what might have been tears. He watched without breaking his gaze. Judith lowered her head and guided Abraham past. But then she left Abraham at the corner and walked back toward the crowd.

"You did this?"

Paulus turned his head toward her and frowned. "Did what?"

"You had him executed?"

"I submitted him to the town's justice. Isn't that what you wanted?"

She shook her head, but she couldn't bring herself to find the words. She hadn't wanted him dead. Or so she hoped. Her stomach shuddered.

"I'm grateful to you for taking a criminal off our streets," he said, looking away toward the scaffold, where she wouldn't look. She wanted to say more, but no words came. She should have expected this.

Behind her, some paces away, Abraham moaned. Judith stared at Paulus for a moment longer then walked back to her brother. No one had noticed him, but the crowd was coming apart.

"We have to leave," Judith said. She held his elbow and eased him over the cobbled streets toward her house. Behind her, she could hear the executioner's steps echo as he descended the scaffold.

Chapter 29

JULY

Maria slept. She slept, woke to parch her thirst, and slept again. She burned, and she shivered, while time flaked and crumbled around her, like the remnant of wood burnt in the hearth. She wasn't sure where she was, on a mattress somewhere, and she thought she heard Judith's voice. But that could have been her dreams. A cool hand against her forehead stilled her tossing body and froze her dreams for a pulsing moment before they resumed to race and whirl about her.

Days passed, she realized later. And she had moved, somehow. Been moved.

One night, finally, she awoke lucid. She tried to push herself upright, but her arm throbbed in protest, and she remembered a little of what had happened. She used her other arm and propped herself into a sitting position on the straw mattress. Her mattress and pile of blankets lay on a rough-hewn wood floor, and any windows in the room must have been covered by shutters, because her eyes could see nothing in the silky dark. But something about the smell of the place was reassuring, something earthy that promised comfort. A tangy smell, too, reminded her of home. Paint, she realized. She was neither hot nor cold, though her forehead was damp with sweat. She lay back down and, after straining to recognize anything in the creaks and scratches of the night, she fell asleep.

She awoke in the morning, judging by the soft light and the bustle of noise from the street outside, below. She had thought the night before she lay in someone's bedroom, but now she saw the close eaves of the roof and the planking of the walls. It was an attic loft.

Someone walked up the stairs, and Maria gathered the blankets to her chin. Again, that smell, and her breathing slowed as the woman came into sight in the stairway. A servant, probably, in simple clothes with a discolored but clean apron over her brown skirts.

"Well, that's something. You're awake," the woman said.

"Where am I?" Maria kept the blankets to her chin.

"You don't remember? Judith Leyster's house and workshop."

Maria sighed and closed her eyes. Safe, finally. "Is Judith coming? To see me."

The servant regarded her. "I'm sure she is. But I don't know when. Here's some broth for you. Drink up. You'll need it to get better."

She sat up, wincing when she moved her right arm. She did not have the courage to pull up her sleeve to look at the wound, but she was glad the arm was still there. She sipped the broth from the warm bowl, although it was difficult to do with one hand. She watched the servant, who had taken a seat on a footstool by the wall.

"I'm Carolein," the woman said. "I'll help you as much as I can. I—we—want you to get better. But it is a busy house, you know." Carolein stood, brushed her skirts with her hands, and turned away.

Maria nodded. She was glad Judith had herself a busy house. Hopefully that meant her workshop was selling a lot of paintings. She sipped the broth, and the warm liquid spread its fingers down into her stomach. She wanted to see the paintings, to see what scenes Judith had turned her sharp eye toward. Or emotions, really—it was emotions Judith excelled at capturing. The ephemeral quality of a celebration, with death looming behind. Or the covetous glance of a friend.

Maria put the bowl on the floor. She pulled up her sleeve and looked at the wound.

"Carolein," she called at the woman's back. She walked back up the stairs and looked at Maria with eyebrows raised. "I'm sorry, but would you mind getting me some . . ." Maria tried to remember one of Sara's basic salves. "Lard? And sweet clover too? Please. A lot of it."

Carolein regarded her, impassive at first, but then she nodded. "I'll see what I can do."

"I know you're busy. I'd be very grateful."

Carolein nodded again and gave a soft smile. "I'm good at what I do, Maria. I heard about what happened to you, and I respect another woman who knows her purpose. I'll help where I can." She descended the stairs.

Carolein's words had seemed like praise, and yet Maria's cheeks burned at the thought of Carolein knowing what had happened to her, how she had ended up so sick. She wondered if Judith knew.

The salve required more than lard and clover, certainly, and Maria laid back on her straw mattress and tried to figure out what else Sara had included. Where was Sara now? Far from Haarlem, Maria was certain. Sara was not the sort of person to wait around for anyone. Maria both resented her and envied her for that. She shifted in her bed and grimaced at the pain. Below, the house creaked, and the fall of footsteps sounded on the wood. The house was filled with mysterious life.

She dozed off again, and when she woke, her legs and hips ached from lying down for so long. She swung her legs off the mattress and, tentatively, pulled herself to her feet. She stood, keeping her hand on the wall for balance, and slowly straightened her back and arms. Her vision swam. Maria shuffled closer to the wall, and groped for it with her other hand. She closed her eyes and held still, hoping the fit would pass. The rising humors of her illness, most likely. She should open a window to let them waft away from her. She twisted her stiff, weak body toward the small window in the gable. Her bare feet protested the rough wooden planks as she covered the few steps as quickly as she could.

She reached for the smudged glass and then looked outside. The sky was bright, but the pavement was dark with recent rain. She gasped and gripped the casement. Below, in the street, was her father, staring up at her.

She gasped and pulled herself away from the window. Her pulse pounded in her ears. She took a breath and looked again.

The man was still standing there, but he wasn't her father. He had the same silver beard and square torso, but he was younger. He walked away, and she could see his gait had none of her father's languor.

Maria eased herself back to the floor. She was dressed in a nightgown, most likely Judith's, and she picked at the rough cloth stretched across her knees. She had told her father she had succeeded, but really, her trip was another failure. She leaned her head back and closed her eyes. She knew her father would be worried about her, certainly. Probably worried enough to forgive her. But her shame pressed in upon her, not just at failing but for running away, and dark humiliation seeped into the raw, painful edges around her arm, heart, and breath. She would speak with Judith. Judith would know what to do, and how to present herself to her father. She knew she needed to go to her father. But a few more hours, or days even, would not make a difference to the man. Assuming they had not already told him.

She must have dozed off, for after some time, she opened her eyes, and her neck ached. She had forgotten to open the window, she realized. She stood again, and the same fierce cloud accosted her vision. Slowly, she reached for the small window. With two weak pushes it swung open. Someone must have had it open recently, she realized with gratitude.

She took a deep breath. The dank ocean salt wafted up to her, and she smiled. The smell of home.

Below in the street shuffled a hunched figure clothed in a tunic with torn seams and breeches so threadbare one cuff hung, barely attached, above his ankle. The man was a beggar, but there was something, a tenderness in the way he held himself, that caught Maria's attention. He limped slowly down the street along the edge, afraid of something, and held out his left palm. As he came nearer, Maria saw his right arm, clutched protectively at his chest, was missing below the forearm. He was a leper. The crowds mostly streamed past him as if he were invisible, but every so often a woman with a basket or a man in a fine doublet would look closely, and then recoil.

Then, two men walked down the street with more urgency than the rest. The leper shrank even more deeply into the shadowed edge of the lane, but they strode up to him. After a brief exchange, each man took one side of the leper and dragged him away, toward the center square. For a moment, Maria feared they were hauling him to the scaffold, but then she remembered the leper house. Before her travels with Sara, Maria had rarely seen a leper, and even on their journey, she had seen only a handful, like the brother and sister begging along the side of the road on the way to Den Haag. All the lepers were locked up, for their own well-being and the safety of the towns. The arrangement gave the sick a place to stay, at the charity of each city's leading residents. Yet there was the sharp fear on the faces of the children who had approached Sara's wagon while camped outside a small village. The boy had whispered to Sara, who showed no fear of him, and gestured toward the village. Sara nodded, unwrapped the bandage around his sister's ear to look at some rash or lesion, and gave the girl both a salve and a draught. She did not charge them, something Maria had otherwise never seen her do.

"Some illnesses are too unfair to add the burden of payment," Sara said when Maria had raised a questioning eyebrow. "What other malady comes with the curse of imprisonment?"

"But they are taken care of."

Sara shook her head but did not argue. "Let me show you the recipe to that salve. I give it away, so you may as well help make it."

It was the only recipe Sara had shared with Maria during their time together. Now, Maria pressed her face to the glass but could see nothing more of the man who had been dragged away. She remembered that recipe though.

By suppertime, Judith had still not come up to visit. Maria, with Carolein's rough help, dressed herself and descended all the way to the main floor to join the household for supper. The two boys looked at her with wide eyes. Judith, already seated, smiled to see her.

"Feeling better?"

Maria scrutinized her friend, looking for some indication the younger woman had changed in their few months apart. Judith's face still glowed with self-possession, and Maria smiled. "Yes, I suppose I am. It's all still, well, strange though."

"Strange? I would have thought you'd be in pain." Judith gestured for her to take a seat.

"There's pain, of course. It's more like I haven't collected all my pieces yet."

The older of the two boys opened his mouth, but then closed it and sat down next to her.

"Are you missing a piece?" The youngest boy ducked his head under the table for a moment then raised himself back upright. His dusky blond hair was tousled from the inversion. "You have both legs. Are you missing something else?"

Maria closed her eyes for a moment. "I don't think so."

Carolein placed a platter of roasted carrots and parsnips on the table, and the sweet, rich smell drew their attention. They fell to eating, pulling hunks of bread and cutting slices from a wheel of soft white cheese. The bread was flimsy and stale, and Maria wondered if Judith noticed. They ate accompanied by the rhythm of their tearing and the clatter of passed dishes.

When they finished, Maria slid her chair closer to Judith's.

"My father, has he—"

"Davit, Hendrik. Go finish tidying the workshop, and then you're free until bedtime." Judith wiped her mouth with the back of her slim hand and watched as the boys skittered out of the kitchen. Carolein took her time moving the plates from the table over to the washbasin.

"Your father doesn't know you're here," Judith said. She kept her eyes to the table and ran a paint-stained fingernail along the grain of wood. "While you were sick, you seemed to worsen if someone mentioned him. When I first saw you in Den Haag, you recoiled from me, do you remember? You didn't want to see me. Or didn't want me to see you. It seemed like you wanted to disappear. I thought I should ask you first about your father."

"I'm glad. Thank you." She watched Judith closely, but the other woman kept her gaze lowered.

"Maria." Judith closed her eyes for a long moment. "Your portrait. Why did you do that?"

Maria tilted her head, cautious. "I did what I had to do."

"How can you say that?"

"It was an offering." The words felt bitter in her mouth. Her feelings seemed to turn to dust and crumble when she tried to explain.

"No, that's just it. Don't you understand?" Judith looked up, her expression bright and angry. "That isn't what we're doing. Painting it isn't some sort of transaction. Art and beauty are what fix everything that's so ugly here." She waved her hand around, at the small clean kitchen with two shining copper pans hanging from the wall. "Why would you destroy that?"

"You don't understand." Maria wished she had the energy to explain herself, but her shoulders sagged with fatigue. If she could have, she would have argued that for Judith painting seemed nothing more than a method for transforming pigments into coins. But she had no spirit for a fight.

Judith gripped the table and looked like she was going to argue, but she collapsed back into her chair. "I'm sorry, I didn't mean . . . it's been so much. You and then Abraham." She shook her head. "What about your father, Maria? What should I say?"

Maria put a hand to her mouth. "Abraham? Has he come back?"

"He's been injured." Her voice was low, almost extinguished. "He'll be fine. I think."

"What happened? I might be able to help."

Judith looked up at her.

"I learned some healing. A little, I was only with Sara a few weeks. With the healer, I mean. But I was paying attention."

"His hand was branded, and he was flogged. His back is torn to bits." Judith returned her gaze to the table and blinked back tears.

Maria bit her lip, mostly to keep the questions from spilling out. "How long ago was this?"

"Yesterday."

She didn't know what to say, and the exhaustion was creeping up her back like a clawed demon.

"I'm sure he'll be all right, Judith," she said finally. "The flogging will heal. Scars, of course. But he won't get sick." Maria wasn't sure she was speaking the truth, but she wanted it to be true. She forced her arm across the table and squeezed Judith's hand. She couldn't bring herself to mention Abraham's branded one.

Judith pulled away and looked up. Her bright eyes were red and rimmed in tears.

"You don't understand. He's a criminal. They read his name in the square, and now there's a D on his hand in case anyone has any doubt. How am I going to sell paintings now? To those same people. Who will want to buy art from a family proved to be degenerate? Things are hard enough as it is. God dammit." She slapped her palm on the table.

"I . . . I'm sorry." Maria tried to keep her words soft.

Judith shook her head and stood from the table. "I know I sound selfish, but you don't understand." She cleared her throat. "We'll see what happens. I'm going to talk to Jan Miense Molenaer tomorrow. On our journey—with you, I mean—he mentioned he might have some extra linseed oil. There was supposed to be a sale, but it hasn't happened yet, I guess."

Maria opened her mouth to ask, but Judith spoke before

she could.

"I forgot that you missed all that. You can hardly find any oil now, and when you do, it's nothing my coins can manage. But I'm sorry, I don't mean to go on. You should go to bed."

"That's strange." Maria looked over at Carolein, who had her back to them as she scrubbed the dishes. She wondered how long Judith could afford to pay the servant's wages. And now with herself and Abraham, two additional mouths to feed, the budget must be scraped down to threads. Maria's limbs felt heavy, as if she could sense her weight upon Judith's small frame. There were too many people to support, it was obvious. And yet, Maria could not return to her father's home. She couldn't face his disapproval.

"Judith, I have an idea. About how I can help, I mean."

Judith, standing in the doorway, shook her head. "You're kind to worry. It's just I don't have room in the workshop for another full-fledged painter. But thank you."

"No, that's not it. I'm thinking of the healing recipes I learned."

Judith gave a half smile. "I appreciate the offer. But I don't see how that could make a difference."

"I have to do something, Judith. I know it's a burden to have me here, but I can't go back to my father now."

Judith took a small step forward, toward Maria, and then stopped. "Why can't you? I'm not saying you should."

Maria pressed her lips together, and she looked again at Carolein in the back of the kitchen. Over the clang of the pots in the sink, the servant was unlikely to hear anything, but her presence still made Maria pause. "I failed him." As she spoke, she blushed. She was lying, and she knew it. Yes, there was her shame, but there were more reasons to stay than that. Still, the truth lay too deep inside of her, and it would hurt too much to dig it up and expose her selfish vulnerabilities. How much, more than anything, she wanted to stay here. How she wanted to fix what had become strained between her and Judith.

Judith nodded. She turned and left the room.

Chapter 30

JUDITH USED HER SLEEVE TO wipe away the sweat from her brow. The heat, so unusual, made it difficult even to breathe. She blinked, tried to focus, and checked her arithmetic in her ledger book. There was still not nearly enough money, and she had not found any linseed oil that she could afford. She'd heard nothing of a sale, either. She rested her head in her hands and closed her eyes. Upstairs, she could hear the muffled voices of the boys joking as they worked. That, at least, was a balm.

She lifted her head. She needed to visit Jan Miense Molenaer. They had barely spoken since the afternoon he had seen her with Willem, and though each time she ran into him in the street or at an auction she wanted to clasp his hand and explain, she couldn't. She had no explanation that did not lead to the black stain of Lachine's death or her own foolishness. But this was business. She stood, went to the kitchen to splash some cool water on her face, and left the house. As she was shutting the door, she paused. She ran back inside, grabbed her pomander, and sniffed the cloves she had added two days earlier. Still fragrant. She attached the chain to her waistband and went back to the street.

When she knocked on Jan's door, a servant answered. The woman, older and more worn than Carolein, pursed her lips and regarded Judith before inviting her inside. The servant called for Jan and then left Judith standing in the bright entry hall. The light here was gorgeous, Judith admitted. Even better than she had expected, based on his description. She knew he paid more in rent than she did, especially since his partner had moved out, and maybe the light was worth it. She held up her arm and examined the way the light drew her black wool into different shades. A touch of silver here, midnight black there. Not bad.

"Have you come to cast shadow figures on my floor? I hear that's a respected entertainment in the Indies." Jan stood in the doorway to the left and wiped his hands on his painter's smock. He was smiling.

Judith snapped her arm to her side and then wished she had not.

"If only that was what I had come for." She gave a soft smile, and a knot in her chest softened. "But I've really come to ask you a favor. You said you had a fair amount of linseed oil. I hoped I could buy some from you. A little, to hold me over until the shipment gets in."

"There's a shipment planned?" He took a step closer. She could almost touch him.

"Well, no. I mean, I don't know of one specifically." She blushed. "But I assume one is coming. With so many painters here, someone will want to sell to us. Right?"

Jan nodded and regarded her for a brief moment. His eyes flickered to the window behind her, and a woman laughed in the street. Judith didn't breathe.

"I'll give you a jar. No, don't argue, I don't want you to pay, and that's not negotiable. I'll give you a jar. But that's all I can spare. I don't know when I'll find any more either."

She held his gaze, but he did not smile. "Thank you," she said, and her blood warmed even more than the day's heat should have allowed. He wasn't going to make her talk about Willem, she realized, and she wanted to kiss his cheek in gratitude. She hesitated. "Can I ask . . . where you found what you have?"

He crossed his arms and looked at the floor. "Frans Hals. He helped me out. I can't say more than that, Judith. I'm sorry."

"Something is going on, isn't it?" She took a step closer to him. His golden mustache glowed above lips that were both soft and firm. She had known his face for so long that it had gone from novel to commonplace to, now, something new. She clenched her jaw to focus her thoughts on the oil. "There is something, I'm certain."

He kept his arms crossed. "Look, I can't say anything else. I don't know anything else. But you can try talking to Frans."

Judith crossed her arms to mirror him. "Certainly. I'll ask him to kindly return my student while he's at it. Did you know I had to pay a fine for that? We're not exactly on the best terms."

"Then talk to Frans de Grebber. I've heard his name mentioned. And he doesn't seem to be having any trouble with supplies."

She nodded though her stomach sank. She didn't want to lie to her former master about Maria. And she dreaded learning he might not hesitate to lie to her, if doing so would protect his workshop and his prized independence. Jan raised a hand to indicate she should wait while he stepped away. When he turned to leave her, she noticed the muscular swell of his calves, and she blushed.

He returned in a few minutes with a stoppered stoneware

jar, probably about three weeks' worth of oil. He handed it to her, and she gaped in mute gratitude. His fingers brushed hers as he passed her the jar, and she couldn't make her tongue form her profound thanks quickly enough. If she mentioned the new painting she had in mind, he might understand. It was to be a merrymaking picture of a gambler laughing while, perhaps, cheating his friends. She might ask him how he would represent the delicate, easily broken ties of loyalty. Jan would understand what she was saying if she asked for his thoughts. Few people would, she realized.

"This will help," she began. He held up a hand and dismissed whatever she would say, and then made as if to leave her.

She shifted the weight of the jar in her arms, and glanced in the direction of his workshop. "I wanted to ask you—what are you working on now?" she said.

He turned to look at her. "Would you like to see?" He smiled and swung his arm wide, inviting.

Judith placed the jar on the floor by the door and walked past him. As she did, she noticed a stray hair high on his cheek his razor must have missed a few days in a row. It was darker than the mustache above his lips, and she smiled. She was about to ask him the color of his beard when she remembered herself. She clamped her mouth shut.

They entered his bright workshop, and Jan pointed at a canvas strung up on its stretcher on his easel. The grinning figure of a boy glowed in the center, and he held a cat in his hands. The left side of the painting still only had its dead coloring in, but Judith knew what image would emerge.

"That again, Jan? You're fond of those children." She touched one finger, ever so lightly, to the painted boy's sleeve.

He smiled. "Hans is such a good model, I have to make the most of him before he outgrows me."

"I'm glad you haven't lost my hat." She pointed at a fur cap resting on a table. In the painting on the easel, the boy wore it.

"Never," he said in mock horror. "I will give it back, I promise."

"You do?"

"What, you don't trust me?" Again, that smile. Judith looked away.

She pointed at the cat in the boy's hands. "A cat held tightly makes strange leaps," she said, quoting the adage.

He raised an eyebrow. "What do you mean by that?"

"Nothing. It's something I tell myself often. Maybe too often." She looked at her hands. She was talking too much. "You're right, I had better speak with Frans de Grebber. Only, I don't know what to say about Maria."

"Will you tell him?" Jan took a step back and leaned against the wall.

"No. I don't know. She doesn't want me to. But maybe I should."

"If it helps you get your oil, you mean."

Judith flinched as if he had slapped her. "How could you say that?"

"I'm sorry. That was cruel." He pressed his lips together and looked down at his thumb. "That's not what I meant. I didn't mean to say that."

She pressed the jar to her chest and looked at him. So he was still angry. Or Jan, like everyone else, had confused her fixedness of purpose with selfishness. His mouth was open, but he said nothing else. She turned to walk out.

"Thank you for the oil," she said over her shoulder. "I'll repay you however I can. If you need props, anything."

He stayed inside the workshop. "I'll think about it," he called in a weak voice.

She let herself out.

She walked home, where she stashed the oil under a table in her workshop. Downstairs in her bedchamber, she unhooked the pomander, placed it in its box, and buried the box at the bottom of her clothes chest. Then, without a word to anyone in her house, she left again to go to the De Grebber home.

Chapter 31

JUDITH TOOK THE SHORTCUT THROUGH the echoing Grote Kerk, where she could hear the prelate arguing with the man who swept the floors. What did it matter, she thought as she clicked her way across the stone floor, if dust collected in the corner? Surely such a small thing would not offend God, wherever He was. When so much filth accumulated elsewhere. The prelate, now behind her, argued strenuously to the contrary. She listened to the few words she could catch. Maybe she was wrong, and God did need perfection. Or at least the attempt. She stepped out into the muted light, dimmed by low, warm clouds, and she wondered what Maria's God required. How much effort was enough. It was like asking how bright a candle ought to be to illuminate a model for a painting.

She knocked on the green De Grebber door without having yet decided what she would say, and a fog of unease washed over her. Her stomach twisted. It was unlike her to be so unprepared. She took a step back, and felt a sharp stone press at the sole of her shoe. The sound of footfalls came from inside as someone approached the door, and she straightened her skirt.

Frans de Grebber opened the door. He was wearing a threadbare dressing gown that doubled as a smock, judging by the stray smatterings of paint at his sleeves. He frowned, and for a moment, Judith feared he had forgotten who she was.

"Frans." She was determined to address him as an equal, no longer an apprentice. "I'm here to talk about linseed oil."

He groaned and dropped his head back toward his shoulders. "It's not for sale." He looked at her and exhaled. "Not even to you, Judith. I'm sorry." He put his hand to the door.

"No, wait please. I'm not asking to buy any. I mean, I would, if you were willing, but that's not why I'm here. I want to talk about the situation, that's all. I heard you might know why the price is going up."

"Shouldn't you be painting? Look at this light you're missing. Perfect. Now, if you'll excuse me. Even if you don't have painting to work on, I do." He moved to shut the door.

"What! No, I—wait!" She thrust a hand out to stop the door from closing, and behind her, a cat hissed. "Maria. I have Maria."

He swung the door open, and his drawn face fell in upon itself. "What? Maria?"

Judith's shoulders sagged. She was detestable, and Jan was right. Her loyalty hadn't lasted a minute. "May I come in, please?"

He stepped back.

She walked into the large entry room, the display space and family gathering room that had once felt more familiar than home, and she noted little had changed. A strange bit of nostalgia and loneliness filled her. The same paintings lined the dun-colored walls, and the same light fell from the large windows. But then a second glance revealed many of the paintings were crooked. All the frames were muted by dust.

"What do you mean you have Maria? Is something wrong? You're not holding her against her will, are you?" He took a step closer, and she could smell the bitter decay of his breath. He had slippers, usually only worn by women, on his feet.

"No, no. That's not what I meant. She's staying with me. She was hurt. No, she's fine now." Judith's stomach curdled with self-disdain. Jan's words echoed through her head, and she pressed her hand against her temple. "Why don't we sit somewhere, where I can explain?"

He nodded slowly and led her to the set of chairs he used to host guests who came to view his paintings. Frans had never, in Judith's experience, tried to even pretend to comply with Guild rules on selling only through approved channels. She took a moment to look around more closely. The paintings in the room, flanked by a window to the street and a fireplace, were nearly all the same history pieces and sample portraits she remembered from a few months ago. She had never liked the one of Daniel in the lion's den, which still hung next to a window. The formalized figures, the fresh face of Daniel, and the glorious jeweled sky all diminished the horror Judith thought the real historical moment must have produced. Glossing over that authentic horror to produce something beautiful was more grotesque than any painted corpse. That was why she didn't produce history paintings. She did not have the mind for it.

They sat in a pair of straight-backed, wooden chairs, and Judith folded her hands. She cleared her throat and looked again at the paintings. She was wrong, she realized. There were at least two new ones. A portrait of Maria done a few years earlier, judging by the overlarge lace ruff at her neck, and a genre painting of drinkers at a table, an unusual theme for him. She blinked and leaned forward in her seat. One of the models was Gerard Snellings.

"Is that Gerard Snellings? In the painting there. Peeckl-haerring?"

"Who?" He drew his eyebrows together and tried to follow her gaze.

"In the merry company piece you've got there. The drinker. Is that Gerard Snellings?" She tried to keep the urgency from her voice.

"Him? I suppose so, I don't really . . ." His voice trailed off, and then he turned to her with a fierce gaze. "Look, I don't want to talk about my models. My cursed models. Tell me about my daughter. Please."

"All right." Judith took a deep breath. "Maria is fine. She was sick when I went to get her, when she arrived at my house. But she's better now. She hasn't been with us for long, only a week or so."

"A week you've kept this secret?"

Judith's cheeks burned, and she looked down at her hands, folded in her lap. "Yes. She asked me to keep silent. Though she was going to tell you soon. She said so."

Frans sagged in his chair. Gray stubble gave his cheeks a shimmering, ghostly look. Judith reached out to pat his hand, but he drew his arm back.

"I don't know what I did," he said, his voice so low she could barely hear him. "And you know what, Judith? That relic? That cursed piece of bone, Heaven forgive me. The priest sent it back three weeks after she left. She got what we sent her to get, Judith, and she still fled. I don't know where I went wrong."

They sat in silence. Outside, a passing mule's hooves struck the paving stones, and somewhere nearby the tap of a hammer sounded. His pain was palpable, and she was helpless.

"Can I ask about the linseed oil?" Judith said hesitantly. If Jan was right about her venal character, she may as well try to save her workshop.

He took a deep breath. "Right. The oil. What a holy mess. Those fools."

"What do you mean?"

He cocked his head and regarded her, and some of the color came back to his face. "If you haven't figured it out, I'm not sure it's worth it to discuss it with you."

She bit her lip. "Someone's driving up the price. That much is clear. They're limiting availability of the oil so people like me have to scrounge around and risk our workshops to buy the stuff. People who aren't famous and are just trying to make it."

"And who would want to do that? No, who could do that?"

She thought about the meeting she had overheard. "Well, lots of people use linseed oil for various—"

"No. Don't be foolish. You know this is about painters, you practically said as much. About too many painters trying to sell their art to a public flush with cash but swamped with options for spending it. Why buy a panel of painted wood when you can have a pewter stein? Or a map, to make you look worldly. Or, even better, a blossoming tulip, to make you look rich."

Judith picked paint off the inside of her wrist. Outgert von Akersloot had been at that meeting. "It's the Guild leaders, isn't it? They need to have everyone join the Guild, but they can't have all of us selling."

He gave a crooked smile and crossed his arms.

"How do you get by, then?" she asked. "Is it true you have oil?"

"Listen. I don't abide by this nasty plan. But I'm not getting involved one way or the other. I sniffed the fools out months ago. They tried to distract me with the relic and, I don't know, maybe it worked. After a fashion." He looked at his hands for a moment. "But I figured it out, and they had to sell to me. At the usual price. I'm not helping them buy it up, but I'm not printing pamphlets on it either. Not my business."

"Why didn't you tell me before? I thought . . ."

He shrugged. "Why didn't you tell me about Maria?"

From somewhere else in the house, a boy called for him, but he ignored it.

"What can I do?" Judith asked. "I know I can't report them. I realize my family has no credibility in this town. No one would believe me over Frans Hals and Pieter Molijn."

"And you have no proof."

"And I have no proof." A story about snatches of a conversation overheard while crouched next to a known criminal would do her no good.

He sighed. "Look, Judith. Like you said, people use linseed oil for a lot of things. There's plenty of the stuff out there in the world. It will make its way to Haarlem. These men have bit off more than they can chew. Wait it out. You'll make it. Try some walnut oil instead, if you can afford it. This won't last forever."

She closed her eyes and tried to steady her breathing. She wasn't worried about forever, she was worried about three weeks from now, when her jar from Jan would be empty.

"And, fine. I'll sell you a little of what I have. But I can't go too far. I don't get unlimited supplies, and I'm on a tight budget too."

Some tension dissolved from her shoulders. "Thank you."

"I'll be by, soon, to see Maria," he said with his eyes fixed firmly upon her. Judith nodded.

Chapter 32

AFTER WALKING A BLOCK FROM Frans de Grebber's house, she stopped. Standing in the cobbled street, she pressed her fingertips against her closed eyes and cradled her head. It didn't matter who was watching. She could paint, yes, and that was a relief. But for how long? And to what end, if someone else would have control over her ability to do so? Her workshop was supposed to bring independence, not bind her to the whims of men who meant her ill. Or, even worse, who would barely acknowledge her. And for this knowledge, she had broken a promise to her friend. She pressed at the flesh below her eyebrows, then took a deep breath and continued walking.

A man in a floppy cap and a wool vest pushed a wheelbarrow of cabbages and a few artichokes down the street ahead of her. Distracted, Judith dipped her chin in polite greeting, but then jumped when she felt her foot connect with something soft. A cabbage tumbled across the street and landed in the muddy gutter. He had been chasing after the produce that had fallen from his pile, she realized. The peasant opened his mouth as if to curse, then closed it and glared at her. She apologized and grasped at her pocket for a penning, but he ignored her as he picked up the rest of his vegetables. She walked on, her breath ragged.

At home, she set Hendrik to mixing paints with the new supply of oil. While he heated the first batch of oil in a small copper dish he held with tongs over the fire, she began painting on the one remaining prepared wood panel. She should tell Maria, of course. Judith had to apologize and prepare her friend for her father, who would surely be coming. But the words escaped her. To simply tell the story she would have to admit how easily she gave way. She needed to compose the scene, as she would for a painting.

"Davit, sit there, I need you to model. For the dead coloring." Later, she could hire models for portrait part of the work. But now, she needed to rough out the spacing and figures in the conceptual phase. Children listening to and playing noisemakers, enjoying both their freedom and disharmony. After this, if she could find the coins for another prepared painting support, she could start on the gambler picture. The pleasure of watching someone else sin would surely earn that work a buyer. Perhaps that tailor whom she had finally managed to speak with while Maria was recovering. But one painting at a time.

Davit ought to be holding one of the instruments, she decided, and she went to get the rommelpot, a pig bladder stretched over a bowl and punctured by a stick, when she heard her front door slam. She frowned. Carolein knew how much she hated the shudder of a loud door. She paused and wondered if she should call to Carolein, but then she looked out the window. She turned away and was about to hand the pot to Davit, but then spun back. There, down in the street below, were Maria and Abraham, apparently headed toward the center of town. Judith nearly dropped the ceramic pot. If they were going to the De Grebber house, Maria would find out Judith had betrayed her trust. Or perhaps Abraham was up to something, some repeat of the disaster that had sent him out of Haarlem and flayed his back. Judith thrust the rommelpot at Davit who, startled, bounced it between his hands before clasping it to his body. She hurried down the stairs and out the door.

She followed them at a short distance—easy enough in the busy streets, especially since their progress was slow. A linen merchant she had known since childhood called out to her from across the street. She flinched, but Maria and Abraham did not seem to notice. Judith nodded at the merchant, who hurried over to grab her elbow and ask after Judith's father, about whom she had nothing to say. She expressed a few pleasantries and by the time she extricated herself, she had lost sight of them. She hurried down the street and wondered if she should try to rush ahead to the De Grebber home. But then she saw them turning down a side street toward the canal. A sick feeling of relief poured over her. That wasn't the way toward Maria's house.

The street was quiet, and she hung back until they had nearly reached the other end of the block. When she emerged into the open space by the canal, she saw Maria and Abraham walking up the curved back of a bridge sloping over the canal. On the other side they stopped next to a gate in a long brick wall. Maria knocked, then exchanged a few words with the modestly dressed woman who opened it. They crossed the threshold, and the gate closed behind them.

From the other side of the stone canal, Judith could see the property behind the wall was a large house, but she was not familiar with the street and did not know who owned it. She stepped out of the alley, rested her hand on a slim chestnut tree, and then approached the gate. Next to the gate hung a plaque, which read, "Haarlem Leper House." Judith read it twice and ran her fingers over the brass. She frowned in confusion. Were they visiting someone? Or maybe Maria had gone to peddle her supposed healing lessons. No matter what Maria hoped, a few weeks dabbling with plants alongside a woman who had apparently left Maria for dead could not have taught her much. Judith clenched her fists. Why hadn't they told her, asked her opinion? She kicked a rock into the canal. Then she walked back home, and the sweat dripped down her back.

Chapter 33

THE WOMAN WHO HAD LET Maria and Abraham inside the gate at the leper house raised a hand to indicate they should pause. She was shrunken and old, with signs of the disease spotting her neck and cheeks, but she had answered the gate door with a defiant look. Maria willed herself not to flinch. She wanted to help those people.

"Thank you for letting us in. I didn't want to talk in the street. I'm here to see the Leper House Administrator," Maria said. She didn't know who governed the house, but whomever he was, he would be the one to grant her permission.

"The magistrate?" the old woman said, one eye narrowed in skepticism.

"The Administrator," Maria repeated.

"Paulus van Beresteyn is a busy man," the old woman said. "But you're lucky; he's here today. Wait." She held up a gnarled hand.

Maria and Abraham stood silently as the woman hobbled into the large house a few roedes away. From that distance,

Maria could hear no sounds coming from the house. A few dun-colored sheets flapped on a line in the breeze.

The Administrator, a slight man with a winged brown-and-gray mustache, fiddled with a shining button on his doublet as he approached.

"I've just got a minute, I'm in the middle of some record keeping," he said.

"Thank you for your time," Maria said. "I'm here to offer mine. I have some training as an herbalist, and I thought—"

"That's no use here," Paulus interrupted. "It's kind of you to offer, really. But they'll be better off with your prayers." He began to turn away but then paused, as if his eyes had snagged on Abraham.

"You there. How old are you?"

Abraham stood up straight and clasped his hands behind his back. "Twenty years."

"You strong?"

"I worked at the docks some time."

"Yet you send your wife to find work now?"

Abraham furrowed his brow in confusion.

"We're not married, magistrate," Maria said. "He's my friend's brother, that's all."

"Fine," said Paulus. "The point is, boy, are you looking for a job too?"

Abraham glanced at Maria, who raised her eyebrows in an encouragement she did not feel.

"It's mostly hauling privy buckets and putting sheets out to dry," Paulus said. He inclined his head toward the sheet on the line. "But, every once in a while, I have need of a strong back. And it seems you're not afraid to spend time with the sick."

"I'm not," Abraham said, and Maria saw a twitch at the corner of his eyes before he stilled his expression.

"Good," said Paulus. "Nothing to fear, really. I've got to

get back to work, but come tomorrow. I'll pay, don't worry." Without waiting, he turned and walked back into the house.

They let themselves out of the gate, and it closed with a click behind them.

"I stole your job," Abraham said. "I'm sorry."

"No, not at all. I didn't want that job. Hauling privy buckets? Look at me, I can hardly carry a canvas." Maria forced a smile on her face. "And I'm glad you'll have some coins for yourself."

"I had to take the job before he realized what I've been punished for. No one else will hire me, I'm sure." He traced a finger over the bright pink welt on his hand.

Maria didn't know what to say, so she nodded and fixed her gaze on the streets while watching for any dog excrement or mud that servants in nearby homes had not yet washed away. She had failed again, and again she had to return to Judith's house to hide.

They emerged into the lower end of the main square and walked past a man playing a flute for coins and a tight circle of young women giggling and bobbing their heads as they eyed a man on a horse. The scaffold still stood to their left, blocking the municipal building, and Maria felt Abraham quicken his pace.

Then, he stopped. They had reached the corner where Judith's street split off from the square, and Abraham held out his hand.

"Maria," he said.

She looked past the pastry vendor with his tray of sweet-breads and down the street. In front of the brick face of Judith's building stood her father.

If he had not been looking right at her, she might have turned and walked away. The sight of him, his arms crossed over his chest as if in anger but his eyes wide like pools of water reflecting the moon, made her feel as if a line fractured down her breastbone. How she had missed him, and wanted him to miss her.

She took a few steps closer. Behind him was Judith, who was biting her lip as her gaze jumped between Maria and the ground. That was guilt playing across the woman's face. Judith had told him, she realized. And then a throbbing in her arm reminded her of her wound, and how far she had traveled. Only to return to where she began.

"Hello, Father," Maria said softly when she approached. She did not reach for him, and they stood an arm's length apart. The sun broke through some clouds, and a bright ray made the wrinkled skin at the outer corners of his eyes look nearly transparent.

"You're coming home with me," he said roughly, and then his face seemed to soften in apology. But he said nothing else.

"So I gathered. Judith, how much did you sell me for? Or were you glad to get rid of another mouth to feed?"

"No, I . . ." Judith's shoulders drew up in anger as if she were going to protest, but then she clamped her mouth shut. "I am truly sorry to see you go."

Maria shook her head. "I have nothing here," she told her father. "We can go."

He folded her arm into his. As they walked away, Maria waved to Abraham, who stood a few paces back. "God be with you," she called to him softly. Then she pinched her eyes closed and let her father guide her for a few steps, before she opened her eyes to the sights of bustling Haarlem. She followed him home.

Chapter 34

It was a hot Sunday morning, and Judith stayed in bed past sunrise. When Carolein came to inquire, Judith rolled over toward the wall. She could not face Carolein and lie to her.

"I feel dreadful," Judith said quietly. It was true enough. She hoped her voice was low. "I'll have to let you go to church without me."

"Should I send for Maria? She might have something you can take." Carolein had mentioned Maria's name often since Frans de Grebber had come to take her away a month ago. Judith suspected she had some hope of helping the women repair their friendship.

"No," Judith said, more sharply than she intended. "I'm not one for those physics. I'll rest a bit. Thank you, Carolein."

Carolein looked at her with eyebrows raised over her dark eyes, and Judith closed her eyes. She knew it would look like the pain she was suffering was physical, and she pressed her lips together in regret. She missed Maria, she could admit as much to herself, at least. But she also knew that she deserved Maria's anger, and that was too much to say out loud.

When the servant shut the door, Judith felt a dark guilt gnaw at her chest. It fed upon both her lie and her impending absence from church. Only Catholics and Jews were permitted to miss the Reformed service. But then, she told herself with a grimace, a little bit more shame heaped upon herself and her family was of little consequence at this point. It was the linseed oil that mattered. If only Judith could get her workshop on the right footing. And maybe those other things wrong in her life would rearrange themselves, once she had the freedom to paint. To snatch life and style it as she pleased upon her painting support. Frans de Grebber had said she didn't have proof. She would find some.

When the streets quieted, and the church bells finished tolling, Judith hurried out of bed and into her shift and skirt, a light one to account for the heat. Even still, by the time she closed her house door behind her and stepped onto the paving stones, she was sweating.

She made her way, head down, through side streets and over to Pieter Molijn's house. He was a prominent painter, a Guild leader, and a suspect easier to start with than the famed Frans Hals would be. A long row of newly built houses with matching black shutters rose up from the street, and she hoped no one was looking out the windows. Adjacent to Molijn's house was a gate. The latch was unlocked, and Judith stepped into the walkway before the gate slammed closed behind her. She gritted her teeth at the sound.

Molijn's workshop was, she assumed, inside his house, but she wanted to see what the garden held. If he were storing large amounts of linseed oil, he might not have the space for it inside the building. And barrels of oil might attract attention in his workshop, especially since he had recently shifted his work away from painting and toward ink-and-pen drawings. To appeal to different buyers, he said. A smart move, if the painting market was glutted. That might be his assessment, but Judith refused to believe buyers would abandon honest, evocative paintings. There were still people willing to pay for art by new artists. She hoped.

The brick pathway led her to a small, enclosed garden. A brick patio filled most of the space, but there were a few plots of vegetables and herbs, and a small apple tree filled the back corner. There was far less space here than she had imagined. And no linseed oil.

She could hear no sounds beyond the casual chirping of a few songbirds from the garden next door. Judith took a deep breath. She climbed the brick steps leading up to the kitchen entrance, and tried the door. It was unlocked.

Barking erupted as soon as she swung the door open, and a small dog ran toward her. Its tawny snout snapped as it yapped at her and lunged at her ankles.

She shushed the dog, batted it away, and closed the door. He kept barking. She tried to open the door again to get herself out, but the latch stuck. Still the dog barked. Finally she lifted her foot to aim at its side, only in hopes of keeping it away while she squeezed back out the door. The dog whimpered and fell silent. She lowered her foot.

She stood still, her hand on the door, and listened to the house. There might be an apprentice home, sick, or maybe Molijn was a Catholic. Her stomach plummeted at the thought. His parents were from the south, she remembered, though he himself was born abroad. He might well be Catholic.

Her blood pounded in her ears, and she could hardly hear beyond it. The dog growled, but backed away.

"Well, if I'm this far," she said to the dog, her voice trembling. She walked inside.

Chapter 35

Maria knocked at the leper house gate. It was Sunday morning, and Abraham was not working. A rat scratched and scurried along the edge of the wall some paces away, and she hoped someone would come to the door. She knocked again.

She had spent weeks thinking how to spend the hours that dripped past her window, first in Judith's attic while she lay listless, with only Carolein to talk to when the woman brought her food, and then at her father's. In the attic, Judith came in the evenings, true, but Maria now saw that as a meager consolation, some sort of assuaging of Judith's guilt rather than a real gesture of friendship. After Judith had betrayed her and sent her back to her father's house, Maria resolved to listen only to her own convictions. When Abraham came sheepishly to her door, to ask if she would still help even if it meant concealing her work from the magistrate, she knew she would.

She knocked a third time. Abraham had told her to come today, at this hour, because Paulus and his wife, Catharina, would almost certainly be at church services, along with the rest of Haarlem. Excepting, of course, the lepers.

Finally, the same old woman answered. The late morning air was already heavy, and Maria felt the sweat running down her back as she explained her appointment to the woman, who stood blocking the entrance, as if strangers regularly sought entry to her domain.

"You're sure you're here to see him? Gerrit?" Her voice was raspy.

"That's right." A wash of panic came over her, and she wondered if she had Abraham's friend's name wrong. But she clung to her recollection.

The woman harrumphed, considered Maria for a moment, and then stepped back to let her pass. The tension at the back of Maria's neck eased, until she began to worry that she would be introduced to the wrong man. A mistake might reveal how Abraham had broken the rules in inviting her, and maybe he'd lose his position here. No, she would say whatever she needed in order to protect him. Maria, unlike some people, knew how to protect her friends.

A small yard and dull but tidy garden lay between the gate and the brick house, and somewhere inside the house a child shrieked. A second child followed, and then both voices dissolved into giggles. The idea of leper children laughing struck Maria as so strange she almost turned to search out the sound. Perhaps the playmates were healthy children. No, even if they had the disease, they were still children. They might laugh, and they deserved to be cured. She walked around the house to the kitchen garden, where Abraham had suggested she might find Gerrit.

The sun shone strong against her skin, and she could feel its heat suffusing her face. She stepped back under the shade of an aspen. As she did, an old man wrapped in a loose garment, perhaps a linen nightgown, walked out of the house. His gait was uneven and his shoulders rounded, ordinary for an old man perhaps, and she saw no sign of the disease. Then, once he was closer, she noticed how he wrapped his hands into the loose folds of his long sleeves.

"Maria de Grebber?" he asked in a clear voice.

"Gerrit?"

"The same. A pleasure to meet you. Will you come inside, out of the sun?"

She hesitated. Surely the leper house was filled with stale air, the sort of miasma that might transmit the disease.

"Of course," she said, more graciously than she felt. She would grow her soul to fit her behavior. She hoped.

They sat in the kitchen, with the door open to catch the breeze, and Gerrit poured her a cup of small beer.

"We won't be disturbed?" Maria glanced out the open door to the small garden wilting in the heat.

"Paulus and Catharina never come on Sundays, if that's what you're thinking. Or rarely enough that I'm not worried. And I'm allowed to entertain guests anyway, so don't trouble yourself. We're fine." He smiled, a soft expression that didn't show his teeth. Maria looked more closely at his face and realized his fine cheekbones and arched eyebrows must have been handsome when he was young.

"I'm not sure where to start," Maria said.

"Wherever you like. I'm here to listen and see how I can help. Abraham said you had an idea."

"It's me who should be doing the helping. That's what I want, really, to help. To find a way to help you."

"I'm fine. This cursed sickness is one of the many ways my soul might find its way to rid me of this old body. But it's the little ones." His gray eyes clouded over, and he looked at the floor. "I don't like to let myself hope for something better for them. But when Abraham said—"

"Are there many children here?"

He shook his head. "We're not a crowded house. There are five children, including my two grandchildren. A few more of us older people. The rest look my age, but they're some ten or twenty years younger. Anna, I think she's got some other sort of sickness. But she's welcome here nonetheless."

"Anyone's welcome," Maria suggested.

"The Administrator has the final word, as he pays for the food, on top of what the city provides. But that seems to be the rule. It's just that not many, even the most desperate, want to take their chances with us."

She nodded. "I'd like to see what I can do to ease your burden. Though I don't know if I can remove the disease. I don't want to promise."

Gerrit reached his hand toward her but let it fall short, still wrapped in his sleeves. "I'd be grateful. Even if you help them breathe a little better, that would be a relief."

"I should see them, I guess. To see what I can do." Her stomach clenched at the thought. It was easier to consider the agony of the sufferers in this house if she had only her imagination to conjure their lesions. But if she was to be a healer, she had to face the sick.

"Magdalena, Jacob, come in here," Gerrit called.

The children materialized almost immediately, like they had been lurking outside the kitchen. The girl, taller than her brother, gave a guilty smile as she looked up under her long eyelashes. The boy ran toward his grandfather and then skidded to a stop when he saw Maria. Both children were thin, with dull hair the color of winter grass, but their blue eyes sparkled with life. The only sign of the disease on their faces was a pale smudge ringed by a pink rash on Magdalena's left cheek and a mottled white stain on Jacob's upturned nose. Maria exhaled the breath she hadn't realized she was holding.

"Come here," she said and held out a hand. Both children stepped closer, but they remained out of reach. What a selfish person she was, she thought, to fear these creatures. Her guilt uncoiled from her chest like a snake reaching down from a tree branch. She closed her eyes. When she opened them, she stood and approached the children. She crouched down and took the girl's arm in her hand. It was fine to feel fear. The girl was scared too.

"May I see your arms?" she asked.

Magdalena nodded and rolled up her sleeves. Beneath the coarse linen were white sores like fine scales burned into her pink skin. Maria took a deep breath and pressed one with her fingertip.

"Does it hurt?"

Magdalena shook her head. "I barely feel it," she whispered.

"I see." Maria pulled the girl's sleeve back down but continued to hold her hand. Magdalena's eyes grew wide and then filled with tears. How long had it been since an adult had held the child's hand? Even Gerrit, with his fingers as they were, might not want to grasp his granddaughter's hand. Magdalena squeezed, first gently and then with a fierce intensity that reminded Maria of Judith. She pulled the girl into a hug and then reached out an arm for her brother. She held the two children quietly as they sobbed into her bodice.

"I can make you something to ease the discomfort," she said, her cheek alongside Magdalena's bound hair. She looked up to Gerrit. "I'll need to go to the apothecary to get some quicklime. I'll slake it with water." She hesitated.

"I've grown some black hellebore," he said, his face still but his eyes bright. "And chamomile, calendula, and sweet flag."

She leaned back a bit from the children, though she didn't release them. "Where did you get such plants? And how did you know?"

"I was a horticulturalist, once." He shrugged. "When we moved here, I brought some of my plants with me. Particularly the ones I thought might be of use. Do you think they could help?"

Maria squeezed the children once more and then stood. "The black hellebore, certainly, and perhaps the sweet flag. I was thinking first a plaster of the slakened quicklime and then a poultice of the herbs. But I'll need oil—linseed oil is best, though I know it's hard to find. Beeswax to bind it."

"There's loads of oil here," Jacob said, speaking for the first time. His voice had the bright ring of fine glass.

Magdalena and Gerrit glanced at him, and Gerrit pursed his lips. "We're not supposed to talk about it," he said. "But. Damn the man. You say you need linseed oil?"

"It's the best, as far as I know."

"Then you'll want to see this."

Confused, Maria followed him deeper into the house and then up the cramped wooden stairs. The children trailed behind them, first whispering, then giggling. Another younger girl joined them.

When they reached the third story, Gerrit pulled out a stool, reached up, and swung open a hatch to the attic. A cloud of hot air poured out, and he pulled a sliding ladder down.

"Careful on your way up."

Maria hesitated, unsure about how to climb in her skirts and whether this deeper violation of Paulus van Beresteyn's regency was worth the risk. But she had come this far. She put her hands to the roughly hewn wood and slowly pulled herself up the ladder. The children stayed below.

In the attic, the steeply pitched roof hung close to her head, and she had to crouch to avoid the supporting rafters. There was hardly any room to stand, for the floor was filled with small wooden casks. Nearly every inch of planking was packed, two or three high, with casks bound by iron bands and displaying seared brands of the Van Beresteyn insignia. Many had additional markings, which Maria could not recognize. By her feet lay a pile of dark rags, and she picked one up. Gerrit, who stooped next to her, watched as she inhaled. The heavy scent of linseed filled her nose, and she dropped the rag.

"There was a leak when they loaded the last ones up here," he said.

"They?"

He shrugged. "No one I know."

The sweat ran down Maria's temples, and the space grew stifling as though she and Gerrit were sucking out whatever air the heat had not destroyed. Her thoughts seemed similarly congealed. She knew the painters were suffering a shortage of linseed oil to bind their pigments, and yet here was enough to supply the whole town. She grew nauseous as the meaning dawned upon her.

"You knew this was here?" She narrowed her eyes as she stared at Gerrit.

He seemed taken aback. "Yes, of course, I saw them load it up here."

"And you didn't tell anyone? Why didn't you tell Abraham?"

Without exposing his hands, he wiped a bit of sweat from his forehead. "I don't understand. Why would I tell him? The Administrator made it clear that this was a private matter of his, not to do with the leper house. Abraham has no need to clean up here or manage any of these casks."

"I apologize." She pressed a hand against her forehead. "Of course you don't understand. His sister and the other painters. They need this oil."

"His sister? I know nothing of painting, or why she or

anyone else would need these barrels. Until you mentioned oil, I hadn't thought of this at all."

Maria plucked at the neck of her shift in hopes of generating a breath of breeze against her chest.

"Can you help me with this one?" She bent down to lift one cask lying on its side atop a second.

Gerrit approached, hesitated, and then wrapped his covered arms around the heavy barrel. It was small, so his arms encircled the barrel below hers. They seemed to breathe the same air until Maria, though ashamed, held her breath, and they heaved the cask from its side to upright.

"We'll have to get Abraham up here to open it," she said. "I don't trust myself to hammer off that top band and not send the whole thing flying. He'll know how to put it back and make it look like no one's touched it."

"That's fine," Gerrit said. "Though if this is related to painters, are you sure that's wise? I mean, his sister, and . . . I am not fond of Paulus van Beresteyn, but I live here. It's the best leper house in the United Provinces, in my opinion. I don't want to take the children anywhere else."

Maria wiped another rivulet of sweat from her forehead and briefly touched his shoulder.

"Abraham can keep a secret," she said. "Until we can figure out what the story is with Paulus and the oil, it's no harm if it sits here a little longer. Particularly when we can borrow a little."

He nodded and, after a pause, gestured toward the exit. Without further discussion, they descended. Maria breathed the relatively fresh air of the second story with a heave of relief. It was strange that the heat of Hell should accumulate in the rafters rather than down below, but then perhaps that made Hell itself all the more terrifying.

Magdalena and Jacob stood on the landing waiting for

them, and Maria smiled to clear her thoughts. The girl gave a shy smile in return before they both ran down the stairs and out into the yard.

"I'll be back soon with Abraham," she said to Gerrit.

"Today?"

"Perhaps. I'd like to get started. These children need all the help I can offer, and there's no sense in waiting a minute longer than we need."

He nodded, and Maria thought she saw a tension in his shoulders fall away. Then he turned to store the ladder and close the hatch to the attic.

Chapter 36

In a corner of Pieter Molijn's empty, sun-filled workshop, Judith found a barrel of linseed oil. A large one, a generous supply for one workshop, but nothing that could explain the citywide shortage. She took its measure, nearly full, and then she left the barrel as it was. The little dog followed her around the quiet house, its nails tapping along the wooden floorboards and bright tile floors as she moved from room to room.

She was in the kitchen at the rear of the house, checking again in the pantry for any sign of a false wall or other concealment, when she heard the front door open. The dog ran, gleefully yapping, out of the kitchen and toward the front. She could hear a voice, muffled by the intervening rooms, greeting the beast with a bemused tone.

Judith rushed to the back door. Her heart pounded, and as she ran, her hand clipped the edge of a pewter plate. It flipped up and clattered to the floor.

Silence engulfed the house. Then, footsteps.

She leapt to open the back door. She ran out, and it did not latch behind her, but she kept running down the small flight of stairs and into the patio garden. Behind her she heard a deep voice calling out.

"Who is that? Stop, you!"

She skidded around the corner, hopefully before the man, presumably Pieter, could exit the kitchen. She ran down the narrow pathway between the houses, out the gate, and into the street.

Upon entering the street, she froze. Men and women were walking home from church, and they stared at her, taken aback. She thought for a moment, then she ran.

When Judith arrived home, she was damp with sweat and shaking. Upon closing her own door behind her, she sagged against it, her boots muddy. She sank to the floor, giggling.

"Judith, I—" Abraham walked up and then paused, regarding her. "What are you doing?"

"I can't believe I made it, it's just . . ." She took a deep breath and tried to calm herself. "I was running and then walking, but no one saw me. I mean, no one saw me leave Pieter's house. I broke in, Abraham! Can you believe it? But listen, what I saw proves it, you see?" She grabbed his sleeve. "He had a barrel of oil. A full barrel! No one else I've spoken to has that much. That proves there's something going on, some sort of conspiracy, like Frans said. And I'll find the proof of it. I'll find it and expose them."

"Judith, you what? You broke into someone's house?" He lowered his arm out of her grasp.

"Not really. I walked inside; it wasn't locked. But are you listening? The other painters, the Guild leaders. They are conspiring. To squeeze the rest of us out of business." She glanced around to make sure neither of the boys were listening, and she saw no one. She hoped they were visiting their friends, the other young apprentices, as they usually did on Sundays. The rowdy boys she had never fit in with.

"You broke in. You entered someone's house." He rubbed the scarred back of his hand and took a step away from her.

"Abraham, I . . ." Her voice grew quiet. She looked down at her feet and then up to meet his gaze. "I never criticized you for what you did."

"You didn't need to, Judith. You were ashamed of me." His face grew pale.

"It was different, what I did now. No, I mean, what you did doesn't matter, it's all fine." The lie she could offer hung at the back of her throat, but she could not force it out. She could not deny her shame.

"I dishonored our family name, whatever was left of that. And then you go out and do nearly the same thing. Really."

Abraham narrowed his eyes as he considered her. Then he pushed her to the side and walked out the front door. When he slammed it behind him, the house shivered and fell into silence.

Chapter 37

AFTER SHE LEFT THE LEPER house, Maria walked around town, delaying her return to her father's home. She had been back at her childhood home a month now, since the day he took her home. When they arrived at his house after walking silently through Haarlem that day, he stood in the entry hall where, with the midday light shining down, his face held the shadows. He looked old. It was the first time Maria had thought of him as old. It was as though she could feel the fragility of his life, like an eggshell newly drained of its egg and resting lightly in her palm. Each night since returning, she brought him his pipe. One night, after delivering the tobacco, she wandered through the dim workshop. A few paintings stood propped on easels or drying against the wall. A shallow bowl of linseed oil lay next to the grinding stone, awaiting pigments. She had imagined taking the stone and crushing her fingers beneath it, pulverizing her skin, bone, and blood to make a paste. But she reached a hand inside her sleeve to caress the tender scars there, and she walked away.

Maria sidestepped a puddle of horse urine. In the heat, the odor wafted up more strongly than usual, and she grimaced. She wondered how all that linseed oil would smell if someone spilled it all out and let it drip through the floorboards and rafters through the house. Maybe such a shower might prove curative for the poor lepers. She tried to calculate how many guilders an attic full of linseed oil would fetch, but her mind quailed at the effort. A lot, certainly. More than Judith could hope to earn in five years, or maybe her lifetime.

Maria tucked a sweaty strand of dark hair back behind her ear. Did Judith intend to spend her lifetime painting drinkers and dreaming of unattainable commissions? She didn't know anymore what Judith wanted.

She should tell Judith about the oil. In spite of her smoldering bitterness, she owed Judith that much. Maria walked past a woman sitting by her open entryway and mending a sock while a child in a dirty smock tapped a cup with a stick. There were greater problems in the world than Maria's pain, and she needed to learn to release her pride. Though perhaps Judith should sacrifice hers. Maria had sacrificed so much already. She bit her lip.

After a few hours of walking, she turned toward Judith's house and could nearly see it from across the broad main square when she spotted Abraham hurrying across the paving stones. She hitched up her skirt and rushed to catch him.

"Abraham!"

He paused and squinted as he looked across the square. She gave a small wave and ran a few steps before calling out his name again.

He recognized her, she could tell, and he stood to wait, though his features still twitched with some sort of restlessness. With anger, she saw when she reached him.

He shook his head as if they had already been having a

disagreement.

"There's nothing left to say to her, Maria."

Maria nudged his elbow and walked in step with him, moving away from the curious basket vendor leaning over his wares to listen.

"Judith?" she asked, though she knew.

"She takes me into her house to make me feel guilty about what I've done, the crime I've already paid for. More than she knows, Christ's blood. I came back to Haarlem on my own. Simply to apologize to the man who owned the tulip bulbs. But Maria, you've seen how she looks at me. Like I'm some filthy secret to hide away, as if the blacksmith on Lombartsteeg were going to turn his nose up at her paintings because of me. I didn't even steal anything, Maria! I broke into a house, same as her."

They were walking past the high walls of Grote Kerk, and Maria stopped. "Same as her?"

"It's incredible, isn't it? She has the gall to make me feel like sewage for breaking into a man's house, and then she sneaks right into an artist's house. I think she was looking to take a jug of the oil or something. And she tried to laugh it off, as if what she had done was nothing."

Abraham looked up at the cathedral's single tower, and they stood too close for Maria to see the crucifixes upon its pinnacles. When he looked back down, tears shone in his eyes.

"It's not right of her to be so cruel," he said softly.

Maria laid a hand on him and ushered him into a chaste embrace.

"She can't see anything but her painting," she said. The words felt like a condemnation and, at the same time, a relief.

Abraham stood back and nodded. "I know."

"I have an idea. I could use your help with something. And I know someone who'd be glad to see you today," she said.

"That's hard to imagine."

She pressed against his arm and turned him in the direction of the leper house. "I went to visit your friends today, to talk about how I could help them. And I think they've got the materials for some curative ointments and poultices. I need your help gathering everything."

"That sounds simple enough."

"Wait until you see the task," she said with a small smile.

They walked in silence. As they passed the familiar brick houses and green-painted doors, an anger hatched from the flimsy shell in her chest that she had tried to use to contain her feelings. The anger crept and circled, feeding itself upon her thoughts. It was one thing to have ambition, but it was another to forget those who loved you. Or once did.

She used her sleeve to wipe the sweat from her eyes, and she turned her thoughts to the other ingredients she might need. Some ground pig's hoof most likely, which would be easy enough to find. And though she would not tell Abraham, she would take a cupful of the oil to be consecrated by the priest currently lodging in town, in the house where they had held their clandestine Mass this week. A blessing from the Lord could not hurt. She glanced at Abraham, who seemed lost in his own thoughts. He fingered a bit of thread that had come loose from his shirt cuff, and almost collided with a cart of onions and carrots.

The sky was bare, and the sharp sun pricked them mercilessly. The crowds were starting to thin as people turned inside to eat their midday meal or rest from the heat. A calm seemed to unfurl, like a fog drifting over from the lake, and she tried to unclench her jaw.

Maria had not asked Abraham about his time in Amsterdam, but while she tended to his back one morning he had told her a story that someone had told him. The man was a veteran of the war with the Hapsburgs, and he had seen the sack of Magdeburg, a Protestant town on the wrong side of some river in the German states. Maria had listened only partially as she dabbed the ointment on his wounded back, but when Abraham described a street, vacant except for the blood running down its gutters like the rain after a storm, she paused. They had both held still that morning, in reverence of the horror. Now, at the thought, the afternoon peace seemed to quiver. She wondered if cities elsewhere had lanes weeping blood now.

They rounded a bend and could see the trees lining the canal up ahead. The smell of smoke wafted toward her. Some poor woman had burned her family's food. Abraham glanced over but said nothing. When they reached the top of the bridge arcing over the canal, she stopped. A tendril of smoke curled out from the top window of the leper house, which she could see above the high wall. A bird cooed behind her, and she almost turned around to look at it. But then a plume of flame burst through the window, followed by the explosion of shattering glass.

She screamed, a short gasp of terror. Maria ran toward the house, but then she stopped. She turned around and saw Abraham running toward her, then past her, toward the house. She had to alert the fire brigade. She ran, her skirts pulling unevenly at her waist and thumping against her legs, slowing her stride. A burning scent chased her.

A man, his belly round under his fine linen doublet, stepped outside his house on the busy Kleine Houtstraat, which led to the southern gate.

"Fire! There's a fire," Maria said, gasping and ragged. "Go tell the watchman!" She pointed south.

His face clouded in affront at her command, but then his eyes widened. "Fire? Where?"

"At the leper house. Hurry, please!"

The muscles in his face relaxed, probably in relief that the fire was on the other side of the canal from his home, but he nodded and ran down the street toward the gate. Usually, the watchman was the first to spot flames, since fires most often sprouted at night. He would sound his trumpet and point his lantern in the direction of the fire. But today, there was no such alarm. Perhaps the sun glittered too brightly for the man's eyes to discern the smoke.

Maria wiped the sweat from her brow and resumed running toward the town hall, only a few more blocks away.

Her cries of "fire" attracted attention, and within minutes, a crew of men was hauling the city's two large sail cloths from the shed behind the Stadhuis and dousing them with water. In the distance, she heard the horn blow, and she knew the townspeople would be filling their required leather buckets with water and forming a line to pass them toward the burning house. She hoped relief would come quickly enough. A fire threatened everyone. And inside the house were those adorable children. Her throat began to close in panic.

The men bundled the sails up and ran off; they would wet them more thoroughly closer to the house in the fetid canal. Around her, people emerged from their houses, curious and concerned, and she pointed east toward the burning house. She saw a few of them grab their mandatory leather fire buckets and run toward the conflagration. Maria ran after them, her hands empty, and her heart pounding. She needed to help somehow.

By the time they reached the canal, the smoke was billowing up above the brick wall. Two lines of men, peppered with a few stout women, stretched out of the gate. The lines convulsed with the frenzy of passing full buckets toward the house and empty buckets away, and the din of their yelling nearly rose above the roar of the fire and the calls for help inside. One of the sail cloths rested on the roof, and men on ladders continued to douse it with water as the buckets arrived. Flames twisted and reached out the windows.

A scream pierced the air. Maria cringed and scrambled toward the gate. A wave of heat pushed her back. Breathless from the running, Maria turned toward the canal. She could help lift water into the buckets, or at least pass the sloshing pails. But there was no place for her, and the ground began to spin. She stumbled to the bridge's low wall and leaned against the bricks. When she looked up, she saw Judith running along the canal toward the fire relief efforts. The street was crowded now, and she didn't see Maria.

More cries for help rent the air, and Maria squeezed her eyes shut. Her head was swimming, and her lungs burned from the smoke. By the gate, the water-bearers drew apart to let a child, bundled in rags and coughing, pass into the street. One of the lepers. It might have been Magdalena, though she couldn't tell with the smoke. Maria tried to stand, but wobbled and fell back against the wall.

She coughed. The smell of the smoke shifted from rich to acrid as the thick clouds gathered and rolled further away from the building. Judith walked over to the girl and knelt down. She said something Maria could not hear then reached an arm out. Judith paused, but then she rested her hand on the child's shoulder and drew her in. The little girl's face wrenched into a sob.

A man, Abraham, emerged from the gate carrying a body between his arms. When he stepped clear of the billowing smoke, he set the woman down. She rubbed her eyes and hacked a gasping, ragged cough into her dirty clothes. Abraham stood up and walked over to Judith, who threw her arms around him. Behind them, the building groaned and cracked, and the water-carriers yelled down the line for more buckets.

Abraham pried himself free of Judith, whose face had gone pale, and he ran back beyond the walls. Inside the burning house.

Maria stood, but her knees buckled, and she leaned against the wall edge. A loud crash sounded from behind the brick walls, and screams joined the cacophony. Some of the rescuers streamed out from the gate then turned to stare back at the smoke. The roof had collapsed.

Chapter 38

The fire raged on through the day and into the night. It ate at the house's masonry shell, and the night sky glowed a sullen orange against the clouds of soot. The town poured bucket after bucket upon the flames, and as Judith passed sloshing full pails down the long, frantic line, she thought they might scoop the entire canal up and splash it upon the burning house. She hoped they would. She had to save Abraham.

When he had run away from her, protesting that he had to save someone named Gerrit, Judith had screamed, demanding he return. She tried to follow him, but a woman with calloused hands and worn clothes pushed Judith into the bucket line. And then she saw the roof collapse. She stood, stunned and suspended, until someone pushed a full pail into her hands, and she had to pass it along to the next person. Then came another bucket, and another, and soon she surrendered to the rhythm and the blisters that bubbled under her palms.

By morning, the largest and most ravenous flames had

dimmed, and the house smoldered in tame fury. Judith collapsed onto a stone wall near the canal and pressed her raw, aching hands against her cheeks. Once she closed her eyes, she heard all around her a soft, crescendoing sobbing. The air grew saturated with mourning, as cries of anguish crept into the silence left by the defeated fire. Her own chest constricted, and a painful grief ripped through her. She had not seen Abraham since he ran into the house. She knew what that meant. She opened her eyes and saw children in rags with tears washing the ash from their faces, and women cradling crying men against their chests.

She might be wrong. She ran to the demolished front gate. Inside the courtyard, the wrecked house radiated heat, and the lingering flames ate slowly away at what beams remained. She grabbed the shoulder of the first man she saw.

"Abraham, have you seen him? Abraham Leyster. Tall and thin. Have you?"

He shook his head, and she ran to the next man. And the next. And the next. No one had seen him.

An old man in a long gray robe hobbled over to her. He looked at her, and his red eyes spilled over with tears. When he raised his sleeve to wipe them away, she saw he had knobs in the place of a few of his fingers.

"I . . ." He started to speak, but his throat swallowed the words. He pressed his eyes shut, and his cheeks gleamed in the dim morning sun. "I'm sorry," he managed finally. He reached out as if to touch her, and then he stepped back.

"No," Judith said. But her throat closed over her breath.

She nodded at the man. She could manage no more response than that, and she stepped away. She walked around the courtyard, calling softly for Abraham.

The colors around her faded, as if bleached by the sun, and she blinked her eyes, burnt by the ash. She left the enclosure and walked back into the street. Still she called his name, and the few townspeople nearby looked at her with pity.

Judith could see his face perfectly in her mind's eye. She strained to fix her thoughts on his details, to pin his expressions.

"No, you can't go," she said, not caring that she spoke out loud. She would not let herself cry though. If she held back her tears, she might still find him. If she behaved as she ought to, calm and reasonably, Haarlem might unearth him unharmed from some corner of the wreckage. She wanted to argue with him, to convince him to stay home. To never have left, never have ran out after they fought. No, she should have stopped him earlier. So much earlier. She had been so ignorant. She conjured his image again, as if it were a portrait. His smile brightened then melted. She felt as if someone was prying her ribs from her body, one by one, and raking her chest with talons. Judith knelt in the street and pressed her palms against her dry eyes.

Three days passed before the workers could remove enough of the wreckage to find the bodies. Judith spent her time waiting seated on her stool and staring out the window at the gray street below. She gave the boys the time to do as they pleased, but she heard them lingering about the house. When Judith wrenched her thoughts into the present, she was surprised to see that Carolein had set them to scrubbing the hearths, and her apprentices had obeyed. They hunched on their knees and scoured the hearthstones. She sometimes thought the rivulets of sweat running down their sooty faces might be tears.

The workers brought Abraham's body, wrapped in a linen shroud, to her house. They laid him on her bed and backed out of the room without a word. Judith stood above the tall form and reached out a hand to touch the fabric. It was colder than she had expected. Behind her, in the entryway, she heard Carolein talking to the men. Slowly, Judith unwrapped the body.

His head and torso were charred and brittle, and one of his arms was bent across his chest. His legs were almost untouched, and his brown linen pants were streaked with soot. One shoe had fallen off. Judith turned away for a few minutes.

Then, gingerly, she undressed Abraham's body. Carolein came bearing a bucket and cloth and, without speaking, they washed what skin they could. Judith stayed away from the charred areas, though once she got too close, and black greasy ash smeared across Abraham's unburnt skin. She fought back the urge to retch.

They draped a fresh shirt around his torso and put clean pants on his legs. Carolein wrapped his head in fine linen, and then left the room to send Davit to find a scribe who would write out the public death notice. Judith pulled a chair over and sat beside the bed. She could see his scarred hand, the D etching the pallid skin. She pressed her eyes closed and waited.

Carolein returned and crouched down on the floor next to Judith. Carolein's brown skirts pooled out around her like stiff paint on a palette. She cupped Judith's elbow in her hand.

"The head worker left this for you, from Paulus van Beresteyn. Abraham's wages, those that hadn't been paid yet." She dropped a small leather pouch in Judith's hand. The weight of the coins caught Judith's attention, and she looked first at Carolein's face, her eyes wide with empathy, and then at the pouch. She opened it and counted the coins inside. Thirty-two guilders.

"That's as much as he'd earn in half a year. Or more," she said in a low voice. She couldn't marshal any more sound than that, and she realized she didn't want to talk about Abraham's earnings in front of him. As if he would think less of her for considering money now.

Carolein nodded. "It's about as much as a funeral will

cost." She stood, gave Judith another brief caress on the shoulder, and left.

Judith counted the coins again. Carolein was right. Abraham had no guild to pay for his funeral, and Paulus van Beresteyn must have known he had little in the way of family either. The magistrate, as ambitious and rigid as he was, meant well. She knew about ambition. Tears rushed up and blurred her sight. How undeserving Judith was of any family. She was both grateful for the gift and angry at herself for having to accept it. A better sister would have been willing to spend her last cent to send her brother on his way properly. She knew, even now, that she couldn't do that.

She stood. She did need to plan a funeral, no matter where the money came from. Judith walked over to lay her hand upon Abraham's still chest, and then she left. The list began forming in her mind: coffin, a black shroud, food, beer. Flowers, for his youth. She had little time, and yet the litany of tasks closed over her thoughts with the relief of an embrace. She closed the door to her room and called for Carolein.

Chapter 39

JUDITH THANKED THE MAN, WHO smelled of brine and whose name she had already forgotten, and stepped out of the crowd of mourners. She leaned against the cool plaster of her wall, straightened the black lace covering her hair, and watched as the knot of men dressed in the traditional black robes shuffled past one another to give their respects to the coffin. She and Carolein had decided, against the pastor's wishes, to place the top upon the wooden box. Her brother's covered face was too intimate in its description of his death and last pains for Judith to leave him to others' eyes.

She didn't know many of the mourners gathered now in her house. Men from the docks and Abraham's life before he fled, she imagined. She had wanted the lepers to attend, but Carolein pointed out that if they did, the sick would be the only mourners. Judith thought that would be fine, but in the end, she conceded to tradition.

A good number of the painters from St. Luke's Guild had come too, ostensibly out of sympathy for her, but she suspected it was more to demonstrate guild cohesiveness. They had never met Abraham. In the crowded overflow in her entry hall, Judith saw Frans de Grebber and Maria, but she stayed away from both of them. They had come for Abraham and would have nothing kind to say to her. She couldn't bear any more reprobation, no matter how much she deserved it. And she was grateful, in a way, that Jan Miense Molenaer was in Amsterdam still, where he had traveled before the fire to set up a relationship with a dealer and meet with a merchant who wanted to commission a portrait for his daughter's wedding. She had sent Jan a letter about the funeral but heard no response. That was fine—good even. Bearing her grief alone seemed fitting. Judith spoke only in soft thank yous and mumbled affirmation of whatever anyone said to her about Abraham, though few people spoke to her at all.

The pastor cleared his throat, and the low murmur of conversation drifted into silence.

"We are here to mourn the passing of the brave young man, Abraham Leyster, who died before his time. A few words from the Holy Bible." He bent his gray head over the few pages he had brought, verses copied from the holy book, and read them in a voice that rolled up and down First Corinthians, then a brief selection of the Psalms. Judith's attention wavered between the pastor's palsied hands and the closed coffin. Why would her brother never grow old and complain of aches in his joints or dim hearing? He had left her alone. Or she had driven him away, into the flames?

She'd heard no word from their parents. The full room swayed slightly under the spell of the pastor's words, and she imagined her bowed and bewildered parents cutting their way through the crowd. She had waited three days to write them, for it had felt too final to see on paper the words confirming that Abraham was dead until she could see him for herself. But by the time she had the funeral announced, she knew she had to tell them. Now, she exhaled a jagged breath and tried not to think about why her father and mother had not arrived or written. Perhaps the letter had gotten lost.

Outside, church bells tolled three o'clock and then the funeral tones. The pastor put away his verses and indicated for the pallbearers to screw the coffin lid tight. The young men had been easier to find than Judith had expected. After she sent the death announcement to those names that she knew, these men came to her door, one by one, to offer their help. She assumed they had been friends with Abraham, though she didn't ask. It didn't matter now.

The six pallbearers lifted the coffin onto the hand bier and laid the black shroud over it. Judith stepped forward to lay a bunch of lilies upon the coffin, and other mourners added the white roses and other flowers Carolein had bought. The men then hefted up the laden bier and carried it out. Judith fell in line first, followed by Frans Hals, the most prominent citizen in the room. Everyone else took their place, though she didn't turn around to watch. Against her will, her eyes flooded as she watched them carry the coffin out of the house. His final departure from her home. They bore him feet first, as if to suggest he might walk to Heaven on his own. That was a relief. She had said nothing to the pastor about this part of the procession. Only criminals were carried out head first, and she was glad the pastor had decided Abraham was not one. She wiped the tears from her cheeks and choked back the urge to sob. It was unseemly to grieve noisily.

The procession inside the Groke Kerk and the following brief service went quietly. The summer heat still weighed upon the city, and Judith was sweating beneath her black dress, even in the cool shade of the church. The sensation of moisture on her skin was a welcome distraction. She didn't want to think about the moment when she would have to turn from the grave and leave Abraham behind. At the front of the Grote Kerk, the pastor's voice boomed, but she hardly listened.

After the service, the pallbearers moved the coffin to the side of the church, where the heavy paving stone had been slid to the side earlier. Judith narrowed her eyes, trying to shrink the range of her sight to avoid seeing what lay in that dark hole under the church floor. The pastor led the pallbearers and a few other observers in the customary circular passage around the grave site before lowering the coffin all the way to the bottom. Abraham's head pointed east. Judith leaned over to bid him farewell, and a few silent tears fell onto his coffin. His body was already too distant. She watched as the rest of the group gave their prayers. Then, she handed a coin to each of the pallbearers, mumbled her thanks, and turned toward the house. She tried not to think, but still a part of her screamed that with each step she was again abandoning her brother and leaving him behind. She squeezed her hands into fists and focused on the feeling of her nails against her palms. Her feet felt rubbed raw with each step.

Carolein had stayed back at the house, and when the group returned, the house was filled with benches and chairs. She had pulled the kitchen table into the large space of the entry hall, and it was laden with peaches, breads, and cheese. Four barrels of beer lined one wall, and the mourners set to filling their cups. Carolein guided Judith to a chair against the wall and handed her a mug heavy with beer. Judith took a sip and puckered her lips. This was, to her surprise, potent double beer. She thought they had agreed to serve the standard simple beer, to avoid trouble as the evening wore on. She watched as a middle-aged man she didn't recognize opened the tap on the barrel to her left and poured the beer into his tankard. The liquid was golden, not bread-brown like hers. Carolein must have set aside something for her. Judith took another sip and relished the quicksilver feeling it sent to her head. This was better than the black wound in her chest. She drank again.

Across the room, Frans Hals stood nodding in conversation with Outgert van Akersloot and Frans de Grebber. Maria sat behind them, obscured by the crowd. Judith could barely see her, for which she was glad. Frans Hals seemed to be saying something flattering about Judith's paintings, for he lifted the traditional black cloth covering the wall hangings and indicated some detail beneath to Frans de Grebber, who nodded. Ordinarily, Judith would have flushed with pride, but now she watched them. Pieter Molijn hadn't come, but as she watched Haarlem's leading artists lean their heads toward one another and chuckle, she imagined he would have stood there with these men. Sharing the same secrets. They were hoarding linseed oil, and even Frans de Grebber knew at least some part of the story.

Beneath the heavy layer of her grief, a radiant anger stirred as she watched the older men. They wanted to pretend to include her, yet they tried to force her out. She didn't know how they had set up the scheme, but she might find out. Paulus van Beresteyn had obviously played a role, and who else? She closed her eyes for a moment. None of that mattered. She opened her eyes and looked at the artists again. Frans Hals was laughing at something Outgert had said, and Dirck threw an arm around his brother's shoulders. They would never embrace her like that. She wanted to paint, but she didn't want to paint alone. And yet everything she had done seemed to make her only more alone. Her workshop would only last a few more weeks if she couldn't find more oil or money. She looked away.

Judith drank a few more sips then rested her mug beneath her chair. The beer's warm hum was pleasant, but she didn't want anything pleasant right now. She watched her guests eat, drink, and speak more and more loudly. She nodded when people came to express their regrets or say some kind words about Abraham. The house grew stifling, and Carolein opened all the windows. The front door hung open to the street, and a ray of sunshine slashed through the doorway to fall upon the one bare spot of wooden floor. No one wanted to invite the extra warmth by standing in the sun.

Staring at the sunlight, Judith remembered a time when Abraham had visited her at the De Grebber house. She was young, thirteen or so, and had only been there less than a year. Abraham was ten. That day, like today, was filled with glittering sun, and they had spent the afternoon sitting in her loft bedroom and making shadows against the circle of sunlight on the floor. Maria sat with them, smiling as the younger children played and chattered. Judith loved her for not mocking their game; a game that Judith already realized she herself was too old for. But it was the best way she and Abraham had found to talk to one another. The three of them had been so happy that day.

Judith stood. She felt sober and empty. She wove her way through the crowd, past a long bench, and over to the other side of the room. There was an empty stool next to Maria—Judith's painting stool, she realized before she sat on it.

As if exhausted, she took a few breaths and listened to the conversation swirling around them. Maria kept her eyes fixed on a spot across the room, or perhaps on her father, who was refilling his tankard. She took a small sip from her own cup.

"How's your father?"

"He's well."

Judith pursed her lips and tried to think of something else to say. "Are you planning to leave Haarlem? I had heard from Abraham that you were interested in Amsterdam."

Maria glanced at her and narrowed her eyes for a moment.

"No, I'm not, not yet." She paused, then looked at her father, who was laughing alongside Dirck Hals. "Once you realize how much someone loves you, you find you have a lot of power over them. I can't, I wouldn't, do anything now that might hurt him."

Maria took another sip, and Judith stared at her hands crossed in her lap.

"Every day I think about how I should have kept my word to you," Judith said. "I'm sorry."

Maria nodded. She swirled the beer in her cup.

"You're angry," Judith said. It was obvious, but she didn't know what else to say. Silence was worse.

Maria exhaled. "Mostly at myself. For expecting anything different."

"What does that mean, Maria?" A part of her relished the opportunity to defend herself, and Judith sat up straight upon her stool.

Maria turned to face her, and she had tears glistening on her red cheeks.

"Do you want to know? I shouldn't say this, Judith, not today."

"You've gotten this far."

"Judith, you think only of yourself. All you wanted was to have your workshop, and no one else mattered. What does your success mean, really, if you're alone?"

It was as if Abraham had spoken too. Judith's anger flared then collapsed like a bit of kindling quickly consumed. She nodded. Maria looked at her as if expecting a fight, but Judith had nothing to say. She slumped against the wall. Around them, the men and women in black drank and told stories and laughed.

She took a deep breath, and let herself release the dike she had built inside her chest. The wooden slats behind her breastbone that held back the sorrow, anger, and fear gave way. She let herself cry. When the tears turned into sobs, and people began to glance at her, she didn't try to control herself. She didn't care. Maria was right in a way. Judith had thought of her workshop, though not only of that. She had missed her friend and her brother, and she had forgotten how to tell them. If she had been able to paint Abraham, to show him how well she saw him, how she noticed the pinch in his cheek when he smiled, or swirl of black hair over his ears, or even the way the D on his hand bent over his veins, he might have understood. And she had thought Maria understood that, too, but Judith had never asked.

"I'm sorry," she said through her tears.

Chapter 40

CAROLEIN APPEARED THROUGH THE CROWD and bent down to whisper in Judith's ear.

"You need a break," she said. "It's understandable. Come with me." She reached under Judith's arm and pressed her up. Carolein's cornflower blue eyes were rimmed red, as if she had been crying, but her cheeks were dry.

Judith complied, and as she stood, she glanced back at Maria. The other woman's face was a mask, but her eyes followed Judith.

Carolein parted the crowd, many of whom regarded Judith with pity tinged by condescension. Grief was one thing, weeping was another. Frans and Dirck Hals seemed to shake their heads as if her misbehavior only confirmed some judgment. None of them understood. Carolein held her hand and guided her up the stairs. Judith felt no shame for showing her emotions. It was not doing so that injured more.

They entered the workshop, and when Carolein shut the door, the noise from the funeral gathering below dulled. "You need a moment," Carolein said.

"Thank you," Judith said. She hiccupped through a sob and wiped some tears away.

"It's nothing." Carolein turned to leave.

"Wait. Carolein, tell me. Who have you lost?"

Carolein faced her. She lifted her dry, chapped fingers to Judith's jaw. "Too many. And it never gets easier."

She closed the door again before Judith could say anything.

In the softening late afternoon light, the white plaster walls lost their ridges and pockmarks. The uniform white space seemed to wrap its arms around Judith, and after a few minutes, her crying slowed. She breathed in the comforting smell of crushed ochre, Cologne earth, bone black, and the rest: the blended perfume of all her pigments. The wooden boards creaked as she walked through the room. There was her easel, untouched since the day Abraham died. There was Davit's panel, where he was working on a study of the violin. And there was the mortar and pestle Hendrik had been using to grind charcoal into pigment fine enough for a gentle gray paint. She ran her fingers over each brush, bowl, and table she passed. She picked up the shard of crockery Lachine had given her when they made their deal. Over the months her thumb had worn the sharp edge down, a little. She placed it back on the table.

By the window hung the painting of a man offering a woman some coins. She loved that painting, and when the dealer at the auction house expressed his concerns, she decided to keep it for herself. The woman in the dark scene fixed her eyes on her needlework while the man in the fur cap bent over her shoulder, trying to distract her. A flame illuminated them both. Judith loved the focus she had captured on the woman's smooth cheeks and downturned eyes. Yet the painting would not be complete without both figures. The brown in the man's fur hat echoed the brown in her hair. The gold of the coins in his palm contrasted with the sky blue of her skirt. While preparing the scene, Judith had scratched perspective lines into the white grounding, outlining how she would guide the eye from the woman's knee to hand and setting the woman's chair just that much farther in the illusory distance. But instead of boasting of her skill with perspective, instead of painting tile grids to show the viewer what she had done, she painted over the lines. It was the woman and the man who mattered. This painting had achieved the elusive balance of positioning and light that she strove for. Had she focused too much on the woman or too much on her technique, she would have thrown the painting askew.

She looked around the workshop. Under the grinding table sat the jug of linseed oil she had purchased from Frans de Grebber. It was more than two-thirds gone, and she didn't know where she would find more. Perhaps she would go knocking on Pieter Molijn's door, she thought bitterly. And how to explain that?

She shook her head. Maria was right. It was her brother's funeral, and still she was thinking of the cursed oil. None of her labor mattered if she didn't have a life worth living. She picked up the jug, then she grabbed the rommelpot from the prop table with her free hand. Carefully, she opened the workshop door and walked out to the landing. Below her, the mourners ate, drank, and raised their voices to be heard over the din. Paulus van Beresteyn stood arguing with Frans Hals and Outgert van Akersloot. His stiff lace ruff radiated from his collar, and his deep black tunic drank in the light. He did not wear the mourning gowns of the others, and yet somehow he didn't look out of place in his finery. Paulus van Beresteyn. She would have to thank him for Abraham's wages, if she could think of the appropriately graceful words.

"I'm owed something," he said, his voice sharp.

"It's not our fault you can't protect your investment," Outgert replied. Judith listened and pressed her lips together.

A man with curly golden hair under his broad hat rushed in the open door, and Judith froze. Jan Miense Molenaer. He looked up at her with eyes wide in sympathy, and she wanted to run down and greet him. But if she did, she'd never get this courage again.

Judith placed the jug of oil on the floor. Then she pulled the rommelpot's stick slowly through the pig bladder stretched over its opening. A loud groaning sound echoed across the room. She repeated the motion a few times until everyone in the room was looking up at her with startled faces.

"Neighbors and friends, thank you for coming today. I know it's unusual that I would address you at a time like this, but I hope you'll have patience with me." A murmur of voices rippled across the crowd and then faded. Judith watched their upturned faces, and a cold panic gripped her throat. She had walked out without thinking, really, and now a black fear washed away whatever words she had held ready. She stood in silence. At the back of the room, Carolein held a hand over her mouth. Maria sat where Judith had left her, her arms wrapped around herself as if she were shivering.

"Thank you for coming," Judith said again. "Abraham . . . he would have been grateful. Surprised too, probably." Her voice caught, but she pressed forward. "I'm a little surprised. But I forgot to see the people around me. Awful, isn't it, for a painter not to be looking? Not to see the hidden details? And for that, I'm sorry. I'm sorry, Maria." Judith put the rommelpot down and picked up the jug. "I learned, recently, that some other master painters don't want the rest of us around. I understand why. It's hard to make a living. They're hoarding this stuff," she held up the oil, "to squeeze the rest of us out." Below, there was a sharp intake of breath and a few low murmurs. Judith didn't look to see who was speaking. Her stomach was twisted in an anxious knot, but she kept talking. "Maybe there's some sense to it. Still, I'm finished worrying about it."

She unstoppered the earthenware jug. Carefully, she lifted the jug over the balustrade. She tipped it and poured a thin stream of heavy oil down onto the floor below. It splattered onto Dirck Hals's black leather boots, and she smiled. A few people exclaimed and whispered, but mostly the crowd stood in shocked silence. She wondered, for an instant, if anyone would ever buy her paintings after this display of madness. But she had had enough of fretting over what Haarlem thought about her.

She stopped her pouring and held up the brown jug.

"There's enough left here for one painting. I'm going to use it to paint my friend Maria, if she'll let me. It's something I should have done for Abraham too." She blinked back a tear. "And then, if there's not enough linseed oil for me to buy, I'm going to talk to the younger masters in town. We'll find our own. And we'll talk to the Vroedschap." She knew the painters in the room would understand the threat. If the St. Luke's Guild wouldn't represent the interests of all of its members, the men of the city's governing Vroedschap might be less willing to recognize the guild at all.

Her hands trembled when she finished speaking. She tucked them, one hand still holding the container, under her crossed arms. She had no idea if she could follow through, but judging by the panicked glances exchanged by the Guild leaders standing below her, she had hit upon something.

She put the jug down. When she straightened, she saw Maria climbing the stairs toward her. Her blue eyes glistened with tears, and her brown hair had come undone under her cap. She reached the landing and held out a hand.

"I'm sorry, Judith," she said, her voice so soft it was almost impossible to hear. "That was cruel of me to say. That you only thought of yourself."

"But true," Judith said, her two hands holding Maria's one.

"Not entirely," Maria said.

"Yes." Judith sighed and stepped away. She smiled as she wiped away a tear. "Not entirely."

Chapter 41

IN THE ENTRY HALL BELOW, Frans Hals and the other men of the Guild pushed their way through the crowd to the door. They left without another glance at Judith, and she felt a chill of fear. Even Frans de Grebber left with them. A few other mourners followed, though to her surprise, the room stayed full. Paulus van Beresteyn stayed, gnawing on a peach and chatting mournfully with a trader from the docks. Carolein must have found good beer indeed, Judith thought with a small smile. She realized he had provided the funds for the painters' scheme, but she found she could not blame him. He did not know her, and he had never pretended to welcome her into a guild. As she and Maria descended the stairs, Jan raised a hand in greeting.

"It seems you're glad to see him," Maria said with a soft smile. Judith blushed.

"I'm happy to see any kind faces," Judith said. She found Jan's gaze, and then looked down at her feet.

"Go on." Maria nudged her at the small of her back.

Judith wove through the small crowd to where Jan stood. His face was red with heat, and he wiped a bit of sweat from his temple.

"Thank you for coming," she said.

"I only received the message yesterday," he said. "I left as soon as I could, but the horse I had threw a shoe, and then . . . That's all to say that I'm very sorry, Judith. I'm sorry Abraham has left us."

He wrapped his warm arms around her and pressed his lips to her cheek. It was a customary greeting, and yet Judith felt herself relax into his embrace like she had never done in any other. He held her a moment longer than traditional, and then he released her to grip her slim shoulders between his hands. They were strong hands, used to grinding pigments and wielding a brush with precision. She softened against his shoulder, and her tears threatened to break through again. She pulled back.

"Thank you for writing to me," he said. "And that was brave, what you did now. You know I'll support you. Always."

"Of course." She couldn't muster any more, and her voice quivered with emotion. She laid her hand over his upon her shoulder, then stepped away. There was no rush. She would speak to him again, soon. It didn't need to be now.

She found her way back to her chair by the wall, alongside Maria, though they said nothing else. That seemed right. She knew their wounds would take time, but she was relieved to hope they would heal. She watched as her brother's friends and neighbors drank themselves to laughter and tears. Paulus van Beresteyn filled cup after cup of beer, until he wept on the shoulder of a spice merchant. "I'm ruined," Judith heard him say, through the crowd.

She stood and walked over to him.

"Thank you for Abraham's wages," she said. "That was

generous."

He ran a finger around the pewter edge of his tankard. "He was a better man than I."

"You're kind." Her throat caught, and she had to take a deep breath.

"The artists were wrong to think they could restrict talented artists from painting," he said. "I'm glad to see their scheme ended, and I'm sorry I took any part in it. It seemed like a good investment." Paulus kept his gaze upon his hand.

"I knew the Frenchman a little," she said. "He was kinder than I expected."

Paulus shook his head and drained the tankard. "As was Gerard. It's all over. Now, I'm going to avail myself of another drink. My condolences again."

Judith raised a hand to stop him but let him go. He was right, there was nothing more to say. The men were gone, and whether Lachine had meant to murder Gerard or accidentally gave him a mortal injury didn't matter to either man now. She returned to her seat, where Maria was speaking quietly to a neighbor. Judith closed her eyes and tried to remember Lachine's face. One day, she would have to find those urchins of his. She could pay them to model.

The gathering lasted until before nightfall, by which point the final drop had been drained from the barrels, and the mourners had shuffled home. Jan and Maria stayed until the last guests stumbled out the still-open door, and then the three of them helped Carolein and the boys with the cleaning. Judith swept a broom across the wooden floor, while Carolein and Maria took turns scrubbing out the tankards and cups they had borrowed from the neighbors. Jan and the boys replaced the tables and benches.

Finally, the household grew still. Jan collapsed next to Judith on a bench in the kitchen, and he squeezed her hand. A warm shiver ran up her elbow.

"I'll talk to my father about the oil," Maria said as she dried a tankard and set it on a sideboard. She rested her hand upon it and seemed to hesitate. "Judith. I should have told you this earlier, but I was so angry, and then Abraham . . . I'm sorry. I'm so sorry. Before the fire, one of the men at the leper house showed me the attic there. Paulus van Beresteyn was storing dozens upon dozens of casks of linseed oil in his attic."

Judith blinked and, in spite of her fatigue, sat up straighter upon the bench. She glanced at Jan, who looked equally surprised. Maria kept her gaze on her rag.

"You knew? And you didn't tell me?"

"I'm sorry I didn't, Judith. My friend there made me vow not to tell, and I thought to use oil for my healing. The fire happened just after I learned." She wrung the rag between her hands.

"Did Abraham know?" Judith held her breath. She wanted to hear Maria's answer, and yet she wasn't sure she could bear it.

"I'm not sure. I don't think so."

"I don't know what to say." She covered her mouth with her hand and glanced back and forth between her friends.

Jan pressed his lips together, and a worried line creased between his eyebrows. He said nothing. Maria exhaled loudly.

"It wouldn't have made a difference, Judith. And I had promised the leper . . ."

Judith held still for a moment. It hurt to learn that Maria hadn't told her. That her friend could know something so important to her and keep it a secret, even if there was nothing they could have done. Judith pinched the bridge of her nose. Yet she could see how, perhaps, she had deserved to be left in ignorance. Or at least how keeping a vow to a friend was honorable.

"The oil is all gone now. None of us can use it for anything," Judith said.

"I know. I think, maybe, that God was punishing all of us for wanting it so badly. The painters, the magistrate, me. We all thought we could control something. But why should Abraham pay?" Maria's voice quivered.

Judith leaned her head back against the wall, and she closed her eyes for a moment. "I can't think of Abraham being punished for anything. He already paid his debts."

"Maria, you didn't happen to see a leak in those casks, did you?" Jan asked.

Maria pursed her lips together. "There were some soaked rags upon the floor."

He shook his head. "The oil catches fire easily. The smallest thing, even the hidden sparks from this awful heat we've been having, might set it off. That could be what started the fire."

Maria gasped. "Then I should have told someone. Right away. I could have stopped it."

Judith shook her head. She was too tired to feel anything but the deep grief that lapped at the hole in her chest. "You didn't put the oil there, Maria. Don't blame yourself for this too." Perhaps someday she might feel angry—but not now. Abraham was gone, and nothing would change that. No matter how much she wished otherwise.

Jan nodded. "It's a good thing that you learned of it at all, Maria. That will help us make our case to the other painters. If we need to. I suspect that if all the oil has gone up in flames, the Guild leaders will have trouble finding the money to buy up more. In a few months, we should get back to normal."

"Whatever normal is," Judith said softly. There had been too much loss and pain for her to go back to anything. Her tears welled up again.

"That was thoughtless of me," Jan said and shook his head in disgust. "Forgive me."

His eyes were wide in pleading. He had forgotten for a

moment about Abraham. His death and her pain had faded behind Jan's concern about his workshop. Judith knew how easy it was to let one's own worries blind.

"I know what you meant," she said. "And you're right. Our livelihoods depend on that oil." She wiped the tears from her cheeks. She glimpsed a smear of ash upon the back of her hand, but when she looked again, she saw nothing but her glistening skin.

Jan, sitting next to her, put both hands on her shoulders.

"Judith, I'm so sorry. Sorry for Abraham's loss and for you. For my idiot words. I hope you'll give me the chance, someday, to prove that my heart thinks of more than my livelihood," he said. Then, before she could respond, he stood. "Maria, I won't let you walk home alone. I brought a lantern, but we shouldn't wait too long."

Maria nodded and dried her hands on her skirt. "Thank you, Judith." She bent down and gave Judith a kiss on the cheek. Judith could feel a lingering hesitation in the gesture.

Maria followed Jan out the kitchen door into the entry hall. Judith was too tired to follow them, but she listened as Jan used a flint to strike a flame for his lantern. She heard the tin lid of the lantern settle over the cylinder, and she could imagine the light falling through the punched holes of the body. The front door closed heavily behind them.

Judith stood and bid Carolein good night. When she walked out into the darkened main entry hall, a flash of reflected moonlight on the floor caught her eye. She walked closer and bent down. It was a small pool of thick linseed oil, missed in the cleanup. She dipped a finger in it and lifted it to her nose. The rich scent rode her breath down into her body, and it was as though Abraham were whispering in her ear. Like he did the day of the fire, when he embraced her and refused to stop trying to rescue the lepers. "But I love them," he had said.

Judith walked quietly up to her workshop, where she gathered a knife, a palette, and a stoppered jar. She tucked a brush behind her ear. Then downstairs, in the near dark, she scraped what remained of the oil onto her palette. She unstoppered her jar and tapped some ground ochre onto the oil and used her knife to blend it as best she could. The paint would be too dirty to use properly, but that didn't matter.

In her bare feet she stepped out the front door and paused on the threshold. In the dark, the customary green of her front door turned black, as if it had swallowed its own color. She gave the paint another stir then began guiding her brush along the door, a handsbreadth above the handle. She worked for a few minutes, laboring more by habit and instinct than sight. Every so often, a tear welled up and fell down her cheek. She let them.

When she finished, she cocked her head and tried to make out the small design. The flash of wet paint suggested a few lines. On the right sparkled a small star. She gave a slight smile and used the back of her hand to wipe away another tear. Her monogram now marked the building as her own. She dabbed a bit more paint onto her brush and added a flourish to the looping J. Judith of the leading star lives here, she thought. No, she paints here.

Epilogue

MARCH 1643, AMSTERDAM

JUDITH SAT AT A TABLE and guided her brush down the vellum. The carmine lit up the curve of the tulip's petal, and she smiled. She had done little painting in the past few years, and she was relieved to see her skill unfurl from her hands again. She wished Abraham, now ten years dead, could see what his sister was still capable of. He had once asked her if she could paint a tulip, and she never had a chance to show him.

The tulip, a watercolor of a single plant, was for a collector who wanted a book to catalogue his precious specimens. Judith would execute two of them. It was the perfect work for her now. She bent down from the table and gave the cradle a nudge. Inside, the baby grunted and slept on, her rosebud mouth parted slightly.

Six years had passed since the crash of the tulip market, and six years had seen the births and deaths of her two sweet boys. Their absence was a sickness that she could only hold at bay, never conquer. But little Helena, who nursed with her fists curled tight against Judith's breast, helped. The girl seemed fierce and determined to live. Judith prayed she would.

Jan was painting in the workshop, but she would show him the tulip when he came to eat. She had painted with him some, rendering the dead coloring or the fine textures of fabrics, but she had mostly occupied herself with the record keeping and business side of things, which she had learned over seven years of marriage that she did better than her husband. Between the log books, the pregnancies, the babies, and the sadness, she had little time for painting. Or, really, little heart left over. But the release now, the rising confidence that swelled up from her fingertips, was a joy. She smiled and rocked the cradle again. She was anxious to finish and sign the piece with her starred monogram.

She had seen Maria only a few times since she and Jan had moved to bustling Amsterdam shortly after their marriage. But they had nurtured their friendship through a regular correspondence. Sometimes Judith struggled to find anything more than her daily business to report, but she knew Maria understood. Maria, for her part, had given up painting entirely. It was too painful, she wrote, something Judith understood, a little. Now Maria was about to marry a potter from Utrecht, Wouter Coenraetsz de Wolff. Judith feared that the marriage would take Maria even farther away, but she knew, no matter what happened, that she would see her again.

The light softened, and Judith glanced up. A silent spring rain had started. She hoped Carolein, who had moved with them, had taken in the wash.

Helena gurgled in her cradle and blinked her large, peat-colored eyes open. Judith smiled and gave the cradle another nudge. Only a few more minutes' delay, she silently promised the baby. She needed to paint a little longer.

Historical Note

Judith Leyster was born in Haarlem in 1609, and she became the only woman to attain master status and operate her own workshop in the city at that time. Even as a teenaged apprentice, her work caught the attention of a local chronicler of the art scene, Samuel Ampzing, who praised her "good, keen sense." She likely spent at least part of her apprenticeship in Frans de Grebber's workshop, but the limited contemporary documentation on her life makes it difficult to know much about her training and career. She did petition the St. Luke's Guild with a complaint about an apprentice abandoning her workshop for that of Frans Hals after only two days. Other than that, the documentary trail of her artistic career is faint.

The trail was so scarce that only years after Judith's death in 1660, collectors began attributing her few surviving paintings to other artists. She signed her work with only a beautiful, stylized monogram, and once she vanished, credit for her paintings went to Frans Hals, Jan Miense Molenaer, and others. It was only in 1893 when Cornelis Hofstede de Groot, while investigating a monogrammed painting attributed to Frans Hals, rediscovered Judith (and in doing so, reduced the price of the painting by more than a fifth). Over the next century, scholarship and recognition of Judith's work slowly gained momentum.

I first learned of Judith from a 2009 National Gallery of Art exhibition celebrating the 400-year anniversary of her birth. The self-assured young woman gazing out from her own portrait floored me. I wondered how Judith had managed to find a place for herself in a world that we think of as dominated by Rembrandt, Frans Hals, and, later, Johannes Vermeer.

A Light of Her Own is a work of fiction, and I have taken some historical liberties, more than I can list here. Samuel Ampzing was both married and dead by 1633, and may his spirit forgive me the creative license I've taken. Judith's lawsuit against the family of Willem Woutersz, her pupil, was not the same year she gained entry into St. Luke's Guild but rather in 1635. She was the eighth of nine children born to Jan Willemsz and Trijn Jaspers, who later changed their name to "Leyster" or "leading star," likely in reference to the North Star. Abraham was the youngest child. For simplicity, I left Judith's elder siblings out of the story. Her parents did flee their Haarlem creditors in 1628, and they very likely did not return to the city. As I hinted, Judith married Jan Miense Molenaer in 1636, and the young couple may have already faced financial difficulties from Jan's assumption of his recently deceased father's debts. Money worries appear to have periodically dogged Jan and Judith the rest of their lives, though they also had sufficient prosperity to purchase property, including a country house. Judith's astute business management probably facilitated what success they had, and Jan's paintings were popular and likely sold well. Together they had five children, though only two outlived Judith, and only Helena survived to marry and have children of her own.

Today, Judith's self-portrait is part of the permanent collection in the National Gallery of Art in Washington, DC. It hangs a few rooms away from a self-portrait by Jan Miense Molenaer. I like to think they would be happy to be so close still. The one extant painting by Maria de Grebber belongs to the Museum Catharijneconvent in Utrecht. I invented her friendship with Judith, and yet I suspect it is not much of a stretch. Judith likely studied in Frans de Grebber's workshop—quite possibly because he had a daughter a few years older who also painted, as we know from Samuel Ampzing's account. With so few women who shared her skill and interests, Judith may well have found a kindred spirit in Maria de Grebber. May we all find the same.

Acknowledgments

I ENVISION MY WRITING JOURNEY PERHAPS as Judith might—a dark path lit by the flames of those who have loved and helped me along the way. I could not have found my way here, to this book, without their help.

My dedicated and insightful agent Shannon Hassan both shaped this book and found it a home. Her faith in our beloved Judith has meant so much to me, and I couldn't have had a better champion.

I'm deeply grateful to Dayna Anderson and Kayla Church for inviting me into the Amberjack family, where Cassandra Farrin and Cherrita Lee kept me and my words in line.

Whatever semblance of order my words have owes to the lessons I've learned from my fellow writers. My thanks to Mary Aceituno, Richard Agemo, Felix Amerasinghe, Tara Campbell, Jeanne Jones, Terri Lewis, Kseniya Melnik, Britt Peterson, Beth Wenger, and Kate Wichmann. Particularly, my undying thanks to Mara Adams, Meredith Crosbie, Suzie Eckl, Rosalyn Eves, Michelle Lerner, Andrea Pawley, Dorothy Reno, Lisa

Schultz, and Heather Webb for reading an early draft of this novel.

As much as I like to play a historian on the page, I am not one. I'm so fortunate and grateful that actual historians and experts helped me compensate for my ignorance. Melanie Gifford at the National Gallery of Art provided crucial insight about painting materials, and Frima Fox Hofrichter of the Pratt Institute was this book's historical fairy godmother and the source of tremendous expertise on Judith and her times. Thanks also to Dr. Chrissy Macken and Dr. Lindsay Kim for their medical expertise.

Finally, I'm thankful to so many in my family. Particularly my father Ronald Callaghan for teaching me to read in the first place, and my mother Elizabeth Barry for encouraging my writing and this novel. My children for pardoning my distraction and even urging me to "work upstairs." And my husband, Patrick. Without you, there would be nothing.

About the Author

CARRIE CALLAGHAN IS A HISTORICAL fiction author living in Maryland with her spouse, two young children, and two ridiculous cats. Her short stories have been published in literary journals around the country. She loves travel, seasons of all kinds, and tea. And books, books, books.